Robert Chalmers

The Innamincka Affair

Copyright

The Innamincka Affair
Publishing.

R.A.Chalmers

Wentworth Drive. Felixstowe. IP119LD

United Kingdom.

Published by R.A.Chalmers. 2015

First published in the UK by R.A.Chalmers

ISBN-13: 978-0-9807985-9-3

ISBN-10: 0-9807985-9-0

DEDICATION

… to all that has gone before

Love. Lies. Mortal Danger. A lot can happen with an affair at Innamincka.

Rebecca Boucher loves to get the job done. As a respected junior partner in a London law firm, the brief couldn't be simpler. Fly out to meet the owner of a vast cattle property in Australia, check over some paperwork, fly home. She certainly doesn't have time for love, not even in the gorgeous shape of the property owner Cooper Anders, all six foot something of smiling casualness. Then again, maybe Cooper can change her mind, given time...

But when Rebecca is practically kidnapped by the client over stepping the line, everything changes. Cooper falls under the suspicion of the security services who suspect him of complicity. Unknown to anybody, Cooper has been watching suspicious activity on his vast property. Could this new development be connected to Rebecca's mysterious confrontation with Eastern European thugs?
As events take a dramatic and deadly turn, Rebecca and Cooper must race to uncover the truth - before the sun sets on their future together.

Chapter 1

Rebecca had cleared passport control, picked up her luggage from the carousel, placed it on a trolley, and was now in the customs queue in the Brisbane airport terminal building. Patience was something she had in abundance, and there was nothing else for it but to wait for her turn.

Nothing to declare and light luggage should have seen her through in no time. Like everyone, she was now inching along in the queue.

Since receiving the message in her London office from her client, that Cooper Anders would only deal with a representative of the client company face to face, she had been on the move. Cooper Anders was the owner of a vast tract of land in Australia that her client was particularly interested in, and nothing less than her presence in Australia as representative would do. The Australian had indicated that he did not want to sell, but he was none the less willing to talk. Maybe Rebecca would be the key.

The queue was going nowhere as the customs officers seemed intent on scrutinising every single item that some Hawaiian shirt wearing hippie had stuffed into his bags. All the customs counters were jammed with people, and it was just a waiting game.

Rebecca was vaguely aware of the admiring glances from the men about her, and she was the picture of cool unruffled elegance. She was tall and slim, with regular workouts in the gym giving her skin a healthy glow that no skin cream could enhance. She was not a lean muscle machine, just a healthy young woman in her prime. Her Armani shades were pushed up on her hair line, above a smooth high forehead. Intelligent green eyes shone beneath sweeping natural eyebrows, and long dark lashes. Her dark hair was brushed back for comfort and fell almost to her shoulders in a silken swirl. Her light jacket and pale trousers were immaculate.

The trousers were of a thin material that didn't exactly cling to her, but rather followed every curve of her perfect body from her slim waist, down over her trim little bottom, then falling in a straight line from just above the knee. Just enough movement there to keep the men in the queue behind her transfixed. No one would have thought she had just stepped off a long haul flight from London. Travelling first class had helped of course. She usually flew first class, it was worth the extra, and to those observing her, she looked first class.

Rebecca was heading toward thirty, and while she was active socially, enjoying the company of her colleagues, there was no one man in that life. There just didn't seem to have been time since she had started with Willet, Barber, Links & Boucher - Attorneys at Law, London and New York. That's what she told herself, and any friends who occasionally suggested the company of one or another of the eligible men in their circle.

She was Boucher, the youngest partner the company had ever had. And she was very good at what she did. She had a reputation for being able to see through the cloud of little problems surrounding any case and fixing right to the core of a matter. She was known as a calm, polite, but implacable opponent in the courts. To date, she had never lost a case. This trip was something of a proving ground for her. If she was successful with this mission, her place in the company was assured, and she might finally move up from junior partner.

There had been a young man once. Strong, handsome and honest, who had confessed undying love for her and she for him, before he had shipped out to fight for his country. They had vowed on that last night to wait, to hold a rein on their passions until they could be married. They had shared a

2

dinner the night he left. They had shared a funeral when he was brought home, the victim of a roadside bomb in that far away country. Rebecca drew a deep breath and sighed for lost days. She hadn't been close to a man since. The wound and hurt of that loss had left her feeling so alone and helpless that she had never let anyone get that close to her ever again. She had locked her heart inside a cage and vowed never to let herself be open to such pain ever again.

Her mobile phone beeped with an incoming message from her office. "Cooper Anders waiting for you in the Arrivals Area" was all it said, but she sighed. She had been looking forward to getting to her hotel and finding out what she could about this mysterious Cooper Anders before actually meeting with him. She didn't have a photograph, and there were no other details other than the details of his ownership of this land of interest to her client, and some sketchy personal details. Well, she would meet him soon enough it seemed. He was probably some checked shirt wearing cowboy with a big hat, so he shouldn't be hard to spot in the crowd outside.

The queue inched forward. Finally, the hippie type had been moved on, his tatty canvas hold-all repacked. Within minutes Rebecca was approaching the desk, her small carry-on and laptop hung from her shoulders, and her single suitcase balanced on the unwieldy luggage trolley. The Customs officer waved her through the aisle beside the desk, more intent on those behind her, and she was through and out into the Arrivals area. She was focused on the crowd behind the barriers. Placards raised, hands waving, children crying. Somewhere in that throng there should be a man called Cooper Anders waiting for her. He had better be!

Australia was not a place to be stranded in. Oh, it was safe enough in terms of personal safety, but public transport was abysmal. Taxies were as scarce as hen's teeth and cost an

arm and a leg if you did manage to get one. You didn't want
to take one from the airport into the city. It was a vast
country, and city planners had built the cities as though they
had the entire country to spread out in. So they had.

Rebecca scanned the crowds looking for a placard with her
name on it, perhaps. Or at least the company name. Or even
a country type in a big hat. This was Brisbane Airport, on
the Australian east coast, with a subtropical climate. She had
been here before on business, and once on a holiday that had
taken her to the Great Barrier Reef in the far north. But this
time was no holiday, she was here on business. Her company
specialized in corporate law. Big corporations often had big
problems, and she was very good at smoothing those
problems out. 'This one should be easy' she thought. Just a
cattle station owner resisting a takeover offer from a US
based holding. Her people called it a cattle ranch, but the
Australians called it a cattle station. She knew it was big. She
had done her homework, and the place in question was in
fact larger than a couple of UK counties put together. In
Australia such properties were measured in terms of square
miles, not acres. Rebecca wondered again about three
questions she had as yet unanswered. Why did the US
Corporation want this property so badly, and why was the
Australian owner resisting all offers, friendly and otherwise,
to sell? The biggest question she had personally been why
had the owner insisted on speaking face to face with a
representative, or not at all? Did he want to sell or not? So
she had come all the way out here to find the answers.

She cleared all control gates, and as she moved into the main
terminal area, travellers gradually dispersed and the crowds
thinned.
There was still no sign of anyone looking particularly like a
ranch hand, or anyone with a placard with her name on it.

4

Just a tall, good looking and rather well dressed man approaching her with a smile as open as a new sunny day. His eyes were a dark blue, he had thick dark hair cut fashionably short and his facial lines would make a sculptor cry for their perfection. He was tall - Rebecca realized he was very tall. Easy six foot, and with a few inches on top of that. Broad shoulders and strong brown arms showing from the short sleeved shirt he wore. She recognized a well dressed man when she saw one. Very classy. This man knew how to dress and how to carry himself. He was now right in front of her. Towering over her in fact. She suddenly felt a prickle of reaction wash over her as though someone had nibbled on her ear lobe. Her knees almost gave way. 'Oh My God' she thought, 'what's wrong with me?' Involuntarily she placed her right hand on the man's chest to steady herself, he was that close.

"Are you ok miss?" He said. His rich toned voice washed over her senses. She stepped back in alarm.

"Forgive me. Oh, I'm so sorry. It's been a longer flight than I realized. Please...." Rebecca stopped. Her heart was thumping in her chest as though trying to escape from that steel cage she had it locked in.

She gathered herself together and took a breath. Her normally cool detached self fought to regain control of her senses. He was still smiling at her and had stepped back a pace to give her some room. 'Oh my.' She thought. 'He is one gorgeous man... and here I am babbling like a school girl.' Her skin was still prickling, and she could feel herself responding to him. Rebecca was trying to find something to say that wouldn't sound like babbling again.

He saved her the trouble.

"No worries miss. It's Rebecca isn't it? Your name, I mean. Rebecca Boucher?"

All she could do was stare at him. All of her years of training in some of the best courtrooms in the world, suddenly flown out the window. Her heart was still hammering away in her chest. She was sure her voice quivered when she replied. "Yes, I'm Rebecca Boucher. Do I know you? Ah, of course you must be Cooper Anders." Rebecca fought to regain control of her senses, and set a noncommittal courtroom smile on her face.

"Do you mind if I call you Rebecca?" He said. "I'm Cooper. I believe you are here to meet me; I've been looking out for you."

She was stunned, and Rebecca was not a person easily stunned. Well, this was not going at all the way she had expected, or wanted. It was time to get things back on track. "Cooper. A pleasure to meet you. I wasn't expecting you I must admit. Forgive me for being so… ill prepared, a moment ago. However, I'm sure there will be a hotel driver here somewhere looking for me." Rebecca tried looking past him, but he was too big. Was it just her, or did he really block everything else out of her vision? She took a further step back and looked around.

Cooper turned slightly, so he was not openly confronting her. He exuded self confidence and health, and more than one admiring glance came his way in the crowded hall. He never noticed though. He was totally unaware of his presence. He was watching Rebecca walk away from him along the concourse. He slid his hands into the pockets of his well-cut trousers, thumbs hooked on the outside and casually followed, stepping around some children who had decided that they had done enough walking, and were sitting down right there in the middle of the concourse. Cooper continued to appraise this new woman in his life as he followed her. She was… stunning! He'd never seen anyone like her. He wasn't staring - well not much anyway, he thought with a grin. That cute little behind was something to behold. Just at that moment Rebecca turned around. Her eyes glinting as what she thought she saw. Just another man with lust in his eyes. She did a double take. He wasn't staring or ogling she realized. Simply looking at her. Up and down, with a faint smile of open appreciation on his lips, a smile she noticed that lit up his eyes as well. Now that was a smile. Now that was a man. Rebecca went all prickly again. She spun around and started frantically trying to balance her bag on the trolley. What was it about that man? Suddenly she stopped in her tracks. What had she been thinking? Where was she trying to go? She realized with a start that she had been trying to escape…

She turned to face him again. "I'll be with you in a moment." Rebecca said this as a statement. She had to admit, he was drop dead gorgeous standing there with his thumbs hooked out of his pockets. His waist was the trimmest she had seen on a man, well, forever, and that tight mole skin trouser covered butt was just begging to have her hands clasping him to her. Nice shoes too she noticed as an after thought. She allowed her gaze to travel up the length of him, taking in his muscular body, the solidness of his abdomen evident beneath the light shirt he wore to the broad shoulders of a man used to hard work. She didn't think for a moment he worked out. He was used to working hard and his tanned skin gave his eyes a depth that pierced her to the core. His hair was brushed back and parted on the side and was a lovely auburn-brown colour. The cut looked a little old fashioned actually, but on him it suited. Rebecca smiled. 'A bit like Superman actually,' she thought, without the glasses of Clark Kent. 'Would he be able to perform super human feats in bed?' She shook her head slightly to clear it. 'Get a grip woman' she admonished herself. Cooper seemed not to notice, for which Rebecca was thankful. She didn't want to start off with the wrong reputation.

* * *

She turned suddenly and her suitcase slid from the rattling luggage trolley. Cooper leaned past her, his bare arm almost entwined with hers as he took hold of the suitcase. Rebecca went weak at the knees again. 'What is wrong with me?' She thought in frustration. 'Stop being so stupid.' She suddenly felt very vulnerable and not at all sure that she could carry this negotiation through calmly. All her training had not prepared her for this. A man like this walking into her life. Rebecca looked at Cooper and let him have the suitcase. "Thank you Cooper. Very kind of you." She said. She was sure that the bars of the cage she had welded shut around her heart years before were already beginning to bend.

"It's nothing," he replied. "Would you care to go to your hotel first?" He asked. "I took the liberty of sending your driver away. So I know the hotel. The Sofitel. Very nice. My car is in Valet parking."

"First?" Rebecca almost squeaked. Rebecca didn't do squeaking. She coughed politely behind her hand. "What exactly do you mean by 'first'?" She asked politely.

"Well, I wouldn't want you to waste your time coming all this way for nothing, because as I have already told your client, Innamincka Station is ninety-nine percent not for sale. So I thought perhaps I'd show the place to you first hand. We have a long flight ahead of us in my own small plane if you agree, either today or tomorrow. So I thought you might like to take some time to get over the flight. Have a relaxing meal, and a good nights sleep in a comfortable hotel. The Sofitel is 5 star by the way.?" Cooper ended his little speech with an upward inflection, creating a question of it. Was 5 star good enough?

Rebecca smiled. She liked a man to take charge. Especially when he looked like Cooper, whose smile travelled to his eyes as well as softening the lines of his face. Rebecca found herself gazing wistfully at his lips. Her own lips parted slightly as she licked them with the tiniest tip of her tongue.

Amazing how the aircraft air-conditioning dried the skin. She rummaged in her grip for some lip balm, to cover her involuntary actions.

"Yes, that would be nice. I don't mean you to take all this trouble though." Rebecca smiled to take any sting out of the words. She was not sure of this man, and she discovered that she didn't want to do a thing to give him offence. 'Oh well,' she thought. 'A nice dinner and a good sleep will prepare me for whatever is to come.'

She realised suddenly that he too was probably at the same hotel in that case.

"Are you booked into the same hotel?" Rebecca asked. Well, this was business after all, and it would be nice to have some company over dinner.

"Yes, I am," Cooper replied. "I've had some business in town, and I've been here a week or more now. However, business is finished for now. It's Friday, and no one works past Friday lunch time in this state. So we may as well relax."

They were walking toward the exit doors, and Cooper had signalled the Valet Parking desk to have his car brought over from the valet holding. It should be waiting outside for them when they got there.

Cooper held open the passenger door for her and then put her bags in the trunk. He stepped around to the other side and eased his long frame into the door and sat beside her. The hire car was spacious, quiet and smooth. Especially after the hours of the enveloping roar of the jet, and the noise of the terminal.

Rebecca was taking in the sight of Cooper, sitting there beside her. She was discovering that he was a hard man to take her eyes from. She couldn't keep watching him. He'd surely notice and probably take offence. He certainly didn't say much. A lot of men babbled on, the sound of their own voices filling their ears. Not Cooper. Apparently he spoke when spoken to, or had something of importance to impart. Otherwise, nothing.

Cooper was not especially being quiet though. He was thinking, and he was especially thinking about the woman sitting next to him. 'She is real class. Not just good looking - she is really really good looking.' He could feel the aura of self confidence about her. He knew she would be very good at her job, and although she looked all soft and very ... female, Cooper told himself he had better beware of this one. He found himself lost for how to best describer her to himself. He had been expecting some high-flying tootsie from a sharp New York or London office, all suit and tie, bobbed hair cut and sharp attitude to match her sharp gold nib one-off fountain pen. He had not been expecting this person, and that was for sure. He had been prepared to be polite, but firm and after some preliminary discussion in the security of his own homestead, send her on her way - but now? He was not sure he wanted to send this woman on her way ever. Which was crazy he knew as he'd only just met her less than fifteen minutes ago.

Rebecca settled back in the luxury of the leather upholstery and looked out of the window. She never tired of seeing new places. She never tired of meeting new people, and more like Cooper would be a real bonus, but they were few and far between.

She knew from her pre-trip research that Cooper was not married and had never been married. He was thirty three, just a few years up on her, actually. There was no detail on his current... interests, but someone as good looking as he was would not be wanting for the company of good looking women. She closed her eyes as she lay back against the soft leather. The car was almost silent, the outside traffic noise just a soft shushing in the background. Rebecca was thinking of the soft smile of the man next to her. His strong brown arms and clear blue eyes. The almost neutral smell of him as she had stood oh so close to him in the airport. His lean hard body that seemed to stand like an Oak tree, immovable against her softness. What would he be like in bed? That firm butt emphasised the perfection of the man. Rebecca could feel his stomach muscles rippling under her fingers as she stroked her hand over his midriff, just brushing his leather belt. No fantastic over decorative belt buckle for this man. His didn't need to over state his presence. His upright confidence told all that needed to be told. She let out a soft breath as she saw her finger tips brushing the hardness of his thighs...

Rebecca sprang upright in the seat, eyes blinking open in dismay and the seat belt cutting an unflattering line between her breasts.

"Oh. I.. um, I." She stuttered. Trying to turn to Cooper, she only succeeded in making the seat belt tighten against her. Her breasts were outlined in their perfect proportions, and Cooper was looking straight at them. How could he not? He flicked his eyes back to the road.

"Arrh!" She almost yelled and snatched her hands to her lap to ease the seatbelt. She had dozed off for a second.

"Sorry Cooper. I normally handle jet lag better than this." She didn't even believe the statement herself, but it was the best she had right now. If red was the colour of traffic lights, she would be able to stop whole lines of cars right now. Cooper reached over with his left hand and took her right hand.

"Rebecca, don't worry yourself. The trip has been long and tiring. I know they always are and skipping time zones is very trying. We need to get you to the hotel and rested. After a shower and a nice light meal, you will feel one hundred percent better."

Coming from anyone else, Rebecca would have been alert on the instant. But no, this man meant what he said. She would

11

shower, eat and sleep, while he went to his own rooms. Dam. Did he have to? She knew it was for the best, and there was a lot of work to do. Somehow she had to convince this man that her plans - well, the plans of her client, were the plans he should follow. Never mind what he wanted. For the first time in years, Rebecca felt unsure of her mission.

There was the problem. With a capital P for Problem. One look at this man and you could see that he would never, ever, do what others wanted if it went against his grain, and Rebecca knew that he held onto the property he had because it had been in his family for generations. He was the last heir to a vast cattle property that in any other context would have been called a country. It was all his. No holding companies, no management companies. He lived on the property, in the grand homestead, and he ran it with seeming ease. There were hard men working in the Australian outback, and underneath that smiling exterior sitting next to her she knew lurked a man of iron will. He would have needed it, or the property would have been split up or failed years ago. He was very well educated, with a university degree under his belt, and wealthy beyond the dreams of most men his age. What was it that kept him out there in the lonely central regions of Australia where the country was really mostly desert? Rebecca vowed to keep this in mind. He was 'oh so nice', but she remembered the old adage. Still waters run deep.

The car rolled to a stop outside the hotel doors, and the concierge hurried to open the door on Coopers side. Cooper asked him politely to help the lady first, and amid a flurry of apologies the man hurried around the rear of the car to her side and opened her door. Cooper popped the lid of the trunk so the bags could be retrieved. The bell boys handled Rebecca's small suitcase and carry-on easily. She had kept

12

her laptop with her. Rebecca liked to travel light, and this was her limit. She always travelled first class, so baggage limits on flights were no problem, but it was just so difficult to manage more than one suitcase when travelling alone, so she always did travel light.

Her clothes were all designer labels, but rather than the height of fashion they were more from the business wear end of the market. What ever she wore would look good on her, and she prided herself on looking good when she stepped from the aircraft, no matter how long the flight. Self awareness, confidence, posture, self-assurance, health, minimum makeup, these were all traits that had been instilled into her by her mother and father, and maintained throughout her college days, and were now just a normal core part of her. It had been a good investment, because when she walked into an office or restaurant, or a court room she turned every head. She had the same effect in hotel foyers. The concierge knew class when he saw it. This woman was of the finest and he hurried to escort her to reception. It took but a moment and her bags were whisked away to her room on the fourteenth floor. The formalities at the desk completed, Rebecca turned to look for Cooper. He was no where to be seen. She turned back to reception, noting that it was just after three pm, and she admitted to feeling a little jet-lagged. A freshen up would be nice.

"Excuse me, but did you see where Mr Anders went? The gentleman with me a moment ago."

The girl blinked and shook her head. "I'm sorry madam, I didn't notice." She said.

"No matter. Thank you all the same."

The concierge escorted her to the lift and indicated the fourteenth floor button.

"Enjoy you stay with us madam. I set the lift to take you directly non-stop, for your convenience. Mr Anders has asked if you will join him in the Privé 249 restaurant and bar

13

when you are rested." With that he withdrew, leaving her alone while the lift whisked her up to the fourteenth floor. A short walk took her along the hall to room four, one of the Superior Rooms. There were others on floors above, luxury rooms far in excess of her needs. This was a business trip of course, and she needed space to be in, rather than somewhere to simply enjoy the luxury for it's own sake. The rooms were lovely. Spacious, and with a sweeping view of the city. Entering the bedroom, she carefully slipped off her waist-coat and blouse and hung them in the wardrobe, the trousers followed next, letting them slip to the floor with a whisper of material. The long mirror on the door of the wardrobe showed her to full advantage, and she turned slowly in front of it, checking for blemishes that may have magically appeared during the flight. She smoothed her palms down over her full breasts and on down over her stomach and smoothing around over her firm butt. She liked to wear a thong normally, but for travelling preferred her almost prim cotton-tails as she called them.

Rebecca enjoyed her body and was quietly pleased that she was a beautiful woman. She knew she was, with that confidence that came from her inner core. She looked now at her shape and wondered how it would fit against the solid shape of Cooper. It would be interesting to find out. Suddenly she unhooked her bra and snapped down her panties, tossing both onto the bed as she headed into the shower. The water gushed from a large shower head and fell in a torrent like tropical rain, washing down over her and washing away the tensions of the trip. She smiled as she imagined Cooper sharing the shower with her. What would he be like? Passionate, quick, too fast for her? Or slow and careful, able to bring her slowly to a climax. Well, perhaps she would get a chance to find out.

Rebecca was a little surprised with herself, and her obvious reaction to the presence of Cooper. This had the promise of being a good trip. A pleasant interlude. A very presentable man to dally away the spare time with. The prospects of a good husband even.

Rebecca stood bolt upright in the shower, and switched the control off, ending the water spay immediately. Where on Earth had that come from? A husband. Not on your sweet life. What was happening to her? She stood in front of the bathroom mirror, towelling herself dry a little over vigorously, and muttering.

"What are you thinking of? That came right out of left field. The last thing I want in my life now is a husband. Got it?" She waved a finger at the reflection in the mirror. "Got it!" She repeated.

She went back into the bedroom, and drew her clothes out of the suitcase and began to hang them in the wardrobe, and put the personal things in the side table draws. Her clothes required nothing more than a shake to have them looking like new. They were expensive clothes, and she expected no less from them. She slipped on a pair of her favourite briefs, a bright red rose over pale blue silk. Totally un-business like, but then she never expected she would have to display them at a board room table. The thought made her chuckle. Bra and blouse followed, and she slipped on a modest knee length evening skirt, dark green to match her eyes, and the little blue flowers sprinkled across her blouse. Top button undone? Maybe top two buttons.

She was back on target. Not a husband, but a successful conclusion to her task was the mission.

Chapter 2

Cooper waited patiently in the lounge bar. There had been no real reason to meet with Rebecca, other than curiosity. He knew why she was here of course, and rather than have a room full of his own lawyers deal with her, he thought he would be much better off dealing with this issue directly. He had no intention of selling what was in effect his birth right, but he was interested in the sudden interest being shown by a foreign company. Cooper's father had died after a long illness some years before, and his mother had died when he was a child. There were no siblings, so the property was entirely his. It was not only his birth right, but he loved it. He loved the wide open spaces, the hardness of the land, it's stark beauty. The quietness. On a cold winter night under the stars, when even the insects had been stilled, you could almost hear the earth turning. He had to admit to himself though that he was growing a little tired of being on his own out there. So tinged with his interest in the foreign company, was the vague notion that it might be time to see what a busier world had to offer. A world with Rebecca in it, perhaps? Perhaps put his university degree to some use. He had originally gone back to the property to help his father, but now he too was gone and Cooper had to admit to himself in his quieter moments that it all seemed a little directionless. He hadn't even managed a girl friend for so long now he was wondering how he would manage one now, such was his unfamiliarity with the fairer sex. Familiar people in his life had slowly drifted away with their own lives to worry about, and his life was getting quieter and quieter.

Rebecca entered the lounge, looking casually about for Cooper. She wanted to know what his plans were. She had her own ideas of how any business discussions should proceed and didn't have the slightest intention of flying anywhere with anyone. Certainly not with Cooper Anders.

"Rebecca." She heard her name spoken softly. Cooper stood next to an elegant table to one side of the entrance. "Would you care to join me?" He asked. Rebecca paused and gave him a long steady look and a nod before continuing past him and approaching the small bar. She took in his strong jawline and finely chiselled nose in a face, that while given a pleasant cast by his beautiful eyes, was none the less the face of a strong character. His skin was smooth and tanned. He didn't sport the latest fashion of a few days' stubble growth. Rebecca was pleased about this, for one she thought it an affectation, and two - he didn't need to make any statements about his masculinity. His obvious confidence in himself as a man was all he needed. A slight smile crinkled the corners of his mouth.

Rebecca had forgotten for a moment why she had gone directly to the bar. Cooper's good looks and animal magnetism, his underlying sexuality, had sent butterflies skittering through her stomach. She had never been so strongly, so physically attracted to a man before in her life, not since her lost love, and she hardly knew this man at all. She drew a deep breath and turned to the young woman behind the bar. "Could you pass me any messages to Rebecca Boucher, please? I'm expecting word from London at any time."

"Certainly mam," the girl replied, and scribbled a note for the reception staff as well.

Rebecca walked slowly back to the table where Cooper sat waiting for her. She took her time, moving very slowly. She wanted to take him in visually before she started talking to him. Up to now she hadn't had much chance, having been taken by surprise at the airport, and at that time still very much disoriented from the long flight. He had risen to his feet again, the perfect gentleman.

"Cooper. You do realise that essentially we are not on the same side of this business arrangement?" Rebecca said.

"Rebecca, please. Let's not talk business right now. Come, join me. Enjoy some down time with me." Cooper pulled back a chair for Rebecca.

As much as this man electrified her, she had to remember why she was here. It struck her that he may actually be trying to disarm her. Get her to drop her guard. It was always much more difficult to drive a hard bargain with someone you loved .... liked! Liked. Not loved. Rebecca almost stamped her foot. OMG, he was gorgeous. So no, she would not kick back and relax with him. She would share a table and a drink as any civilised person would be expected to do, and then order dinner.

Rebecca sat on the opposite side of the table to Cooper. She raised her gaze to his intense blue eyes. He was focused entirely on her. Oh, that felt nice.

"Where exactly is your - um... homestead? that is, in relationship to where we are now." She asked.

"Well, basically due west, and a little south of west. We straddle the borders of the states of South Australia, The Northern Territory, and Queensland. Probably a bit of New South Wales as well. You might say the place is in a good position. The homestead is in the South Australian part."

Rebecca couldn't help but look a little puzzled. It sounded like he was describing a small country out there somewhere. Cooper flicked over a coaster and did a quick sketch with his pen. "Do you know the size of the place we are talking about?" He asked.

"Well no, not really. The paperwork seemed a little vague about that. I assume it's an error in transcription. Because the size mentioned is thirteen thousand five hundred and fifty two square kilometres. That's at least six times the size of the largest ranch in the US."

"Yep," replied Cooper. "That'd be about right. It's pretty big, but mostly marginal country. You know, desert, sand dunes, that sort of thing. Of course, I'm not there alone."

Rebecca's heart sank. Here it comes. 'not alone'. He was married, and it had not made it into her paperwork. She didn't know why, but she felt disappointed.

"Oh, well of course not." Rebecca said. She struggled to keep her voice neutral. "I mean, a man needs company, just as a woman does. Which leads me to ask why didn't you bring her with you?"

'That stopped him', thought Rebecca. Cooper was looking at her with a strange look on his face.

"Her?" He asked. "Who her? Bring who with me? " He was now looking confused. 'Was this woman slightly off her trolley? What, or actually who, was she talking about?' He didn't have any female staff out there.

"I don't have any female staff on the station," he said. "And as for female company, well there is no shortage of very attractive young ladies scattered across the outback. Just none working for me or living near me, and none resident... at the moment." He added after a pause. For the first time since he had met Rebecca, Cooper began to see Rebecca in an entirely new light. Why had she suddenly gone all spiky at the mention of other people - other women in fact, in his life. He gave her an appraising look from under his long eyelashes. There was no doubt she was a stunner. Very slim, long straight legs that seemed to go on forever and the cutest bottom he had ever seen. Small waist and well proportioned breasts. Beautiful clear green eyes that were watching him watching her, with lively intelligence behind them. Not over long hair, now swept back in a functional rather than a fashionable style. He was not a man given to day dreaming, but looking at this woman had started his blood racing, and he crossed his legs by the table to hide any sign he felt would give him away in an instant if she noticed. He coloured faintly around the collar of his shirt.

What had he been doing? He hadn't found himself responding so strongly to a woman in a long time. A woman he hardly knew, other than what he had been told. Was she expecting him to have a wife? Surely his file would indicate the lack of one. Perhaps it was not detailed enough to include girl friends, but that hardly counted. He didn't think he was ready for a wife yet. He thought he had his life planned out ahead of him, for himself and the cattle station. There was no where in the plan for a wife. The distraction of a wife. Children, pets, relations, there was too much work to do.

"No Rebecca, there is no little wife waiting back on the station. No girlfriend either. I doubt there ever will be, living way out there where I do. There's nothing. The nearest shops are a few hours by plane away. No hospitals, no schools, no neighbours. No little white picket fences."

Cooper sounded almost apologetic, and not a little sharpness had crept into his tone. But that was life. That's where he lived, and to date the one or two women who had seen where he lived couldn't get off the place quick enough. He had no doubt this one would certainly prove to be the same. He realized for the first time that this was a mistake. Meeting this woman, indeed any representative of the foreign company was a mistake, and one he would now have to put right.

Rebecca simply looked at him. She had noted the rise in colour under his collar, and the hastily crossed legs and thought she knew the reason. His slow appraisal of her had also been noticed. She was not a little girl any more and knew pretty much how things worked. The idea that she had caused his arousal pleased her. It also caused those butterflies in her lower stomach to start fluttering again. It was not going to influence her now though. She had a job to do. She smiled sweetly and said "Are we going to have a drink, or sit here watching each other for the evening. Something light to eat would be nice too. Even in first class the food leaves a lot to be desired." There were very few others in the room at the moment as it was still early. Rebecca stood up and walked the length of the lounge, admiring the view outside. She need to stretch her legs a little and settle her thoughts. She noticed that Cooper had ordered drinks for both of them. 'Good'. She liked a man to take charge without being overbearing, and small gestures like that proved his capacity for being in control.

As she sat back down the drinks were delivered. A Whisky by the smell of it. Teachers perhaps. Or Glen Livet? Definitely Glen Livet. A jug of water, and a small bottle of Dry accompanied the order. Rebecca liked hers on the rocks. Within moments a selection of nuts and sweetmeats appeared beside the table on a small cart. Cooper raised an eyebrow as Rebecca smiled in appreciation. "Is there anything specifically you might like, Rebecca?" He asked. "No thank you Cooper, this will do nicely until dinner later." She replied. She would have loved a lot more, but she wasn't about to blurt that out to Cooper in the middle of the lounge. His voice flowed over her like molten lava, melting her inside, her heart thumping against her chest. There didn't seem to be a lot to say suddenly as they sat there nursing their drinks. As she had guessed, Cooper was a man of few words, but what he had said indicated a love of his home, and if she wanted him talking, then the best subject might just be that. Not only could she listen to his voice for as long as he wanted to talk, it might be good to know just how deeply he was attached to this small kingdom he owned. For it was a kingdom. Certainly larger than some European kingdoms.

Again it crossed her mind, that she had no real idea why the US Corporation that had engaged her services through her company, wanted to purchase this remote cattle property. She determined to find out this very night with a few discretely placed calls later on. There were some unanswered questions about this whole deal. For example, what happened if something happened to Cooper. What happened to this vast property? Who were the beneficiaries? Rebecca leaned forward to rest her arms on the table. "Tell me about your home. About where you live. I'm interested to hear what would keep a man out in such a lonely place at such cost."

"Well," he began "quite apart from the financial side of things, it is my home. Born and raised. My parents lived there. I was born there. Actually born there. A number of generations of my family have gone before me. It's a wild place. There are still nomadic aboriginals living there. Not many, mind you, but we do see them from time to time, and the station workers know generally where they are at any one time and tend to avoid them if possible. Although usually it's the other way around. Most of the station workers are themselves aboriginal Australians. We have a few Europeans - white Australians if you like, in the workshops, and driving the trucks that bring the cattle in to the markets and other work." Cooper sat back and thought for a bit. Rebecca could see in his eyes he was now far away from her.

"Yes, let me see. In the workshop, two tradesmen, a mechanic/engineer and a diesel fitter. A grader driver. We have a helicopter pilot. The head stockman is Darcy, he's a local aboriginal, as are all the stockmen. It was their place in the beginning. There's Old Bill the grader driver. He's an x-stockman. Been on the place since Adam was a boy. He's too old now for stock work, but he can still climb up into the cabin of the road grader."

Cooper smiled at the memory of the old man. He had taken Cooper over most of the vast property during the years as he kept service roads clear and pushed new tracks into temporary stock yards for the trucks. Cooper had loved those days, before he had been sent away to boarding school to finish his higher education, then on to university.

His father even by then had been very ill and was almost incapable of running the vast property any longer. He has issued his instructions from the wide shady veranda of the homestead, and his staff - most of whom were his friends as well, saw that everything moved along smoothly.

Cooper had spent every holiday at home and often flew back home from the city of Toowoomba on weekends to be with his father. He had brought along friends of course, and now and then a young lady. But none had stayed. The girls from other cattle and sheep properties scattered across the vast country either went back to their own homes to take up running their family stations, or they shunned the bush forever. Cooper had never asked anyone to stay, and although he missed their company, he had not complained or bowed to the pressure to move into the cities. He didn't hate the cities. He just didn't feel comfortable in them. No horizons, and too many people.

Cooper spoke softly as he recounted this patchwork of his life in the vast wilderness of the Australian 'outback'.

Rebecca hadn't said a word, just sipped at her drink. She had raised a hand to the waiter and indicated fresh drinks as Cooper spoke. She could listen to him forever. She was jealous of his love for his home. If only he was able to love her as much as that. Rebecca sighed. No man could love two mistresses, no matter what they said, and his land was obviously his first love.

Well, she had a job to do. The sooner she started now, the easier it would be on her, and on him. She had no doubt that he would eventually give in to the offers of the US Corporation she was representing. New World Holdings. What they held seemed to be very eclectic in Rebecca's ideas. Everything from waste management to air freight and a lot of things in between. There was even a small nuclear power plant in Europe in the mix somewhere. Big players with deep pockets. They did have cattle ranches, both in the

US, and in Argentina, and Rebecca could only surmise that this vast property held by only one man seemed like easy picking for them. Hers not to reason why.

This was going to be a tough mission. Cooper had refused to even speak with anyone but herself and only face to face. He had refused the entry of a legal team into the discussion, either his own, or hers. He would talk directly to Rebecca, as the representative of New World Holdings out of courtesy, and no one else.

"Have you heard of New World Holdings before this offer was made via our law firm?" She asked out of the blue.

Cooper snapped his jaw shut and his lips became a thin line. His eyes glittered. Rebecca had never seen this before. Not like this. His eyes literally glittered, with a light like the reflection from the core of a diamond in them. She involuntarily moved back from the table a little. The man radiated danger like a heat wave. Yet he hadn't moved a muscle, other than to stop talking, and really focus his attention on her. A long silence followed. Then he relaxed a little and said.

"I prefer to not talk about this whole thing until you have seen Innamincka. We will fly out first thing in the morning if that's ok with you?" From the sound of his voice, Rebecca guessed that if she said no, then all talks were off, and her entire mission would be a failure. "But in answer to your question, yes, I had heard of them."

Cooper visibly made the effort to relax. He reached for Rebecca's hand across the table. She almost drew it back in alarm. She hadn't got over the sudden change in him moments ago.

"Please. I apologise. I can see that I have upset you. That's the last thing I want to do." The feel of her small hand in his huge palm softened him to the core. No physical reaction this time to her, just overwhelming tenderness. She was so fragile. He had never felt anyone to be as - yes, fragile - as

24

this woman. Oh sure, he had no doubt she had a good business head on her and would take no prisoners in a court of law. However, he doubted if she could even stand up to a strong wind. Perhaps the bush was no place for her after all. Was he compounding the mistake already made? Was insisting she step right out of her comfort zone and into his a mistake? He was beginning to think that perhaps it was. And all because he could feel her softness in that tiny hand. Which he hadn't let go of yet.

Rebecca looked from his face to her hand and back again. His eyes had softened again, and the little smile lines were back. His hand holding hers was huge. She could feel the muscles in it, tense but at rest. His long fingers were smooth and his nails short and clean. For a man who lived alone, he still knew how to care for himself. She had met ranchers in many countries, and those that still worked the land themselves seemed to delight in carrying it with them under their fingernails. Ugh! What was it about men without women in their lives?

This man was an enigma to her. He was unlike any man she had ever met. Nothing at all like the men in her office back in London, or even New York. She let out a sigh.

"Shall we call a truce then? I'm sorry I brought up business at this moment. I shall start respecting your customs as of now." Rebecca withdrew her hand slowly from his. Her skin was tingling as though a small electric current was coursing through her hand. It shook slightly as she lifted her drink to her lips, the ice tinkling against the glass.

"Customs?" He questioned.

"TGIF Cooper. Thank God It's Friday. No business after midday you said." She smiled as she watched his face.

"Ah." Was all he said.

"Is it permissible under these strange new customs to talk about personal things, between a man and a woman?" Rebecca asked with a slightly bantering tone to her voice.

Chapter 3

"Of course Rebecca. May I start in that case? I'd really like
to know more about you."

'Hmmm,' Rebecca thought 'was this a good idea?' She
nodded and smiled.

"What would you like to know that you don't already know?"
She said.

Cooper sat silently for a moment. He was not sure how to
start now that he had made the opening gambit in this little
game that he seemed to have started.

"Well. Let's see. You already know why I'm not married. The
tyranny of distance to borrow a phrase. What is your
excuse?" He smiled broadly and took her free hand again to
take any sting or impropriety out of his words. He held her
hand by the fingers, up in the air slightly and seemed intent
on studying them.

Rebecca was speechless. Not because of the question, but
because of the feeling that surged through her at the feel of
her fingers in his warm hand. 'Oh my this was difficult' she
thought.

"I..." She started. "I was to be married once some years ago.
He was killed in Afghanistan by an IED. We never even..."
She choked on the words, tears suddenly flooding down her
face. She jumped to her feet and rushed for the lady's room.
Cooper was half risen to his feet, staring after her. 'What
have I done?' He worried. 'Stupid. What a stupid thing to ask
a beautiful and sensitive woman. Too long in the bush with
nothing but cattle and flies for company.' He sat back down
and worried at his bottom lip. So she had been about to be
married once. Not all fire and ice then. His question had
really touched a nerve. So her intended had been a veteran.
Cooper felt a little sad at her loss.

He waited some minutes for her return, but she was not
coming back it seemed. He signalled to the waiter to clear
away the drinks and snack trays.

He looked again toward the restrooms, and it was then he noticed the two heavy set men in dark suits, white shirts and dark ties, sitting silently in a far corner to the left of the entry to the lounge.

He did a double take, and they both seemed to be very intent on studying their menus. Although even from here Cooper could tell one menu at least was upside down. There were some strange people about and that was a fact. He looked again for Rebecca. He couldn't very well go into the lady's room looking for her, so he just settled in to wait. He waved the waiter away again. 'Ok, that hadn't gone at all well.' He thought to himself. 'Face it Cooper, you have no idea at all when it comes to high class women do you. She's... too nice to let slip through my fingers because I'm an unsophisticated country bumpkin.' He shook his head in disgust with himself.

Rebecca meantime having fled to the rest room, had been dabbing cool water on her cheeks and eyes, and drying it off with tissue. Luckily she didn't wear much makeup, so she didn't have any repair work to do. Just to her pride. She couldn't believe what had happened. She thought she had got all the crying out of her system years ago. It seemed not. Something about Cooper and his attention, even his looks, had triggered emotions she had kept buried now for a long time.

She couldn't imagine what Cooper must be thinking. Maybe he had left already. It had taken some time for the sobbing to stop, and the tears to stop flowing.

Well it solved one problem anyway she thought. There was no way that gorgeous hunk of a man would ever take her as anything but a bawling, over emotional female now.

Rebecca picked up her grip and left the restroom. To her surprise Cooper was still there. She went directly to him, and without sitting down, suggested they go to the restaurant immediately. Dinner was a quiet affair. Neither of them willing to broach the subject that had set Rebecca's emotions into free-fall. They sipped their wine and made small talk, both avoiding even direct eye contact.

Rebecca finally said to Cooper. "I will go with you to your property. Your cattle station, in the morning. What time do you wish to depart?"

Cooper sighed. He was regretting the decision he had made to get her to look at where he lived. He should have simply said a flat 'No sale' and left it at that. He couldn't understand what it was that had prompted him in the first place. When Rebecca's arrangements were being made to come to Australia, he had decided on the spur of the moment that he would at least have the pleasure of her company for a few days before he turned her clients down flat, assuming who ever she was would accept the invitation.

Well, she was nothing like he had imagined. Indeed, she was stunningly attractive, sophisticated, well dressed, and looked to Cooper like she had just stepped out of the pages of Cosmo or some similar magazine. But a mistake was a mistake and he wouldn't agonise over it. She would never entertain the thought of him as anything other than a client now, after his crass behaviour of a short time ago.

"Rebecca." Cooper looked at the table and swirled his red wine in his glass. He looked up again. "Perhaps you would rather not have to go all the way out there with me now after all?" He didn't smile, and his face had a far away look on it as he was picturing his home being no more than a house again when he got back there - alone again. He couldn't believe how much it was affecting him this time. "I'm sorry I've upset you. But there it is. We can conduct any business we have, right here in this hotel, which has an excellent business centre. Then you will be able to go directly back to the UK, or where ever your business takes you."

'Well, that's it then.' Thought Rebecca. 'I really blew it that time didn't I? Now he's begging off the trip'

"If that's what you think Cooper." Rebecca was disappointed. She found she had been looking forward to spending some time with Cooper after all, apart from business. But she had certainly messed that up. Crying and running off like a teenager.

"We can meet tomorrow morning if you like, in the Business Suite. We can discuss what ever has to be discussed so that I can take the paper work back to the clients. I'm sorry I've ruined your plans." She grimaced slightly in disappointment and pushed her chair back to stand up. A waiter was there immediately helping.

Without further discussion she turned and left Cooper sitting at the dinner table. She kept a stiff back and head held high until she managed to exit the restaurant and approached the elevators. She was crest fallen, and couldn't believe how she had behaved so unprofessionally. It served her right. She should have taken charge of their meeting right there at the airport. She just hadn't expected Cooper to be so, so - so gorgeous. She felt herself flushing with emotion again as she thought of his rugged good looks.

Rebecca stepped into the elevator and turned to face the doors just as two heavy set men pushed through them, forcing them to spring apart again. They stood in the small space, one either side of Rebecca. She was feeling a little intimidated by their size, one either side of her like that. They seemed vaguely familiar, and she wondered where she had seen them before.

Was she hearing things? One of them had spoken to her. She was sure of it. With an unmistakable East European accent, the one on her left had said something to her.

She looked to her left slightly, trying not to make eye contact. "I beg your pardon?" She said.

"Not to beg pardon lady. You will push button to go to basement car park." He said.

A chill ran down her spine. She was being mugged, and here in Australia, in one of it's finest hotels.

She gasped out. "I will do no such thing. Who do you think you are? You have the wrong person."

She realised immediately that it was a stupid thing to say. Obviously they thought they had the right person, but what did they want?

"We have right person." The man said, hardly moving his face as he spoke. Instead of saying anything further he leant forward and pushed the basement button, the moment that the elevator stopped at her floor. The door opened and Rebecca made a dash for freedom. Or she tried. She found herself held either side in an iron grip on each upper arm. There was another couple waiting to get in the elevator, but they stepped back in alarm as the other man, on her right said brusquely.

"Take other lift." Rebecca noticed he too had that East European accent. She had travelled throughout Europe, on business as well as pleasure and thought she could place this pair in one of the 'stans'. Uzbekistan maybe. What was that one the Russians were having so much trouble with? Chechen? In any case, she was too shocked for the moment to be truly scared.

"Let me GO." She said vehemently. "You will regret this. Do you know who I am? My friend will deal with you."

Neither of the men spoke a word more to her as the elevator car sped down to the basement. They hustled her out when the elevator stopped and almost carried her to a long black car that was idling in one of the darker parking bays. The windows were smoked glass, and she couldn't see who was sitting inside. She thought of screaming, but there was no one to hear her anyway down here. The rear window of the car slid down, and a deep voice spoke from the interior.

"You will after all go out to the cattle property of Mr Anders? Good. We require that you personally check him and his paperwork and report back to me with a positive result for the sale."

Rebecca realised in amazement that she knew the person inside. It was her client. She was totally confused for a moment.

"But, its thousands of square miles. I can't possibly do that." Rebecca gasped.

"Not whole property Miss Boucher. Just the paperwork of ownership held there." The window slid back into place. Rebecca realised with a start that he too had that unmistakable Eastern European accent. The window slid down a fraction again. "Put her back in lift. Hurry. Goodbye Miss Boucher."

The two body guards almost carried her back to the lift, and none too gently propelled her into it. She stumbled forward toward the rear as the doors whispered closed.

Rebecca frantically scrabbled for the button of the restaurant floor. Perhaps Cooper was still there. She had to find him and tell him what had happened. There was no way these people were going to get away with this. they had as good as kidnapped her and told her she had to do something she had originally been going to do in the first place. This didn't make a bit of sense.

Frustratingly the elevator sped her directly to her own floor, and the doors opened. To her great relief and obvious surprise Cooper was about to step into the elevator. He looked at her with sudden concern.

"What happened?" He asked, holding the doors open. "I've been looking for you." She was white and shaking as she gripped his arm for support and stepped out of the lift. Rebecca recounted the events since she had left him to return to her room just a short while ago. That she had decided as they spoke over dinner to call this whole meeting thing off, but now? What now?

Cooper paced back and forth, his face like thunder. The rage burning in him directed at the hooligans who had manhandled such a fine woman at this. He remembered the smallness of her hand in his, and his feelings toward her when he had contemplated that fact.

"Perhaps we should rethink that decision to end our discussion here Rebecca." He stated as he swivelled toward her. "There is something very odd going on here, and I'd like you where I can keep an eye on your safety, while I delve into this a bit further. I will not have you rough handled by foreign thugs."

Cooper wished he had taken a bit more notice of those two in the lounge bar earlier.

"I was looking for you to ask you to reconsider." He added. "I really would like you to see where I live." Cooper was almost pleading, and a hint of it showed in his voice, surprising Rebecca a little as it came across, even over her own current anxiety at her recent rough handling.

Rebecca had calmed down by now and looked at Cooper. "I am not doing anything because those people want me to. Not now. And why do you want me out there if you have no intention of selling? Especially after being bullied by those thugs, I do not feel at all like wasting my time on a fruitless journey into the outback, for what I now know to be no good reason." Cooper reached for her as she had by now stepped back a little, regaining her composure.

"… And don't touch me please. This has been a very strange day from beginning to end. I'm going into my room to rest. If you have anything further to add, I will meet you again tomorrow in the business centre at 9am. Good night." Rebecca turned on her heel and went to her room, closing the door forcefully behind her. 'This was not the end of things, not by a long shot.' She thought, grabbing up her laptop she flipped it open and opened Skype.

She didn't care what time it was on the other side of the world; this could not wait. The first call was to her research assistant in her office in London. The girl, Kali Surinam, never slept it seemed, so Rebecca had no qualms about calling her. Finally, she answered the call,

"Yes Rebecca. What can I help with?"

Rebecca drew a small breath. "I want all the details you can get me on the business of New World Corporation. I don't mean company names and the like. I mean the information that can't be found easily by looking at company registration records. Anything at all that strikes you as… of interest to us. To me. Especially information about the company president, Usman Abbas. Can you get back to me within the next couple of hours? It is urgent."

"Shouldn't be a problem Rebecca. You look terrible. Bad flight?" Kali commented.

"No Kali, just something that has happened here since my arrival. This seemingly innocuous brief has just turned into something we may not want to be involved in. Thanks for asking. Get back to me." With that, Rebecca ended the call. The next call was to Charles Willet, the senior partner. It had been through him that the company had passed the brief to Rebecca in the first place.

Charles answered the call. "Good morning Rebecca. My, you look terrible!" He said with a worried look.

"Charles, you're the second person in as many minutes to tell me that. However, it's not why I've called. Well maybe it partly is. What do you know about New World Corporation? Do you have any background on them, anything that may have come to your attention when you considered the case for our firm?"

"Sorry Rebecca." He answered. "The request came in through the front office. The company requested our services, we checked their bona fides and their bank, and accepted the brief. It seemed straight forward enough. Talk a reluctant owner into completing a property sale was the under laying brief, although it was presented simply as representing the company, New World in the transaction. Which for some reason had to be done face to face with the seller in Australia, by us. The brief landed on your desk." Charles hesitated a moment then asked.

"What's happened Rebecca? Anything we should know about?"

"No, not at this stage. However, New World Corporation may not be a company we can do business with. Just so you know."

"What about Mr Anders?" Asked Charles. "What's his position? Do you think he may have had some inkling as to the nature of the people he was dealing with?"

"Well I'm not sure, but if he didn't before, he certainly knows now, and I don't think he is any too happy about it. I have Kali doing some research for me on the company as well." Rebecca tapped her chin with one finger. She was thinking about Cooper and his reactions to everything that had happened, including his reaction to her.

"Charles, I'll get back to you. I have some reading to do." Rebecca poised her fingers over the hang-up key.

"Ok Rebecca, keep me posted. We are happy to go with what ever your decision is regarding this brief. To proceed, or to drop it. Up to you." With that he hung up.

Rebecca left the laptop running, with Skype open. She hoped that Kali would get back to her sooner rather than later. She had to think about what to do next. So far, her role in this whole thing had remained as defined. Talk directly with Cooper Anders. The arrival of the client on the scene was totally unexpected, and she could not even begin to guess at his reasons.

Some thought was required. Rebecca poured herself a glass

of red wine from the mini-bar and kicked off her shoes. She sat on the comfortable arm chair by the window, and took in the night view, swirling the rich red wine around in her glass. First things first. She had to work out if she was even going to continue with this whole brief. The arrival of the client right there at the hotel, and with his thugs doing his work for him, put a whole new spin on the operation.

Then there was Cooper. What was his game really? As nice as he was, and Rebecca thought wistfully of some of those good points, in the end he too was here for a reason. A reason that she was sure hadn't yet been made clear to her. She didn't believe for a moment that he was here simply to tell a company representative to their face that he wasn't interested in selling. Well, her researcher back in the office would track down any information on the client company that might prove interesting, so it was up to her to see what she could find out what Cooper was up to. This didn't seem like an unpleasant task at all, but Rebecca had to remember to keep her wits about her, because his good looks and natural charm could well act as a smoke screen to his true intentions regarding this deal that he was professing so much un-interest in. Rebecca opened Google and searched for the property name. She could only find a reference to a small town out in the same area. Presumably this was where the cattle station drew its name from. Innamincka, population twelve. And the surrounding region looked like pure desert. Well, Cooper did say it was a lonely outpost. She picked up the house phone. Maybe Cooper was in, and she need to talk to him. Tomorrow may be too late.

"Reception, could you connect me to Mr Anders room please?"

"One moment please." Reception replied.

"Rebecca here Cooper. I'm glad you are in. I thought you may have been out on the town, and I only rang on the off chance. Do you have a few minutes?" Cooper replied he did. "Good, can we meet again in the bar? No wait. Can you come to my room please? I don't want prying eyes or ears nearby."

It wasn't until Rebecca hung up that she realized what she had done. It was never a good idea to invite a stranger - and Cooper was a stranger - to her room. It was a rule she had had for years. Only very very good friends and family got to visit where she lived, even if it was only a hotel room.

Well I can hardly ring back now and change the location, and look like a complete fool.' She thought to herself. She put her shoes back on, checked herself in the mirror, and straightened her skirt. This was a business meeting, and Cooper had better realize it.

A knock at the door and two paces to open it, and Cooper stood on the threshold. Rebecca stood back holding the door open. Still, he didn't enter.

"Come in please Cooper." Rebecca beckoned politely. A small wave of a somewhat unsteady hand.

"Are you sure Rebecca?" Cooper looked at her steadily. What was in his eyes she wondered.

"Look, there are things we need to sort out. Not the least of which is why you are here at all insisting on a face-to-face meeting, regardless of who from our company turns up here." Rebecca set her lips in a compressed line. She meant to keep this meeting formal and direct, even if as she spoke she was looking at his lips, slightly parted as though he was about to say something and thus formed into an archers bow that looked oh so irresistible. So... kissable. She spun about and stepped back into the room toward the sofa and comfortable lounge chairs that occupied the window wall side of the room. A wave of her hand indicating to Cooper to pick a seat anywhere.

Cooper was by now right behind her as she stopped. She didn't dare turn around or she would find herself almost in his arms so close could she feel him. She could feel the warmth of his body emanating from him.

Rebecca found herself with only leg space to step around a chair to move across the open space to the single sofa chair on the far side of the little rectangle.

Cooper waited for her to sit down, then slowly settled himself into a chair about as far away from her as he could get.

His face was immobile. Set like a mask. There was no sign of the smiling open man Rebecca had met at the airport. He was determined not to let this far too attractive woman undermine his resolve, and if she thought inviting him to her room would do it, she was sadly mistaken. He noticed her hands. Her right hand was still held slightly aloft from her lap, and was visible shaking. Not much, but it was. 'So, she is not sure of something.' He thought. He was a good reader of people he had found although he was sure this skill did not apply to women in general. Perhaps not to this one in particular. He would wait and see.

Although he was determined not to give anything away in his expression, none the less he couldn't help but look at Rebecca. If she wasn't actually, well, opposition, he may find her company very pleasurable. As it was, he would just have to admire her from afar. But by the saints, she was beautiful. She was in fact everything he admired in a woman and had as yet not found.

"Well let's see, Rebecca. How can I help? What questions do you have for me?"

Rebecca hesitated before saying. "Would you like a glass of something? Wine, Whisky, Bourbon perhaps? Beer even?" She had heard Australians liked beer. She picked up her wine glass trying to steady her minutely shaking hand. "The mini bar is well stocked and you may feel free to help yourself. I am expecting a call back from my office in London, so don't be concerned if you hear the computer making strange noises."

"Nothing for the moment thanks." Replied Cooper.

Rebecca drew a breath. "It seems to me that you have an agenda of your own Cooper." She paused. "I know I'm on the other side of this deal, supposedly. Yet I have the feeling that both you and our client have placed me in the middle of something here. I don't like being in this position I can tell you."

"I don't know that I owe your client any leeway, and by implication nor you." Replied Cooper, his face still impassive, giving nothing away. His mind however was racing.

He added, "However, as you have obviously been sent out here, rather than someone else, to... distract me," and he thought to himself '... and doing a fine job of it', "this whole business is not your doing. With you I will be honest. Those thugs that man-handled you have really made me angry. They had no right to do that. Sit back and let me give you the full story. If you are still talking to me after that will at least be something I can be thankful for."

'Distract me.' He thought. That's exactly what may have been the motives of the Corporation bent on acquiring his place. Was Rebecca party to that deception, to that distraction? He hoped not. He would find out. Now.

"Are you here to distract me?" He said aloud, his tone less than pleasant, before Rebecca could respond to his first statement. "Did you and your client think that by putting a beautiful woman in front of me I could be distracted into making foolish decisions? Decisions I would regret later on."

"I can tell you Miss Boucher," using her surname on purpose to distance himself from her. "I am indeed distracted by your beauty, but I am not and will not be distracted from my determination to retain my home and my property, and at least discuss its future on my terms. If you are indeed party to this idea, then we have nothing further to discuss. I already know that these people have been on my property illegally, prospecting for minerals I think, and I am interested in discovering what they are up to. Now this. What is your answer? Are you… a honey trap?"

Rebecca was speechless and on her feet. She stood with her mouth open, struggling for words. She was enraged at the idea that she had been thought of as a, what had he called it, 'a honey trap'. She prided herself on her honesty and forthrightness in her craft of interpreting the law, and the idea that she would use her charms to persuade a man this way abhorred her. She struggled to regain control of herself. Her face was flushed and she could feel the burning in her cheeks.

The unsteadiness of her hand had disappeared. His pure magnetism had affected her badly as he had entered the room, and she was thankful now that that that had passed. It was replaced now by icy calmness.

"Mr Anders. If we must become so formal. I can assure you that I find such a suggestion abhorrent and personally insulting. How dare you accuse me of using such underhand tactics to gain your trust and confidence? I can assure you that the firm I am a partner with is one of the oldest and most respected firms in London and New York. I represent that firm here and not myself. As a representative of that firm I can assure you that I am not a, a, honey trap, sent by either the firm or the client to distract you."

Rebecca was looking directly into his eyes. Eyes that glittered with a steely light now. He too was on his feet, with his hands at his side, fists slightly clenched. So close to Rebecca that she could feel his breath warm on her hair as he too calmed his emotions.

He stepped close to her and held her by the shoulders. He towered over her, his masculinity such a powerful force that it broke Rebecca's icy resolve and she could feel the butterflies in her stomach. Her face was turned up toward his as she searched his face for intention. His full lips, smooth and well formed, that archers bow that she recognized as purely him. Slowly he bent down and placed those lips on hers and gave her the gentlest yet most passionate kiss she thought she had ever had. She melted against him. He had his arms around her now, her own arms pinned to her side, his body like a granite cliff against her softness. The kiss lingered. She hoped it would never end. Slowly he lifted his head away. Looking into her eyes with a much softer light in them now. "Rebecca..." His voice husky with emotion. "Oh Cooper... Oh Cooper." Rebecca's voice caught. "Please, we can't. What's happening?" She struggled out of his arms, and he just stood there with a look in his eyes she had never seen before. She backed away slightly, almost stumbling over the corner of the lounge chair behind her. What on earth was happening to her? This was most unprofessional. Entirely unprofessional. Nice, but really no way for a partner in a prestigious company to behave. Suddenly she sat down with a thump in the chair. Her legs just didn't want to go on holding her up at the moment.

Cooper stepped back and sat back down in his own chair. Immediately his stood up again and moved to the centre of the room. Turning to her, he said softly. "No Rebecca. You are not a honey trap. I apologize for being so stupid as to suggest it. That's twice tonight I've upset you badly. I don't mean to, but you are..." He stopped and swallowed, and began to pace about the room. Rebecca watched him silently, trying to gather in her emotions. His touch electrified her, and she didn't trust herself to speak just at the moment.

Chapter 4

Cooper looked at Rebecca reflectively and said. "Earlier this
afternoon when we spoke you mentioned New World
Holdings - NWH for short, which caused me to hesitate, and
it was then that I first had an indication that I had no idea of
the depth of your involvement in this business."
Rebecca spoke quietly. "I asked you if you knew of New
World Holdings. You may have only heard from their agents,
in reference to the enquiry about buying your property. You
may not have actually heard of New World Holdings.
However, I noticed your reaction to that question."
"Yes," he replied. "I have heard of NWH. They've left traces
on my property. Oh, they probably don't realise it, but where
they were being indeed on the property, even though its
hundreds of miles across the desert from where the
homestead is."
Rebecca was shocked. The company had no right what so
ever to be on Coopers property, and in fact doing so would
surely jeopardise their chances of a clean sale.
"So you are agreeing to talks with these people because…?"
She asked Cooper.
"Because I want to find out what they are up to out there. As
simple as that."

Neither Cooper nor Rebecca were actually making eye
contact during this exchange. Rebecca kept drawing her
gaze back to Coopers lips, and for his part, he was doing the
same, while also trying to look like he was not looking at
other parts of her body as well, because he was. Short of
turning his back on her, he couldn't help himself. It was as if
they were conducting two entirely separate conversations.
The one on the surface, the mundane business of working
out who knew what about whom, and the one that had them
so actively engaged, the almost overwhelming urge to rip
each others clothes off and tumble into the king size bed

41

occupying the next room.

Cooper shifted his gaze to Rebecca's eyes. "Rebecca," he began. "I'm… not… sorry." He didn't have to explain what for. Rebecca's faint smile and heightened colour told him he had nothing to apologize for. Considering they had only just met, they had both been very surprised by the power of their emotions. Both were people well used to controlling their emotions.

Cooper had had girlfriends of course over the years and had enjoyed the intimate company of a number of them. He had never felt the need to say the magic words "I love you" though, and would not say them in any case unless he meant it. Either the girls left, or he left, usually on amicable terms, and they got on with their lives. Only two had ever been invited out to the homestead, and on both occasions the girls - young women actually by that time, took one look at the place and couldn't get back to the city fast enough. It had apparently never occurred to them that Cooper may have been willing to relocate to please them.

"Rebecca, I may seem like a country bumpkin to you, and probably I am if compared to the sophisticated gentlemen of Europe and London. But I am well educated and well travelled and I…" He stopped talking like a clockwork running down and muttered "Oh what the hell."

"Let me start again." He said, speaking quietly, and seemingly a little sadly.

"The people who are your clients are up to no good I'm sure of it, and on my property. I want to get to the bottom of it. The antics of those goons convinces me that it is not even something as simple as prospecting. I fully accept that you have no part of their schemes and apologize with all my being that I could have even suspected you. I realize as your clients that you must protect their interests, so I will not trouble you further. You may tell your clients that I am rejecting all overtures from them out of hand. Moreover, if I

42

find them on my land again, they will most assuredly regret it. I will be returning home in the morning, very early. May I see you again in the morning before I depart?"

Rebecca held out a hand as if to steady him. "Must you go now? I'm taking in all you have said," she hesitated a fraction and added "and done. If you leave now…" The sentence remained unfinished. She said softly. "Of course. I would love to see you again in the morning, just call to let me know and I will meet you." She couldn't help but think 'He's slipping through my fingers.' and she didn't mean in a business sense. She couldn't understand it, but she did not want this to be the last she would see of him. She did not want this to be the first and last kiss. 'There, I've said it' she thought. Cooper started to move toward the door. He turned and said.

"Don't open your door unless you know who is on the other side. I'll see you in the morning, perhaps." Cooper closed the door softly. All of his plans now in pieces. He found that he had really been looking forward to showing Rebecca around his home. He wanted her to be able to see it all through his eyes. He knew she was different. He had to know that she would never be a part of any underhanded plan to get around his resolve to keep his station property. It had been a moment of weakness, and he regretted it bitterly.

'In any case,' he thought, 'why would she even be interested in me, anyway. She's a sophisticated woman from one of the major capital cities of the world. Wealthy in her own right, and probably with a string of eligible bachelors vying for her attention.' He did recall that kiss though. Her sweet lips responding to his. The feel of her soft and supple body pressed against his.

"Struth." He exclaimed and smacked his hand against the wall of the hall way. Someone on the other side yelled back "Quiet out there." He hurried to the lift to return to his own room.

The doors to the lift slid open, and he stepped in, checking his watch. 9pm. It was early yet, but he didn't feel like going out. He very much didn't feel like returning to his room alone either. In fact, he couldn't remember ever feeling so alone. Not lonely, he knew that feeling from his early boarding school days, but alone. He worried at his bottom lip as he stepped out of the lift and headed to the bar. It was the ground floor bar, and still contained a collection of business types, men and women alike stopping in after busy days in the office. A couple of politicians enjoying life on the public purse. A couple of elderly tourists sitting quietly to one side looking a little like they expected to be asked to move on at any moment.

He hitched his butt onto a bar stool next to a small group of young women from a local office by the look of them. He didn't pay much attention to them, just noticed their chic clothes and careful makeup and cut-glass tumblers with a dash of what was probably Gin by the look of it, the lemon twists a giveaway. They hardly registered on his mind. He sure registered on theirs though.

Their conversation stopped dead when he sat down next to them. The appraising looks coming his way may have been unsettling if he had noticed. After a few moments, when it was obvious he hadn't noticed, and in fact seemed to be ignoring them, their conversation started up again although a little more subdued.

He ordered a Scotch with ice. It came in a crystal tumble and a small ice jar with tongs to pick up the ice and add it as he pleased. There were nuts on the bar in a bowl, and he helped himself, munching away as he mulled over the day's events. He couldn't believe it had only been this afternoon when he had met Rebecca at the airport. 2pm, and here it was 9pm. In those seven hours he had managed to meet, then upset, then alienate, then walk away from the most beautiful woman he had ever had the pleasure of meeting.

'You might say an unforgettable seven hours' he thought to himself.

At least he thought he was thinking to himself. The young woman perched on the bar stool next to him turned and said.

"Some seven hours, that it would cause such a sigh of regret"

Cooper blinked and turned toward her.

"Sorry miss. Thinking aloud. I didn't realize I was." He turned back to the bar, content to sip his drink and think of what he had to do tomorrow.

The young woman next to him spun her chair and sat elbow to elbow with him and picked up her drink. She knew she was safe here. The best hotel in town, all her friends next to her and by now their attention fully on her. She smiled.

"Care to talk about it?" She asked lightly.

Cooper straightened up and replied politely.

"Well miss, it goes like this. I met a beautiful woman, I managed to insult her twice and upset her to tears once and anger once, then kiss her, then walk away from her. Probably never see her again." He put his glass on the bar and signalled for another drink. By now the other young ladies were crowding in close around him, wanting to hear more of the story. He sighed and looked at the scene in the mirror behind the bar. 'Well, maybe life wasn't all bad', he thought. The bar tender just filled all the glasses of the girls and replenished the nut bowls and moved away up the bar. He knew Cooper was good for the tab. The girls were enthusiastic talkers and there was safety in numbers - and this one wasn't gay. They had all heard him say he had kissed a woman. The petite one on his left was not about to give up her place, although she suffered a deal of jostling from her friends.

"What are your names, ladies? Mine's Cooper" Cooper asked.

45

A chorus of names came to him, but the only one he really caught was from the girl who had sat next to him first. Emily. "Nice name, Emily." He said and smiled at the others. He didn't have a hope of remembering the other names, his mind was not on the subject. 'Well one out of five wasn't bad was it.' He thought.

They all wanted to know who the woman was he said he had kissed. Was she in the hotel? Was it his wife? Some suspense when that one was asked. Audible sighs of relief when he replied that he "wasn't married - yet." To the other questions he was evasive, he didn't kiss-and-tell. He was enjoying himself, and his confidence in the company of the women was assuring to them. They would soon have to leave though. For them it was the end of a working day, and homes still had to be got to. Boy friends to meet, mothers to calm and a weeks work to get over in preparation for the next one.

Cooper saw movement reflected in the mirror behind the bar, a splash of red coming in the door. It was Rebecca. He said to Emily, the young woman beside him, "Excuse me Emily." and slid off the stool to turn and face Rebecca who had stopped in her tracks and was staring at Cooper, standing there surrounded by a cluster of beautiful young women, and obviously enjoying himself.

She had found her room too claustrophobic for the mood she was in and decided to go down to the ground floor bar for a drink of something and the company of other people. She didn't know why she was surprised to see Cooper there, and she couldn't understand why she felt so hurt by seeing him enjoying the company of the collection of young women. They were obviously from a local office nearby, and here for TGIF drinks.... and all of them were now watching both her and Cooper. Rebecca collected herself, and walked up to Cooper, trying to ignore the others. The girl Emily had slipped from her bar stool and collected her shoulder bag from the bar and was saying her goodbyes to her friends. She looked sideways at Cooper as she passed, "Nice meeting you Cooper." The others were collecting their possessions and leaving, with subdued goodbyes. Cooper hardly noticed them leaving.

"Rebecca," he said. "I couldn't face my empty room alone, so I came down here for a bit of human company. Those office girls were here, and we got talking…" He suddenly felt like he was explaining his actions like a naughty boy caught with his hand in the cookie jar.

Rebecca smiled and put a hand on his arm. "You don't have to explain yourself to me Cooper. I too felt the need to be amongst others. That's why I'm here." She looked at the now empty bar stools. "May I join you?" She asked. The butterflies were back in her stomach.

Cooper suddenly realised he had been standing there like some country oaf, with his mouth half open. He almost jumped.

"Of course Rebecca. Please. Sit here. Do you want a drink of something? What can I get you?"

Rebecca thought for a moment. She looked at the bar tender hovering nearby. "A small house red please." She didn't really want a drink, but now she was here with Cooper, she had to have something to do with her hands.

They sat side by side nursing their drinks and looking at the array of colourful bottles on the shelves behind the bar. Cooper was not a man normally lost for words, but he realised that for once he didn't quite know where to start. He had really insulted Rebecca earlier and felt terrible about it. He looked at her in the reflection and found her looking right back at him. He turned to her and said.

"Rebecca, I really am sorry that I insulted you earlier. I do hope that you will forgive me. Also, I am sorry that we seem to have got off on the wrong foot entirely since the airport. Can I ask that we… try again? I might add, I'm not sorry

47

that I kissed you." There, he had said it.

Rebecca coloured slightly. She was not sorry about the kiss either. It had been entirely unexpected, but no, she was not sorry about it.

"I agree." She said. "In fact, if we are starting again, may I say that I would love to come out to your homestead with you tomorrow. All business interests aside, I believe we should be able to at least enjoy each other's company on such a personal trip. If you wish to invite me to come with you, I will gladly accept." Her right hand rested lightly on his forearm. His smooth sun tanned brown forearm. She found herself reluctant to take her hand away, and Cooper had not moved his arm away at her touch.

"Of course. Stupid of me." He said. "It just occurs to me that I didn't invite you in the first place, just assumed that you would come with me - flying off into the sunset to a place that is probably completely outside of your experience. So may I formally invite you to come with me to where I live. To fly out in the morning in my own light plane, a twin engine Cessna that I own. You will of course have your own rooms and facilities. En suite bedroom and your own sitting room. It's a very big house. Far too big for me alone. Your company will be most welcome." He waited for Rebecca to respond.

"I'll take great delight in coming with you. It does actually sound like quite an adventure. I have flown over Australia of course, and can see that it's quite an inhospitable place, mostly. To be able to visit such a place on the ground in safety, in the company of someone I love…" Rebecca gulped, and went as red as a beetroot. "Like, like, someone I like. Sorry, slip of the tongue." She had lost her train of thought completely. Cooper studied the bottles behind the bar carefully and waited for Rebecca to recover. She could not know how much he suddenly wanted her first statement to be true, but he knew it was never going to happen. He had burnt those bridges already by his behaviour. Were they fated to fall over each other all the time as they had been doing? He hoped not.

"Excellent. I'll be waiting in the lobby in the morning for you. Say 8am? Not too early?" Cooper carried on as though he hadn't heard her slip of the tongue.

"8am is fine." She replied. "We can have a little breakfast and be on our way. I presume we will return to Brisbane airport and leave from there?"

"Yes, should take about three hours flying time if we are lucky. The weather is good, and there is no air traffic out that way. We land right next to the homestead. Easy." Cooper thought the trip may actually take more like four hours, but he didn't want to frighten Rebecca off, and if he ignored the Economical Cruising Speed rules, he could push the speed up and do it in three hours easy.

"Tell me a little about yourself Rebecca. This time, I'll try not to insult you." He smiled a little ruefully. He sat quietly as Rebecca began to talk. She found herself opening up to this man as she had never done with any other. A little history of her family, her hopes and dreams, her ambitions regarding the company she had found a niche in. The people she worked with.

They had moved to more comfortable seating by now, and the place had gone a little quieter as the office workers had nearly all gone home. The evening crowd would be starting to fill the place soon. Cooper interspersed her story with his own, and they discovered that they had mutual interests in certain areas, one of which was travelling. Cooper had worked hard to build up the cattle business his father had left him, and he had seen to it that the people he hired to run the place were all honest, hardworking and capable of getting on with it without having to have Cooper there all the time. He had then been able to travel to Europe, and the Americas on different occasions as a tourist. To his delight, Rebecca was as enthusiastic a traveller as he had become. She was less able to get away though it seemed than Cooper was, but as they worked out their commitments, it became obvious that they both used their time to maximum advantage when they did get time. Cooper found his travels more seasonal, Rebecca found her travel more available at traditional times, like Christmas breaks, and at the end of a long and gruelling case.

Rebecca said to Cooper, "Of course, I can't leave the law firm that I am part of. Not only am I a junior partner with the opportunity of becoming a full senior partner, but it also carries a fairly strong contractual arrangement."

Cooper's brow furrowed momentarily. He had just been thinking that it would be nice, really nice, if Rebecca could move to Australia. In fact, move to his homestead. He realized as soon as he thought of it that it was impossible. Rebecca had her career to think of. She was on the way up, and no way would she leave those prospects to move out to the remote regions of Australia, and on top of that, have nothing to do when she got there.

"Well," replied Cooper smiling "that means you won't be staying on at Innamincka I guess."

"Hmmm, no not really." Replied Rebecca. "However, I do want to come out with you tomorrow morning, and for that reason, I suggest we call it a night. I'm glad, in fact very pleased, that we have finally agreed to... understand each other."

Without further discussion they rose and headed for the lifts. Rebecca got off first, and with a little wave and smile went to her room, Cooper to his on the next floor. They both had a lot to think about, each for similar reasons. Although they didn't know it yet.

Chapter 5

The plane droned through the vast blue of the sky, heading
almost directly west. The early morning sun rose behind
them, throwing long shadows across the land from low
mountains and hills as it climbed up into the sky. The golden
light of the early sun slowly revealed a land of browns and
dark greens. They had long since left behind them the long
low mountain range that ran the length of the Australian
east coast. It seemed more like the uplift to a vast escarpment
than a mountain range, and Rebecca was entranced by the
vast emptiness of the landscape that unfolded below her.
They were following a main road it seemed. Well, it was the
only feature she could make out below them, and it seemed
to stretch away over the horizon in the same direction as
their travel. There were occasional small tracks, and lesser
roads, and now and then a cluster of building, their roofs
shining in the morning sun. Rebecca looked across the small
cabin at Cooper. He was concentrating on his flying and
only turned to smile encouragingly at her for a moment. He
said, "I'll be with you in a moment Rebecca. I just have to set
the controls to auto-pilot, and we can relax for a little while."
Rebecca didn't reply, just turned her head to look out of the
side window again. They didn't seem to be all that high. Not
like the big jets. She supposed that these smaller aeroplanes
were only permitted to fly at a specified height, to stay out of
the main airline routes. although she didn't think there
would be any passenger services out this way. It was obvious
nobody lived down there. At last Cooper set the controls
after reporting to some unseen air traffic controller
somewhere. He eased himself back in his seat and turned to
Rebecca slightly, the better to be able to look directly at her.
"I was just letting Toowoomba Air Service know who we are
and where we are going. Compass heading, ETA and so on.
It's a safety measure. If by some unfortunate chance we don't
arrive, the authorities have some idea where to start looking

for us. The flight was logged at Brisbane when we left, but that is a very busy airport, and little things like reporting our position somewhere along the intended route can often help in emergencies. This is a vast country, with very little in it out here, and even less where we are going." Rebecca must have been looking a little worried because Cooper continued. "Don't worry Rebecca. It's all just safety measures. We'll be fine. You will love the homestead I'm sure. I hope you will love it. I hope..." He stopped and swallowed. 'No' he thought. 'I must not say anything of my feelings. I can hardly believe them myself. I've only known her for a day. One day! Am I crazy? Have I been alone so long that I'm falling in love with the first pretty woman who crosses my path.?' He smiled weakly and sat back a little hoping Rebecca would say something. He loved the sound of her voice and could listen to her all day. She didn't say anything right away, just took in what he had said. What had he been about to say? What had he stopped himself from saying? She wanted to say a lot herself, but was too confused to think straight about it. Instead, she changed the subject entirely.

"I still haven't heard back from my research assistant in London. I hope she gets in touch soon, there are things I need to know. Decisions I have to make. Oh! you do have internet out there don't you? I never thought. I've asked her to get me all the dirt on New World. There will be dirt. Any company that big, with so many branches, and only one - apparently master, will have collected lots of dirty secrets. Kali will find them out. We have to get a grip on what they are up to. Did I mention I am going to drop them as clients? No? Well I am. Nobody treats me the way I was treated at that hotel and can expect me to continue to represent them. In fact, quite the opposite now Cooper. I am finding out what is going on, and I was only waiting to be as... isolated as we now are, so that I could tell you. No fear of anyone listening up here!"

Cooper was very pleased to hear the news. Up to this point he had still had reserves, remembering that after all Rebecca was a legal person, and representing another party. So he had of necessity, to keep certain information in reserve. He had said in passing that people from New World had been on his property, but he had not said how he knew, or what he had found out they had been doing, other than a vague 'prospecting'.

Rebecca continued, all the time drinking in the sight of Cooper sitting there focusing on all she said. She couldn't remember ever meeting a man in any circumstances who gave his whole attention to what she had to say like Cooper did. It was very flattering for one thing and did nothing for the butterflies she still felt stirring inside every time she focused on him. She was sure she was falling in love with him. Not the rather bland love of the every day, but a love mixed with the deeper passions of lust. For surely the stirrings deep within her in response to his looks, and the memory of his lips upon hers in the hotel were more than simple love. Even now, she was losing focus on what was being talked about, as she was thinking how lovely he looked in every way, and how very fortunate she was to have met him. If only the circumstances had been better. Oh if only. "I now consider myself no longer representing New World. Last night after we parted, I contacted the office and advised the other partners that I was terminating our dealings with New World. I outlined fully what had happened in the basement car park, and what you have told me of their trespass on your property. All partners are now in agreement, and New World have been advised of the termination. Apparently they were not best pleased, but we remain firm. I was advised also that as the head of New World was believed to be still in Australia, we should expect further contact from him They have no other means just yet of approaching you, and apparently still feel that I am the best person to do that.

53

How they expect me to do that, when it is I who initiated the termination of the brief I don't know. Perhaps we will need to be careful, although how they would approach me out here... Cooper, it's so vast and empty!" Rebecca could see far ahead, and almost all around the horizon line in a nearly three hundred and sixty degree arch. There was nothing but parched landscape, as flat as a billiard table, all brown and grey. No real cover other than stunted low bushes that appeared as dots, like dirty green cotton ball puffs on the landscape. There appeared to be dry river beds crossing the landscape, but where they originated or where they went to she couldn't guess at.

Cooper thought he detected a note of apprehension in her voice as she spoke. He thought to himself that it would not be good for anyone to try to approach them out on his home ground. It would go particularly hard on anyone who tried to approach Rebecca without having good reason to do so while she was in his care. He didn't feel he would be able to declare his love for her, but he would protect her with his life if necessary. Perhaps one day...

"You need not worry at all, " he said. "I will make sure no one comes on the place unless by invitation. If you are contacted by email or otherwise, you have the opportunity to ignore such approaches. All phone calls will be taken by myself. So I suggest you relax. I have plotted a track that will take us over part of the Channel Country. You probably haven't heard of it, but it is an area in the south west corner of Queensland into which all the inland rivers and creeks drain in the wet season. Its vast and largely unexplored, but even when dry as it is now being a spectacular sight. We should be approaching the area in about half an hour. We are making good time as I have our speed set somewhat higher than normal."

Rebecca relaxed visibly. She was not a woman easily

frightened, but the head of New World and his henchmen had badly frightened her. With Cooper's rock solid presence beside her, she could face anything. The landscape unfolded below them, and slowly the area they were heading for came into view. It was quite unmistakable, looking like a vast river system estuary or delta. Rivers and streams in very complex branches merging and separating and flowing always toward the south west. The really strange thing was the lack of water. There was not a drop to be seen in the vast dry river system.

"It's only during the occasional wet season in the far north that any water makes it this far down." Said Cooper. He seemed to be answering Rebecca's unspoken question. She felt as though he had been reading her mind. It seemed to go on forever, and as the plane slowly banked around to head south, Cooper added.

"Not long now, and we will start to descend toward the homestead. Keep an eye out for the little township of Innamincka. You'll love it. Population of ..." Rebecca interrupted "Twelve!" and laughed. Cooper looked surprised. "How did you know?" He said.

"Easy," Rebecca replied. "I looked it up last night." She laughed again, pleased with herself for showing Cooper that she cared enough to be interested in the place, or at least the area he seemed so much in love with. Oh how she wished he would have that light in his eyes when he spoke of her. Suddenly, there it was. A tiny cluster of ramshackle houses seemingly adrift in a sea of wilderness. No trees, nothing. A rough track leading in and out. What did these people do out here? There was obviously no industry or business of any sort. A very strange sight thought Rebecca. The plane droned on, and soon Cooper pointed a little to the left.

"There we are; you will see it more clearly soon. The runway is right next to the house."

Cooper climbed the plane in a slow bank out to the south

and came around while dropping steadily toward the cluster of buildings. Suddenly he let out an expletive.

"There is another aircraft n the runway! I don't recognise it either. Rebecca, I don't suppose you know it by any chance? Your people maybe?" Rebecca peered carefully at the other aircraft and the symbol painted on the tail. She recognised it from her paperwork.

"That's a New World plane. I can't believe it. They have all been told that I am no longer managing their case." She looked at Cooper, his face set in a worried frown. "Do you think," she continued "that they haven't found out yet? Or are they going to press ahead with trying to convince you directly do you think?"

"Just a moment Rebecca, I need to study this carefully." Cooper replied, and instead of trying to land directly, he took the plane in really low and fast from the rear of the house a long way out. The house seemed to rush at them and Rebecca ducked behind the dash board in fright as the plane roared across the roofs of the house and sheds, wheels almost touching the shimmering metal. Cooper pulled the controls back, and the plane climbed sharply and banked now to the right coming around in a long curve to line up on the front of the house. They raced toward it again, barely above the ground. Rebecca thought they were going to crash directly into the front door when suddenly the aircraft lifted and roared almost in a direct climb upward. Cooper was twisted around in his seat trying to look back over his shoulder. He levelled off at some altitude, and Rebecca tried to get her breath back. She was trembling like a leaf, and almost unable to breathe for the fear that gripped her. Her hands hurt from gripping the bar on the dashboard in front of her. A 'panic bar' Cooper had called it jokingly when they had climbed aboard. Now she knew why. She had trouble letting it go. She didn't know if she actually should let it go. "Are... are... are you finished Cooper?" She could hardly talk, her jaw seemed frozen. 'What on earth was he trying to do?' She wondered. Cooper had the plane in a wide arc now around the homestead. He looked at Rebecca, his face grim. "Something is very wrong down there Rebecca. There should be people running everywhere after that exhibition. There is nothing. Not even dogs, and there should be dozens of them." That had an immediate calming effect on Rebecca. She asked. "But you have staff down there don't you? Do you have radio contact at all?"

"Yes to both questions. I am a little reluctant to use the radio though because it's not a private channel. I think I will risk it though. I'll see if I can raise the manager, William. He should be there, and he should have come outside in the first case when he heard us."

Cooper tried half a dozen times to raise anyone on the separate station radio mounted on the console. There was no answer. There was still no sign of anyone on the ground.

"Let's land Rebecca. But, be prepared for a quick take off again if we have to." Rebecca nodded in agreement. She was quite happy to get on the ground. In fact, she preferred being on the ground.

Cooper brought the plane into a smooth landing and stopped at the end of the runway, fairly close to the other aircraft. It was a similar model to theirs, built to carry six people comfortably. They sat there for a time with the engines idling, the props a spinning blur in the bright sunlight of mid morning. They were facing the homestead, and only a couple of hundred yards from the front fence around the house proper. There was still no sign of anyone moving about the property, either in the house - the front door was wide open, or about the yards and sheds.

"Hmmm," said Cooper, almost thinking aloud. "Could be that they have all gone for a drive down to the water hole. Although it's a bit early for that. I'm assuming for the moment that this is a friendly visit. they would hardly come out here in an aircraft that is easily traceable if they were up to no good." He sat for a moment longer. Then asking Rebecca he said,

"What do you think Rebecca? You were in fact the last one to have any contact with anyone from New World. Did you think them... stupid? Or just plain ordinarily aggressive?" Rebecca had to think for a moment and try to see the situation from a dispassionate view.

"No, I don't think they or at least, anyone running the company are stupid necessarily. Just aggressive and perhaps ruthless business people. Shall we go and have a look?" She was unbuckling her seat belt as she spoke. In truth, she would be pleased to get on the ground again. She looked at Cooper to see what his thoughts would be. He nodded, not really taking his eyes from the house. He taxied the plane in closer to the front of the house, now just a few hundred feet away. As he unlocked his side door, Rebecca did the same. The propellers were now stationary, but she noticed that Cooper had left everything set for any eventuality, including a quick getaway.

As Rebecca opened the door, she gasped. The hot air assailed her like a physical presence. It was only mid-morning, but already it was so hot and dry that she had trouble drawing breath after being in the coolness of the air-conditioned cabin. The heat of the land was shimmering in the distance like a vast lake and causing shapes and objects to appear as though they were floating in that vast shifting sea. The sun was already scorching the top of her head, even though her naturally thick hair should have provided some protection. Rebecca thought of herself as being reasonably tough, but she had not been prepared for this. She looked for Cooper and saw him already walking slowly toward the house. He looked over his shoulder for Rebecca just in time to see her stumble from the plane, trying to clutch at the wing for support, she had missed her final step on getting down from the plane. He had hardly noticed the heat, but it suddenly came to him that Rebecca was not used to it. He moved quickly back to her and steadied her. He escorted her into the coolness of the deep interior of the house. The air cooler was humming quietly in the roof space, blowing cool slightly moist air throughout the house. The interior of the house was at least twenty degrees cooler than outside. Cooper noticed this as he didn't normally have it this cool. Of course, others had been here before him. He indicated to Rebecca to sit on the long sofa in the centre of the room and pulled a bottle of water from the cooler by the sideboard. He grabbed a hand towel from the bathroom and soaked it with the water, and began to bathe Rebecca's forehead, temples and neck with the cool damp towel.

Rebecca was sitting upright and cooling quickly. She really had been surprised at the sudden temperature change as she stepped out of the aircraft. She looked at Cooper. Then she really looked at Cooper. He was standing in front of her, with his shirt open and his beautiful tanned body in stark contrast to his long white trousers. He had used the damp towel to wipe his own skin to cool it in an almost reflex natural action. Such a muscular powerful body showing his breathing in a very defined movement of his torso. Rebecca gasped in a shock of emotion and powerful desire. As suddenly as the heat had assailed her outside, this desire assailed her again in a much different way. Cooper dropped to one knee and took her in his hands by the shoulders.

"Rebecca," he asked softly in a worried voice. "What's the matter? What can I do?"

Rebecca struggled to regain control, and said in a voice husky with burning passion,

"You can let me go, and do your shirt up, please. Oh Cooper, what is this place? What have you brought me to?" Her voice was a hoarse whisper. She didn't mean the countryside. She could feel his hands on her burning into her flesh like hot irons, arousing her to a trembling state that threatened to engulf her. She couldn't struggle any more, the intensity of his gaze holding her transfixed. Cooper slowly released his hold on her, his hands dropping to rest on her thighs just above her knees. She gasped as another shock ran through her.

"Rebecca, you have me worried, I've never seen such a reaction to the heat out here in the outback. Business can wait, I should get you airborne again and back into the cool air of the aeroplane." Cooper could feel her trembling beneath his hands, totally ignorant of what was truly going on in her mind. It was not desert heat - it was body heat that was causing Rebecca to shake. He had totally forgotten for the moment even why they were out here. He slowly stood up, his attention wholly on Rebecca. She was so beautiful. Her eyes seemed to change colour with her emotions, and her voice now had a husky throatiness to it that was setting him on fire. Was that desire he could see in her eyes; now so dark they were almost colourless with a deep almost black intensity. He could feel a desire responding within him that took him completely by surprise, an emotional response he had never experienced before with a woman. He knew instinctively he was losing the grip he had on his resolve to meet with this woman on purely business terms. He cursed the people who had sent her to him instead of some slick, grey suited lawyer that he would know how to deal with. Within the same thought he applauded their foresight in realising that a young man like himself would be much more inclined to react favourably to a woman of Rebecca's quality and beauty. But what could he offer her? He struggled with the dilemma. It seemed everything he did with this woman caused an adverse reaction. First emotional upset now physical trauma as he had neglected to realise that someone like Rebecca who came from very protected surroundings, air conditioned office, chauffeur driven cars - again air-conditioned, would never last a minute in the oven like climate he called home. He was a fool he thought and cursed himself for his blindness. How could he resolve this situation and for once in his life do the right thing by this so lovely young woman?

The air-cooler that cooled the whole house hummed quietly, exchanging the tinder dry outside air for cool moist air inside, slowly cooling Rebecca now to the point where her mind began to calm her racing heart. The cooling air though was not cooling her burning desire for Cooper as his hands lightly gripped her legs just above her knees. Her lower stomach area was vibrating as though violin strings were playing inside her. She could feel herself responding in an almost uncontrollable way to Coopers very presence and touch. Her fingers found his bare chest, almost involuntarily stroking the smooth, almost hairless skin. She realised with sensual delight that Cooper was not covered in coarse chest hair, but rather a thin down of natural, short hair that was so pale it was almost invisible. There was no mistaking the darker hair that began to gather on his lower abdomen as her fingers trickled down his stomach gently brushing that darker hair of his belt line. She looked deep into his eyes as she heard him groan with a sound such as she'd had only heard once before as her betrothed had pulled away from her to go off to war all those years ago. That memory tried to crowd in on her suddenly as though that lost soul had suddenly entered the room and was demanding what had once been his.

"No!" Cried Rebecca. "No no no, please, go away now. I loved you once, but I must live." She began to tremble all over and slid to her knees on the floor in front of Cooper. Cooper was more than surprised. Was she demanding he move away from her? How could she have loved him once? What did she mean? He wrapped his strong brown arms around her in a protective embrace and whispered to her.

"Rebecca, Rebecca, we must stop, before I cannot stop. I am only a man, and your beauty is overwhelming me with desire. I did not mean to hurt you, yet again, it was unforgivable of me. Those people are going to pay a high price for their schemes that brought you to this place." Cooper slowly stood, carrying Rebecca upwards with him, still in his embrace. Slowly her senses were returning, and her mind was clearing. She still trembled slightly from the raw emotion that had gripped her, and although she knew she should be back on that plane and fleeing from this impossible situation, she knew equally that she would not. She was overwhelmingly drawn to Cooper, and she knew his reaction to her was equally strong - but she didn't know if it was love. He hardly spoke to her and seemed to only be apologising for imagined wrongs when he did. This was not how it was supposed to happen. They stood, both trembling slightly, facing each other in that wide room. Rebecca tried to draw her breath to steady herself. Cooper too drew back slightly from her, a puzzled look in his eyes. He couldn't understand it. He was a man normally in charge of himself, of others, of his life. Oh, he liked women, but in his plans there was no place for a woman like this. Like this? At once tough - he would not like to meet her in opposition in the courtroom, yet at the same time, so intense and so passionate, and physically... He slowly looked her up and down, with no idea what his look was doing to her. 'Yes, this is a real woman.' He thought. 'Should I say something, before she slips away from me.'

"Rebecca, I have to tell you something. I have to..." He got no further as a tap tap tap on the front door frame spun him around. The world around them crashing back in like a tidal wave.

Standing in the doorway was a near naked Aboriginal man, his spears still in his right hand. His worldly possessions. Cooper recognised him immediately as one of the men, part of the Yandruwandha tribe native to this area who preferred to stick to their own ways, who roamed this vast area living their traditional life.

The man was in the shadow with the light outside, his colour making him but a deeper shadow in the doorway. Rebecca gasped and clutched at Cooper.

"It's ok Rebecca. I know this man. Something is up, or he would never have come into the station yard."

"Boss, you better come. Things not right out there." The man spoke slowly, not sure of the words to use, not used to the language, with a deep guttural voice that seemed to have come from a past age.

Rebecca had never seen or heard anyone like this man. He appeared to be so... Primitive, as though just stepping out of a land that time had forgotten. She shivered and clutched Cooper's arm. He put his hand over hers to reassure her. The mutual tension - passion of moments before had evaporated like moisture in this dry land.

"What's up, Yidniminckanie man?" These people used their own language, and as Cooper didn't know this fellows personal name, it was polite to use his tribal name. These men rarely came into the station homestead area. Cooper couldn't remember the last time he had seen any of these people here. The men may come in close to talk with the station hands sometimes on 'tribal' business, but their women and children never did, remaining a mystery to all. That was their way, and in this vast land, it was fine with Cooper. There was plenty of room for all.

The man in the doorway didn't say anymore, just turned and went and stood out in the yard, the scorching sun full on him, seemingly impervious to it. He waited for Cooper.

'Struth!' Thought Cooper. 'This is serious. Something bad.' He looked at Rebecca.

"Stay here. There is a gun cabinet on the wall there. Can you use a gun?"

63

'My God.' He thought, 'what have I brought her to.'

"Forgive me Rebecca, I can't take you with me outside. It's...
'Man's business.' According to their ways. I will be back in a
moment. Unlock the gun cabinet," he threw her his keys as
he headed for the door. "Load the two Winchesters, and
anything else you can. ... You do know how?" Her violent
nod reassured him. 'That's my girl!' He thought and hurried
outside.

Rebecca raced to the cabinet on the wall as Cooper went
outside. Fortunately for her, her father had been a gun owner
on his farming properties in Suffolk, and had passed his
knowledge to her. The guns were slightly different, but she
noted with some thanks that they were basically all the same.
She loaded the magazines, slightly in awe of the size of the
bullets. These weren't 'Friday Night Specials' - These were
heavy duty military size bullets.

She paused at the door. Cooper was standing casually in the
presence of the aboriginal man, his gaze cast slightly down,
yet attentive. The other man was using a mixture of sign and
words to talk. Rebecca really wanted to know what was
being said.

The aboriginal man suddenly looked at her directly. She
knew it as though she had been transfixed by his look. He
raised his right arm and beckoned her to come. So startled
was she that she just stepped through the door and went to
Cooper. She still had one three-oh-eight rifle in her hand
though. The black man looked at it and looked at her.
Directly, in the eye. He smiled. Rebecca was startled, but
kept cool, and just lifted her chin and looked at this ancient
man. He may be ancient, but she was 'woman', and just
knew that he would recognise her place here in this drama.
The man looked at Cooper for a long time. Cooper just
stood there. He knew these people of course and respected
their most ancient culture. When the aboriginal man decided
to speak, he would.

"This," he indicated Rebecca, "your woman?"

Cooper never hesitated. He knew that to do so would have immediately seen Rebecca sent back inside and probably created an unnecessary argument.

"Yes, my woman. She will be my wife." He gulped and hoped Rebecca would understand what he had had to say.

The aboriginal man looked at Cooper, then at Rebecca. He smiled.

"Sure boss. She... No matter. Come. Men's Business. Leave her here, she be ok. Look." He swept his arm out in a gesture and a dozen people seemed to materialise out of the desert in front of Rebecca's eyes. Silent. Stationary, not a movement, bare feet on scorching sand, the wide circle of men with long wickedly barbed spears in their hands stood on the low sand ridges right out on the edges of the homestead property.

Cooper knew this was serious business. These people never, but never came into the station, and certainly never offered help for the people they considered invaders in the first place.

Cooper turned to Rebecca.

"Rebecca, It's important. Please, will you wait here for me? Go back inside immediately, out of the sun. Go now please. Now. You will be perfectly safe. I assure you no one will get past," he swept an arm. "These men."

All Rebecca could do was nod and start back toward the house. Then in a slightly strangled voice said over her shoulder.

"Please, don't be gone long."

Cooper nodded and turned to the tribal man.

"Tell me."

"I show you." Said the man as he turned and started to run at a trot out of the yard. Cooper had no choice but to follow at the same pace. Fortunately, he was fit. Very fit, and the effort was nothing to him. He looked back over his shoulder at Rebecca, standing in the middle of the yard. He hadn't seen them before, but he noticed two aboriginal women now converging on Rebecca. He almost laughed in relief, she would be fine. She would not be alone.

Chapter 6

Rebecca was not so sure though. The two women who had come into the homestead yard to be with Rebecca were the wildest looking women she had ever seen. She had no idea if they spoke English and seemed oblivious to the sun on their near naked bodies. They were both charcoal black and their hair was long and straggly, sticking out from their head at impossible angles. Deep set eyes almost hidden under their thick bushy eyebrows made it difficult for Rebecca to read their expressions. Their mouths were set in huge grins though, and their teeth flashed as white as china in their dark faces. Rebecca was now standing in the shade of the wide veranda while the other two women stayed out in the sun at the bottom of the steps. She had no idea of protocols with these strange people. They made her think of aliens, so different did they seem to her. She looked out to the slight rise where she had seen the men, but could not see a soul. Nobody at all. The two women saw her looking and giggled. Rebecca couldn't help laughing in return. These women sounded rather like only girls, with that giggle. It was a universal language. She indicated to the pair to come join her in the shade. They hesitated, but slowly stepped up the few treads to the veranda, as though it was the first time they had ever been on steps. 'Maybe it was?' Thought Rebecca. As much as Rebecca was fascinated by the sight of these two women, it was plain that they were equally fascinated with her. They were obviously young women, now that Rebecca could get a good look at them. They whispered together in an incomprehensible language, pointing to Rebecca with hesitant fingers, and one of them came close enough to touch Rebecca's upper arm, and stroke her fingers across the skin. They were entranced by Rebecca's paleness, and one of them stood next to Rebecca so their arms could be side by side. They exclaimed over the difference for minutes, their language a complete mystery to Rebecca. Rebecca tried a little language teaching.

"Do you speak English?" She asked them both. The two young women stood silent, now staring at Rebecca as though she were the alien. "Hmmmm." Said Rebecca. She smoothed her hands in a downward movement over her breasts and said "Woman." Then pointed at each in turn, making the universal 'hour glass' shape with her hands, and repeating "woman". The two women nodded and giggled again lightly, all smiles. They repeated a word, at the same time indicating each other and Rebecca, but try as she could, she could not catch nor repeat the word. The language was beyond her. It was just too different. She had no idea what to do now, given that there seemed no way to communicate with these strange people. She decided to finish loading and checking the rifles. The two women could sit in here in the shade of the veranda if they wished, but Rebecca was not going out into that sunshine again, although she was now finding it easier to breathe. The shock of the hot dry air after hours of air-conditioning had been just too much. She would be ok now though. The two young women were already sitting cross legged on the veranda, looking quite comfortable, and watching Rebecca. She smiled at them and went back inside and finished loading the rifles. She put the safety catches on and rested the rifles against the book case just inside the front door. She didn't think she would need them, with those tribal men out there watching for intruders. It was a mystery for the moment as to where everyone had gone. That New World aircraft on the dusty runway said very loudly that people from that company had arrived, but there was no indication of where everyone had gone. Perhaps Cooper would find out. Rebecca hoped he would be safe. She had no doubt he trusted the aboriginal man, but she had had personal contact with those thugs from New World, and she knew without a doubt they would be big trouble for anyone who crossed their path.

Rebecca drew a chair up to the door and sat, gazing out into the day. What a desolate place this was. Not a blade of grass to be seen. Just red dust and sand, and a tufted, spiked grass that seemed to grow in clumps scattered randomly about the landscape. There was some evidence close about the house that the place had seen a woman's touch at some point in the past, but it had been a long time ago. She suddenly felt like weeping for Cooper, growing up in this stark loveless place, with no soft beauty around him. There were old garden beds in evidence, faded and peeled white paint on stones now scattered about only barely marking boundaries. Cooper's mother had died when he was very young she knew, and it looked like his father never married again. Who could blame the few girls he had brought home for fleeing as fast as they could. Cooper was a lovely man, one who obviously appreciated the finer things in life, but didn't know how to bring those things into his life out here. She looked about the large lounge room, almost the full width of the massive house, and seemingly as deep. But she couldn't help thinking that it looked like a well kept workshop. Like a place where only men had lived for many years. Could she bring life back to this place she wondered? Could she make it a place of love and refuge for Cooper and her and their children? She flushed at the direction her thoughts were going. The two aboriginal girls looked at her and whispered between themselves. One got to her feet and came to Rebecca and softly patted the back of her hand, saying something softly in her own language. Rebecca knew she was being reassured and smiled in thanks to the girl.

"Well, there is no denying it." She said aloud and got up. "I had better make up my mind. I could love this man, but could I love this place?" She found the kitchen and located a large jug of water in the refrigerator and some glasses. These she took out to the girls and offered the water and glasses to them. They handled both very carefully, but quickly poured themselves a drink each and thankfully emptied their glasses. They sat down again in the shade, carefully placing the jug and glasses by them. They seemed content to wait. They were there to keep Rebecca company it seemed, and to watch for anything untoward. They were certainly doing that Rebecca could see. Their eyes were never still, scanning the surrounding plains constantly. She didn't know where the men had gone, but could only assume that Cooper was fine. He knew these people and would be safe with them. Rebecca realised that her suitcase and laptop, everything she owned in fact was still in their aeroplane out there on the runway. The doors open and the heat haze shimmering like a ghostly water pool across the runway. She hoped it wouldn't destroy her laptop and other personal effects. The thought of laptops brought her back to earth. Cooper would surely have a computer system here in the house. She went in search of it. She found it in the office toward the back of the house. The room was large, and it was apparent that all the station business was conducted here, Rebecca hoped that the computer didn't require any fancy start-up passwords. Sure enough, a flick of the switch and the screen came to life. She smiled with appreciation as she spotted the Skype icon on the desktop. She could talk to her associates and her researcher and try to get a handle on what was happening. Fortunately, her researcher, Kali, answered on the first attempt.

"Kali, what have you got for me? You wouldn't believe what's happening out here. You wouldn't believe where I am right now." Rebecca stopped as Kali held up a hand to silence Rebecca.

"Thank goodness you called Rebecca." She said, "You have to have nothing to do with New World. They are involved in some very shady dealings, and I have uncovered, that they are trying to get hold of that cattle property, not for cattle ranching, but nuclear waste storage - without the

government knowing. Without any government knowing. It's worth billions to them if they can get the deal through."
Rebecca was momentarily speechless.

"How did you get hold of that?" She asked in surprise.

"You know that arms dealer I go clubbing with sometimes? He's back in town. He really likes me." Kali smiled a cat-got-the-mouse smile and added. "He really likes me. When I casually mentioned New World, he got real interested in them, and not me. So I … uh, steered the conversation back to me, and in the meantime he kept talking in a distracted way about what they were up to. I have it all recorded."

"Kali!" Rebecca admonished her friend and researcher, "You never had a recording going did you? Will I be able to listen to it…" Kali laughed and added?

"I'll send you a transcript, edited of course. But I need your advice now. I haven't told the other partners of course. This is your brief. But this is a matter of national security, for almost everyone. You know if the wrong people get hold of this stuff…"

Rebecca tapped her bottom lip with her finger. "Kali, can you sit on this for a moment please? Just a day perhaps. Cooper has had to go and investigate something here on his property, and I think it's to do with New World. One of their aircraft is here, but there was no one in the homestead when we arrived. Some local aboriginal men came and asked him to go with them to show him something. Meantime, prepare a…" She smiled broadly, "sanitised transcript and make copies. Lock a copy of your recording in my safe and put your copy somewhere safe. As soon as Cooper returns and hears this, I will call you back. Can you also let the partners know that I will be back when I can?" Rebecca sat back and thought. Kali watching her through the video-cam.

"Rebecca, are you in Cooper's office now? I can see it's not your own laptop you are using, and it's sure not a hotel suite. What's he like?"

71

Rebecca coloured slightly, hoping Kali would not notice, as the video signal was not very good. Kali was not her best ever researcher for nothing though.

"Rebecca!" She shouted, "You've fallen for him haven't you? You have, I can see it in your face." Kali was grinning from ear to ear. "Come on - tell me all about him. Do you have a photo of him? What about a photo in the house?" Rebecca looked about the room. She hadn't noticed one in the main house, and there were no photos on the walls at all in this room, other than one of a huge bull over the fireplace. This was a man's house, and men didn't keep photos of themselves on the wall. How fitting, she smiled, that the only photo was a bull.

"No photos Kali, but he is... so gorgeous. He's over six feet tall, dark hair and the darkest blue eyes, with long lashes that any girl would love to have. He is very careful of his appearance. I can see a mother's influence there, and his clothes are the best. I mean, not fashions like we know them, but probably local Australian fashions that look very expensive. He is a working man after all, and until now has had very few women in his life. We've just come direct from Brisbane on the coast, and my things are still in the aeroplane on his runway. Kali, I think I really could love him."

Kali clapped her hands like a school girl.

"Has he kissed you yet?" She was leaning forward toward the camera, and almost whispering, as though others might hear. When Rebecca replied "Yes" she squealed with delight. Kali looked aside for a moment to her iPhone and momentarily frowned.

"Rebecca, that was Momo, the arms dealer. he just sent me a text. He's remembered talking about New World, and he said, I quote 'If you have friends involved with NW, tell them to get out, now.' Rebecca..." Kali was now looking worried. Rebecca replied. "Kali, I can't. I can't get out. I can't fly.

Cooper is not here. No one is here except the two aboriginal women here to keep me company. Left here by the man who came to get Cooper."

"Can't you drive out?" Replied Kali.

"I don't think so." Said Rebecca. "I would get lost in a heartbeat. There is no where to drive to, and anyway, I don't think there are any vehicles here that I could use."

"What do you mean, no where to drive to? Where are you?" Said Kali.

"Kali, I'm in the middle of a desert I think. We flew in here. There is nothing for thousands of miles I don't think." Rebecca was feeling a little nervous now. She knew she had met with bad people now, but she hadn't realised what scale these people were operating on. She was starting to get a little nervous for Cooper too. She knew he could probably look after himself out here, but he had gone off unarmed after all. What if he met up with them?

She couldn't lose him now. She had waited all of her life it felt like to meet Cooper. His arms around her would feel like such a haven, his lips on hers, brushing them. Probing them with the tip of his tongue, his hands on her body. No, she realised with a start, what ever it took, Cooper was hers. She had been alone long enough.

Kali had been watching Rebecca, and could see what was passing across her face. She marvelled at how someone so inscrutable in the court and in business as Rebecca could be so transparent to her, Kali. Kali smiled and Rebecca noticed.

"What is it Kali?" She said.

"Thinking of Cooper again were we? Rebecca, you are hopeless. The first man who comes along into your life and you appear to have fallen head over heels for him. I saw that look on your face, it was almost embarrassing to watch." Kali smiled hugely. "He must be a real stunner to turn your head. You must put him on camera as soon as he returns, meantime, I'm serious. Momo knows what he is talking

about. If he says get away from these people, he means it."
Kali looked at Rebecca for a moment.

"Perhaps I should call someone to come help you. I know
someone here in MI5 who can get the ball rolling. If you say
so, I'll get in touch with them." Kali waited for Rebecca.
"Just a moment Kali. I'll check outside." Rebecca flew from
the desk and looked out the front. The two girls were still
sitting in the shade and turned to smile at her. There were no
other people or even animals in sight. She ran through the
house to the back doors and looked outside. Nothing and
nobody, just the endless desert stretching away from the
remains of an old house yard fence.

"My God!" She thought, "This place is desolate. Oh Cooper,
how can you live here?" She went back to the computer.
"Kali," she said "perhaps you better had call your friends. I
have no idea who to call from here. Can you stay online
while you call? I need your company." Rebecca was feeling
very vulnerable and alone. The two aboriginal women may
have been right at home here, but this was a place she would
never be comfortable in. There wasn't enough money in the
world to alleviate the loneliness of this location. The house
could be turned into a mansion with all the delights of a
modern home - but it would remain an island in this sea of
desolation. Kali had nodded and picked up her iPhone and
stepped away from the video-cam and computer. Rebecca
sat at the desk and fiddled with some papers on the desk.
Numbers of cattle somewhere it looked like. Rebecca was
not given to panic, but she was starting to feel a little
unnerved. The silence of the place was total. Not a sound
could be heard. No insects, no people, no animals. Not even
any wind to rattle the blinds. Total silence and stillness. She
got up and started to pace around the room. She didn't want
to leave the sight of Kali on the screen in an animated
conversation with someone. The sound was off while Kali
made her call. She was very good at her job. Rebecca

thought about a big fat bonus for Kali when she finally returned to London. Kali was a good friend, but she was also the best researcher Rebecca had ever come across. She could see her now, waving some sheets of paper in the air as though the person on the phone could see them. She was pointing in the direction of the video-cam, but of course the person couldn't see Rebecca. Suddenly Kali was there on screen, the iPhone still in hand.

"Rebecca, can you go to Google Maps on that machine, and pin point your location for me." It was not a question.

"But how Kali. I have no real idea…"

"Rebecca, it's an Apple Mac you are on. It has location software built in. Go to Google Maps and click on "My Location" - then send the map to this address…" Kali reeled off an email address for her.

"Wait, wait, wait," shouted Rebecca, "I need a pen. ok, got it, repeat that email please. And Kali - stay on line please." Rebecca clicked on what look like a map on the bottom of the screen. To her immense relief up popped a map, but it was a map of some city centre.

"Kali…" She called.

"Rebecca click on the small arrow on the top, just near the address label on the left. Got it. Good. Has it located to where you are? It should be showing a blue circle. Good. Now click on the up arrow on the little box on the right side, send it as an email, and put in that address. My friend will have it in seconds. They will know what to do." Kali waited. Within moments Rebecca had sent the map. This was very strange. She couldn't believe someone in London would soon know exactly where she was, down to the nearest centimetre.

"Ok Kali. Done. What did your friend say to your request?" Rebecca said.

"Well, he was a bit cautious at first, but when I mentioned Momo, and Coopers remote property location, he became very interested. They're… looking into it." Kali sat back in her office chair.

"Rebecca, are you going to be ok for a little while?" Kali had things to do, and suddenly Rebecca realised it, and knew she should not be holding Kali online just to keep her company. She straightened her shoulders and sat up.

"Kali, I can't keep you. I'll go back out the front and watch for Cooper with the two young aboriginal women. Well, I'm presuming they are young women, because they are… um… built like young women. Firm breasts still. They have no clothes on other than some sort of fibre belt thing around the waist. I'd love to take some photographs of them, but my gear is still in the 'plane and I'm not going out there unless I really have to. It's actually hotter now than it was when we arrived. I can't believe it." Rebecca was about to sign off and just waited for Kali to answer her phone.

"Rebecca, I'm told you will have company soon. Bye for now." Click - and Kali was gone. No further explanation. What did she mean, 'have company soon'? Rebecca thought of the options. It was either New World coming back, Cooper coming back, or because she had seen Kali take that call, it was someone from the government coming. Only time would tell, and she hoped in any case that Cooper would have returned by then. There was absolutely nothing for her to do now but wait, so she decided to look through the house where Cooper lived. She was curious about living conditions in this remote place.

The house as Cooper had mentioned was very large. It was all on one level and seemed spread out over a very wide area. Rebecca couldn't guess at the physical dimensions because every corner she turned seemed to lead to another set of rooms. She soon discovered what could only be guest rooms set on one side of the house, and so self contained that they would allow guests to remain completely separate from the rest of the house if they wanted. Perhaps these were meant to be her rooms, the ones that Cooper had suggested for her.

She hoped not as she realised with a start that she would much prefer to stay with Cooper. There was one problem though. She was not sure that she could stay in this place long. She was beginning to feel some sympathy with the other girls that Cooper had mentioned, who had fled the place as soon as possible. However, it was not likely that she would be staying in any case. She had a busy practice back in London, partners to work with, friends to catch up with. It was also evident that if Cooper was not in the house, the house was eerily empty. "I have only been here a few minutes, and already I'm talking to myself." Rebecca said to no one in general. She completed her wander through the house. It was a beautiful place, or had been. But now it was tired and worn by a lifetime of minimum care from men. First Coopers father, left on his own with only the boy, Cooper, and now Cooper himself rattling around the big old house, keeping a station property going for what Rebecca could see was no good reasons. If he stayed on out here, he would wither and die like the sparse vegetation of the dusty plains and sand dunes. Rebecca resolved that she wasn't going to let that happen. She went back to the front door and out onto the wide cool veranda. She had already noticed, that if she wasn't actually in the sun, the heat was bearable. The deep shade of the veranda had to be quite a few degrees cooler than out in the open.

The afternoon sun was starting to throw long shadows across the yards from the various fixtures that seemed scattered randomly around the area, and the few skeletal trees that still stood, struggling for survival in this harsh place. Rebecca had earlier discovered the hat rack on the wall by the door and now took the widest brim hat she could find and pulled it down over her hair and stepped out into the yard. Immediately the other two young women were on their feet and following. They appeared to be totally at ease in the hot sun, and their bare feet on the scorching earth made

Rebecca winch just to look at them. The fierce heat of midday was now waning, and although it was still hot, Rebecca felt she would be alright now. She really needed to retrieve her things from the aircraft and get back inside to freshen up. She certainly didn't want Cooper seeing her all sweaty and dusty when he came back, regardless of how he looked. 'He would always look gorgeous!' She thought with a smile, but she always prided herself on looking her best in any situation, so she set off for the plane.

Chapter 7

With The two girls following, still looking about them in wariness. Rebecca opened the cargo hatch she had seen Cooper close with a snap when they loaded some supplies up in Toowoomba, their only stop on the way from Brisbane. Her suitcase and carry-on were there, and she lifted them to the ground, and then climbed up the steps to retrieve her laptop from near her seat. The interior was still hot, but the doors had been left open, and the interior was cooling quickly. Rebecca looked around for her bags, but the girls were already halfway back to the house with them. Rebecca hurried after them. She had never meant them to be her bag carriers. She was very embarrassed and tried to take her bags from them and carry them herself. The girls just laughed and waved her away as they went back to the house. The bags were deposited on the veranda for Rebecca and she took their hands in turn and shook them, thanking the girls for helping her. They had no common language, but they understood none the less, and smiled shyly. Rebecca was at a loss now. She badly needed something to eat, and her two companions must be hungry by now. There was nothing for it but to raid the pantry.

Cooper ran steadily along with the aboriginal man in a direct line away from the homestead for some time. A steady mile burning pace that covered a lot of ground. Cooper did think that it may have been better to take one of the station vehicles, like one of the camel chasers. Cut down Landrovers with heavy metal bars welded on all around the vehicle to protect them from raging camels. They were go-anywhere vehicles, and Cooper wished he had one now. He was however not struggling with the pace. He was used to it. His companions for a lot of his lifetime had been the aboriginal children of the nearby camps, and his working life had conditioned him to the tough landscape and lifestyle needed out here in the outback. As he trotted along, he couldn't help but think of Rebecca, a part of his mind on what he was doing and watching the other man, but part of it wondering if indeed it had been a smart move to bring her out here. How would she fare back there in the homestead with him having just literally run off to who knew where?

"How far now?" He questioned the other man. Cooper still didn't know his name. These wild men had a language of their own, and their names were often unpronounceable as far as others were concerned. This fellow spoke some English, so had probably been educated on a mission somewhere at some time in his youth, before he had gone 'back to the bush'. Might be worth a try thought Cooper.

"What name you speak?" He asked in a broken Pigeon English often used by people.

The man looked across at him.

"Billy." Was all he said.

"Ok, Billy. How far now to what you show me?" Cooper was wondering at the sense of this by now.

"Not far now boss. Just over this next hill. We stop this side." Billy replied. "Don't you worry about your woman boss; my girls take good care nothing happens." He added.

The rise they were heading for was little more than that, just a slight rise in the land, and Cooper remembered that there was an old artesian water bore just on the other side, in a shallow depression. It had long since been capped off, and there was no water there now. Suddenly Billy halted and crouched down, his spears flat on the ground. He signalled Cooper to crouch down as well. The afternoon was well advanced now, and Cooper was getting pretty thirsty. He really wished he had not followed Billy so quickly, without thought. He should have realised these men could go all day and more, without a drink or food. Tough men who lived in this desert for thousands of years. 'Well,' thought Cooper, 'I'll just have to put up with it.'

Following Billy's lead, Cooper lay on his stomach and together they crawled over the sand and rock until they could just see over the ridge and into the depression on the other side. Cooper almost let out a yell of surprise and anger. There was a large ex-military vehicle, six wheels with huge desert tyres on. On the far side of it from where they lay in the sand, a large cage like structure had been erected, and inside Cooper could see his station hands imprisoned. Bill put a restraining hand on him as he was about to leap to his feet and rush down the slope to try to rescue them.

"Look boss." Whispered Billy. "They ok. Got shade, got water." He had a huge grin across his face. These men laughed very little, and to see one with such a huge grin told Cooper that something was up, and Billy was going to enjoy it. Meantime, it was also evident that there was a large group of heavily armed men involved in the party that had imprisoned his men - and the dogs he now noticed. They obviously hadn't head his plane arrive, as fortunately he had arrived at the homestead from the other direction, and flown in very low. They would not have seen or heard him arrive. What could they be up to? How had this huge truck arrived here? It must have come up the Strzelecki Track from Adelaide. There is no way it could have come in from the other direction without alerting people in three states. As it was, how they had managed to get here he couldn't imagine. He looked at Billy and, keeping his head and his voice down, asked.

"Billy, what you know about these men?"

"Boss," Billy replied "these men and more bin here 'bout three month. Big camp over that way." He pointed to the south. "They dig holes with machines. Deep holes. They disturb the spirits of our ancestors. Holes very deep. Make landing place for planes. Big planes." He paused and checked the scene in front of him. "This our country boss, but we ask you. You know about this? You send these men?"

Billy was not smiling now. His hands gripped his spears. Long fire hardened shafts with wickedly barbed points. These were not game hunting spears Cooper suddenly realised. These were man hunting spears. He reached his hand out and clasped Billy on the arm.

"No Billy, this is not my doing. These are very bad people; you must not touch them. Too many of your people will be killed." Cooper had realised in the instant what he thought Billy and his men were up to. Billy looked at Cooper with an unreadable expression.

The leaders of the group were set up under a tent flap. stretched out from the side of the truck and had a radio of some sort set up. They were busy with maps and papers, and one was relaying information on the radio. In all Cooper counted twelve men, all of them armed and some with automatic weapons like he had seen the military use. How on earth he was going to rescue his men he couldn't imagine? The New World group had obviously simply taken everyone by surprise, and for some reason now had them penned up as their prisoners. At least none appeared to be hurt, which was a good thing at least, thought Cooper. He wanted to know about the other camp Billy had mentioned. "Billy," he whispered. "Tell me about the other camp. Three months they have been there you say!" Cooper shook his head. He must be slipping to let something like that happen on his place and not know about it.

"The other camp long way, nearly two day - three day for me that way." He pointed past the current camp, away to the south west. "It built in Raven Gorge between two mountains. You know that place boss?" Billy asked. Indeed, Cooper did. A more remote part of this vast property, in a land that was empty to start with, could not have been found. Cooper had seen tracks of vehicles, and abandoned camp sites over the last month or so, and discarded cartons with New World's logo on them blowing about the desert. He had assumed that they were prospecting. Billy continued.

"Big camp boss. Maybe one hundred men. Drilling and opening up big cave into mountain. Also making short place for aeroplane to land. Short, but very wide. Maybe big plane." Billy gripped his spears. "They not ask traditional owners about this. Now I know they not ask you too." Billy was right to be angry. The people of his tribe were the traditional owners of vast areas of this land that the cattle property was situated on. They took it very seriously when unauthorised activities took place. The members of Billy's group chose to live their traditional way out here, and to Coopers knowledge there were quite a few of them. Not enough to take on a hundred well armed men though, and even here, not enough to take on even a dozen well armed men.

"How many men with you Billy?" Asked Cooper. Billy held up the outspread fingers of his left hand. Five men. Cooper shook his head. "Billy, we have to go back and get more help. Nothing we can do here right now, and it's getting late. Almost dark now." The afternoon sun was almost half way below the horizon already, and out here there was no twilight. One minute light, the next dark. Billy flashed a grin and said. "You go back boss. We ok. Have some fun with these people." Cooper looked around, and even in the remaining light, he could see that there were no other people visible other than those in the camp. As Cooper watched Billy gave a low bird call like a magpie's mating call. The men in the camp ignored it, thinking it was just a lone bird of the desert. Suddenly, on a sand ridge on the other side of the camp a lone aboriginal stood up, clear against the westering sun. He shook his spears and harangued the people in the camp in incomprehensible native language, stamping his feet and raising a dust cloud at the same time. One of the men near the caged station hands started to raise his rifle toward the aboriginal when in one flowing motion the man notched a smooth pointed spear in his throwing stick and launched the spear. The man with the gun couldn't believe his eyes. He saw the spear heading directly for him but was too spellbound to move. He let out a scream of agony as the long fire hardened spear point buried itself deep in his right upper thigh. He dropped his automatic and howled in pain. The stockmen in the prison cage laughed at him without mercy.

Cooper was dumbfounded. "Billy, now they be plenty mad, like hornets." He said.

"Don't worry boss, smooth spear. Punishment spear. See, come out real easy. We careful not to kill them. Just punish."

Sure enough as Cooper looked one of the other men easily pulled the spear out of the mans leg and they rushed him to the camp to dress his wound. The man on the ridge who had thrown the spear had disappeared as soon as he had thrown it. There was much consternation in the camp, with men rushing to and fro encouraging each other to go out and scout around. No one wanted to be first though. When three men got together and decided they could watch each other's back as it were, they started out in the direction of the rise where Cooper and Billy lay hidden. They had taken no more than a few steps toward the edge of the camp when they were stopped in their track by a thrumming sound that seemed to be coming from overhead, and with a whoosh a long and very barbed spear buried itself in the sand right at the leader's boots. He stopped immediately. There was no one to be seen. The general direction of the spear's flight could be guessed at, and together they loosed off a dozen rounds in the general direction, to no effect. Other than to have their leader shouting at them not to be so stupid and frightened like little girls. They shrugged and headed back into the relative safety of the camp by the truck.

Cooper couldn't help smiling. Billy thought it was a huge joke.

"Ok boss. We go back now. I show you the way. Dark soon enough. Your woman be worried now. These people not going anywhere. If they try, more spearing." He was not laughing now. The two of them scrambled back down the ridge and stood up. It was almost dark, and they set off at a run to return to the station homestead. Billy unerring in his course, leading the way. They had been running about an hour when Billy stopped, and started feeling around a small rocky outcrop, sniffing as he went.

"Water here boss. Maybe one, two handful. You drink then we go on." He said.

Cooper felt around, guided by Billy, and sure enough, almost beneath a small rocky outcrop was a small basin of water, maybe a saucepan full. He took two handfuls and stood back. Billy took only one and immediately set off again at the same steady pace. It was very late when finally, the lights of the homestead came into view. Cooper's heart swelled with pride for Rebecca. It could only mean that she had worked out how to turn on the generator for the power. The smaller things like the computer would run for days on the battery bank, but fridges and lights and other larger equipment needed a generator. Cooper had never gone fully solar. It was never considered worth the huge costs involved. Maybe if Rebecca came out here? Then he certainly would. He smiled to himself in the dark. "Cooper, you're a fool. What makes you think Rebecca would even dream now of coming out here to live. You bring her here, and the first thing you do is run off." The two men came into the homestead yard still at a trot, with Cooper calling out loudly that it was he and Billy. He didn't want to get shot at in his own front yard. Billy stopped, and his two women came out to greet him, talking and laughing with him. Obviously pleased to see him, and regale him with tales of that strange woman inside the house. She had fed the women, and gave them water, and tried to do their hair. To no one's surprise, that proved an impossible task. Billy was laughing with them, and they all settled down on the veranda in comfort. Rebecca stood at the doorway, looking out at Cooper who hadn't yet come fully onto the veranda. 'Truth is', he thought. 'I'm not too sure of my welcome?' He was staring at Rebecca now though. The light behind her fro the lounge room had her in perfect silhouette now, and the cotton skirt she had on left almost nothing to the imagination. Cooper clutched at the veranda post. His heart was racing and not from the exertion of the day's adventure. He stepped toward Rebecca to take her in his arms and make love to her right there and then. He wanted to shower her in kisses, feel her breath on his cheek, feel the soft suppleness of her in his hands.

"Cooper." She demanded. "Don't you dare come near me with that river of sweat running off your head. I've died here all day waiting for you to come back, and the first thing you do is want to grab me and hug me to that awful sweaty body. Ugh" Rebecca spun on her heel and walked with exaggerated care back into the house. She was ecstatic however. Cooper had been going to. to. he had been going to grab her. Take her in his arms and hug her to him. To that beautiful body. Sweaty sure, but manly beautiful sweat. She spun around to see Cooper coming into the room and looking somewhat sheepish now, his face aflame with the thought of what he had been about to do. He was raising an arm and pointing toward the back of the house, probably the showers she thought. She walked up to him and carefully leaned forward without touching him, put a finger under his lower jaw and closed his mouth, and placed a long lingering kiss on that beautiful archer's bow.

"Good to see you safely back Cooper." She said as she stepped back. Cooper passed silently by as he headed for the bathroom and a much needed shower. 'Good to see you back?' He thought, 'What kind of welcome home is that?'

He shook his head. But that kiss. Wow with a capital W he thought. He stopped at the bathroom door with his hand on the door frame. He had suddenly realised that Rebecca was most likely very upset, and possibly frightened, and he had said nothing as he came into the house. He spun around and headed back into the lounge room. Rebecca was sitting on the single sofa with her head in her hands. The stress of the last hours had finally gotten to her, and Coopers entry back into the house had been such a relief. However, as far as she was concerned she was out of here the first thing in the morning. She should never have come out here in the first place. The man didn't even keep chickens for crying out loud. A freezer full of beef, another freezer full of frozen vegetables, a pantry full of tins of various other foods and condiments, and that was it. No sign of any fresh food at all. Rebecca had realised of course that Cooper spent a good deal of time away from the house working, both on the property itself, and in the cities where he did business, but not even chickens for fresh eggs! She heard him come back into the room and looked up with tear stained cheeks, wiping away the tears with the back of her hand at the same time. "Not even chickens Cooper. How can you?" She exclaimed. Cooper was dumbfounded. 'Chickens? What was the woman talking about?'

"Chickens? What are you talking about Rebecca, what have chickens got to do with anything?" Cooper replied. He stood just inside the lounge room scratching his head. Rebecca continued.

"This house, I'm sorry, but this house looks like a well kept workshop. A house where everything a man could want is within reach - except a good woman. Don't you even have a house keeper?" Rebecca swept her arms out in a wide all encompassing circle. She looked around as Cooper was looking around. The time worn furniture, the old photographs on the wall. The ornaments on the sideboard and on top of the piano, itself with a very fine layer of dust on it's mahogany black surface. It looked as though nothing had been touched in years. It probably hadn't. For a man who took such good care of himself, Cooper took precious little care of his living space. Rebecca could understand his sense of loss at first losing his mother at a young age, and then his father some years later, but he was an adult now. Everyone in the world lost their parents at some point. You moved on. Cooper started to look around. He looked at the old Grandfather clock near the fireplace wall. It was stopped at eight fifteen. Cooper realised he had no idea what day it had stopped, just that it had stopped at eight fifteen. He looked at his watch. He had been gone the better part of the day. He took up the water jug that was on the table and drank most of it in one long draught. His stomach growled loudly, and they both looked at it as though it was some unusual event. Cooper again started to look about the room. He was seeing it as though for the first time. He understood now about the chickens. Rebecca was telling him something, and he had better listen, or he would lose her forever. The place was tidy, and clean apart from the fine layer of dust, unavoidable out here, but nothing had moved. In fact, he realised with a start, nothing had moved since his mother had passed away some thirty years ago. Everything was still in exactly the same place as she had left it.

"How have I never noticed this?" He said aloud, a sad look in his eyes as he focused on Rebecca. "Rebecca," he said. "Let me clean up and find something to eat, and I will tell you what we found. You can tell me what has been happening here at the same time. It will only take a moment. I'm sorry Rebecca, you have no idea how sorry I am to have brought you into this..." He couldn't finish, he was lost for words to describe something that was both his family home, and a place he no longer recognised as a home. Within minutes he was in the shower, the water cascading down over his body, washing away the sweat and dust of his long journey. Rebecca stood in the doorway of the bathroom and tried not to look at Cooper partially hidden behind the steamed up glass of the shower screen door. She could however see his superbly proportioned body, muscles rippling over his frame as he quickly lathered off the dust and washed his hair in a cursory manner. He was getting rid of the dust and sweat, not taking his time over the finer necessities like shampoo and conditioner.

"Cooper," she began, and he looked up to see her there, nearly dropping the soap. "I spoke to my researcher in London. She contacted some people she knows, and told me that the people who are here on your property are, amongst other things, involved in nuclear waster disposal, arms dealings, and probably drugs. It's the nuclear waste disposal that has everyone hopping, because apparently New World have solved one of the great puzzles of how to contain such waste in very small containers that show no radiation footprint. In other words, you could wave a Geiger counter over one, and it would not register. What they haven't solved is where to store them, because being so small, there are a lot of them." Rebecca paused. The sight of Cooper stepping out of the shower only feet in front of her was too much. Cooper was listening intently and had stopped what he was doing so he could.

"Oh my God Cooper..." Gasped Rebecca. There was a distinct note of longing in her voice. Cooper visibly started and quickly wrapped a bath towel around his waist. He went a slight shade of red.

"Sorry Rebecca, I forgot for a moment, I was so intent on what you were saying." He came to stand only inches from her in the doorway. 'He is so tall,' thought Rebecca as she looked first up into his eyes, then down at the bath towel with it's very obvious rise over his sex. She wanted to reach out and stroke that rise in the towel, to feel it harden and try to escape the confines of the material that held it. Her breath was getting shorter, and she was starting to weaken at the knees. It may be the early hours of the evening, but she had already showered and eaten what she could put together for her and the aboriginal women. She was now wide awake and her senses were zinging at the proximity of Cooper's nakedness. Rebecca felt herself becoming very aroused, her wetness alerting her to what she wanted to happen. She reached up and put a hand on Cooper's upper arm, not trusting herself to move otherwise.

"Cooper..." She almost croaked, clearing her voice quickly. "We don't actually know each other very well do we. And I don't think you like me very much - not really. Let's stick to business, then we can decide if we stay here or leave at first light." Rebecca sighed and turned to go back into the lounge room. Cooper didn't hesitate now, he reached out as she turned and wrapped his arms around her, pulling her to him so her back was against him. His arms almost around her, as his hands cupped her breasts, her nipples instantly erect, her whole chest fluttering at the feel of his hands on her. She could feel the hardness of him against her bottom, the thin cotton dress she had on absolutely no guard against such feeling as this. Cooper whispered in her ear.

"Rebecca, stop talking for one minute will you." His breath on her earlobe raised goose bumps all over her body, almost alarming her as her own inner place started to pulse with a desire that she had never, ever felt in her life before. 'Oh my God...' she whispered only half aloud. Cooper slowly and softly massaged her breasts and began to move slightly from his hips, softly pressing against her then allowing himself to ease back. She could feel the hardness of him at each press and it was lighting her up like the Blackpool tower. Slowly Cooper turned her around to face him, his hands now cupping her either side on her bottom. His towel fell to the floor and Rebecca could feel his nakedness, his pulsing hardness, pushing against her dress and trying to find a way between her thighs. Rebecca was gasping with emotion and desire, and a soft moaning deep in Coopers throat had her trembling from head to foot. He bent his head down and kissed her with a burning passion that took her breath away. It had been a long long time since anyone had kissed her, and for Cooper, he couldn't remember the last time he had kissed a girl and had her kiss him back with the desire and passion that he was now feeling from Rebecca.

What was he doing he thought, amidst the tangle of emotions that flooded his mind? 'It doesn't feel as though she dislikes me.' Cooper was beginning to lose his self control, as surely as Rebecca was losing hers. He swept her up in his arms and carried her down the hallway to his bedroom. The door was shut but Cooper wasn't about to put Rebecca down as they still struggled to continue the kiss while he walked— lurched really from side to side—down the hallway. With one swift kick the old wooden door crashed open and banged against the side dresser, spilling the few ornaments and photographs onto the floor. They hardly noticed as Cooper placed Rebecca none too gently onto the massive old carved frame bed, its soft mattress and duvet cover almost enveloping her completely. She struggled to sit up and Cooper helped her lift her dress up and over her head. He was suddenly startled at the sight of her near nakedness, her breasts straining against a small bra and what appeared to him to be little more than a G-String covering her. Pink material with a deep red rose stitched into its surface he noticed in one distracted moment. Rebecca flicked off her bra in one swift movement as Cooper lowered himself onto the bed and raised on one elbow looked deep into her eyes. She couldn't hold such a direct gaze as Cooper seemed to looking into her very soul. 'What was he seeking there?' She thought briefly. His huge right hand slowly brushed down over her stomach until it reached the waist band of her thong style panties. As his fingers travelled slowly over the distance, she could feel her stomach lurching as the muscles throbbed and tightened alternately as though a huge wave of desire were breaking over her.

"Oh yes Cooper, please please please .... oh Cooper, pleaseeee." Rebecca was almost shouting by now as Cooers hand pressed against the mound of her sex. Not for nothing was this called "The Mountain of Venus" she thought as stars began to burst inside her. Cooper slid her panties down over her ankles and dropped the tiny particle of clothing on the floor. He gently slid his hand back up her legs and at her knees slowly put a little pressure on them to move them apart. He moved his hand all the way up until his finger tips just touched the swollen and glistening lips of Rebecca's sex. She let out a moan of ecstasy as he began to brush her swollen parts, alternately slipping a finger just inside then out again.

Rebecca's hand found Cooper's swollen sex, and he almost collapsed onto his back when she took him between her thumb and forefinger and gently began to draw back and forth along the length of it. He was gasping and shuddering with pleasure, his desire evident in the far away look in his eyes as he began to dwell in some inner place where only pleasure and desire lived.

"Take me with you." Rebecca whispered as she urged him to rise above her, her legs wide and knees raised slightly now as Cooper poised himself just above her. Rebecca could feel herself opening ready for him, the wetness intensifying every movement of her muscles. Slowly Cooper entered her. He knew it had been a long time for Rebecca as it had been for him. He was determined not to rush into her and ravish her in the madness of his burning desire to take her. As he entered her ever so slowly, Rebecca could feel the air rushing out of her, a long drawn out sigh was coming from her mouth and she thought she was going to drown in depths of the pleasure that was overwhelming her. Her hips rose up to meet him, as repeatedly he drew back then forward again, each movement drawing a longer sighing moan from Cooper and an increasingly frantic wail from Rebecca. Suddenly Cooper began to grip Rebecca's shoulders frantically as he fought to hold on long enough for Rebecca to reach her zenith. With a scream that could have been heard in the far way campsite, she suddenly lurched upwards, her whole body flailing against Cooper as she tried to take every particle of him inside her, against her, all around her. Coopers blazing body felt her release surging through her, and the resulting spasms of her body pushed him over the cliff that he had been teetering on. Cooper felt himself falling into the abyss of pleasure that Rebecca had drawn him into. He hurtled forward, crashing against the walls of the pleasure temple of Rebecca's desire, until finally all movement stopped, and he lifted his head in wonder to find himself with Rebeca clasped tightly in his arms, an expression of pure contentment and wonder on her face. While they both waited for the eddies and currents to subside, Rebecca was drawing tiny circles on Coopers face with one tiny fingernail. Cooper moved to lay down beside her, but Rebecca locked him in place with her legs wrapped around him, and just smiled and shook her head slowly. Her movement had been like an electric shock going through his whole body, and Cooper was instantly erect. Rebecca smiled and began to move slowly against him.

The darkness outside was absolute, and the two aboriginal women and Billy could not be seen as they quietly padded away from the homestead to return to the deep desert country and plains that were their home.

Chapter 8

The morning sun was streaming in through the wide front door and lighting up the spacious lounge come living room. Dust motes drifted in the still air as not a breath was stirring yet. The old house creaked and cracked, and the iron roof was popping as the sun warmed it. Cooper and Rebecca were both fast asleep still. Slowly the sun crept across the floor of the bedroom until it was shining full on the bed. This was the full on Central Australian desert sun. So it was immediately hot. Cooper blinked awake in shock as the sun hit his face. He had forgotten to close the curtains last night and now he tried to extricate himself from the tangle of sheets and legs and arms to get up and close them. He was also desperately in need of the bathroom, so he continued on past the window to the bathroom after flicking the curtains closed, and was soon back on the bed. It was already too hot in the house to stay in bed, and Rebecca sprang out of bed, coyly hugging the sheets to herself, and went into the bathroom closing the door behind her. Presently Cooper heard the shower running, so he rummaged around for some fresh clothes and underwear. 'Chickens?' He thought. Almost the first thing he was thinking about, and he turned it over in his mind trying to grasp the meaning of it. 'I don't even have any chickens?' He couldn't pin it down, but he knew it was important. So now he had two things to worry about. People trespassing on his property, upsetting the traditional owners, as well as himself of course, and in addition to that a lack of chickens. Hmmm. "Which," he said aloud "is the more important of those two?" It didn't take him long. The illegal entries he could deal with in a number of ways. Some less pleasant than others. But Rebecca had suddenly become the most important person in his life, and if she wanted chickens, by God she would have chickens.

"Rebecca." He called softly through the door now that the

shower had stopped.

"Yes Cooper." She replied.

"You mentioned something that you had found out from London, last night before we, um, er... became distracted." He actually flushed slightly, his cheeks reddening. He felt like a schoolboy caught out with a cigarette. This was silly, he was a grown man for goodness' sake.

"Yes, my friend in MI5 told me he was taking care of those people. When I mentioned Momo the arms dealer, they became very worried. I could hear phones ringing and people rushing about in the background. He did say someone would be here very soon. I'm not too sure, but I got the feeling that they would not be coming out here on a commercial flight via two or three stopovers. It sounded much more urgent than that."

"Well to hell with them." Said Cooper out loud. "We have things to do this morning. My station men are being held prisoner about twenty five or so miles from here and I have to rescue them. I think Billy wants to spear the intruders. I hope he doesn't. Well, not yet anyway. But he and his people are very upset. These people have really offended them, and I am sure, although he didn't say, that something else has happened as well. I know the local people, and it takes a lot to draw them out of the desert fastness now."

Rebecca came out of the bathroom door, drying her hair with a towel. She looked at Cooper with a grave look on her face. She was obviously worried about the whole thing, and she had been thinking. If she hadn't come out here, would these people be on Coopers property in the first place? If she had conducted the business - insisting on doing so - from her London office, then maybe none of this would have happened. She voiced her concerns to Cooper as she went and found her suitcase and dragged it into the bedroom. Cooper went and stood just outside the door, his back turned while Rebecca got dressed. He didn't feel at all comfortable being in the same room while she did this. They weren't married, and disregarding last night, 'How can I disregard that!' He thought in amazement, instantly becoming aroused again as his thoughts momentarily dwelt on their activities, but never the less, he knew that a girl needed her privacy. He was not sure what for, but as the aboriginal women called it, 'secret women's business', it was better he didn't ask, so he removed himself and gave her her privacy.

"You needn't worry on that score my darling..." His voice choked a little. He hadn't ever used that word to anyone, and the surprise of it gave him pause. Rebecca came out to stand before him. He was about to begin apologising as Rebecca looked up at him, but her smile was wistful and soft. She put a finger on his lips.

"Don't you dare apologise my big Aussie? It's the nicest word anyone has ever called me, especially as I know you mean it. She brushed a kiss across his lips, thinking as she did so that she had become very attached to his beautiful mouth and that wonderful arches bow. And there were now a few other things she was very attached to. 'Like his whole body.' She smiled as the thought of it. Cooper was very relieved, he thought for sure he had upset her again. He had had enough of upsetting her. Instead of answering her he bent down and returned the kiss, lingering as long as he was able to without wanting to carry her off to the bedroom again.

"Cooper, behave..." Rebecca admonished him gently. They both smiled and headed for the kitchen by mutual consent. Cooper got to the door of the kitchen and stopped dead in his tracks. It had suddenly hit him. Chickens. Of course chickens. Chickens laid eggs, and he had no eggs. A 'full English Breakfast' - which he was sure Rebecca would want, required eggs. All he had was powdered eggs like some Antarctic explorer. He smacked his forehead in despair and frustration. He had brought Rebecca all this way without even thinking about what they would eat. Rebecca stood watching him. She could almost see the wheels turning. She was very good at reading people, and she loved this man and... Rebecca's thoughts lurched to a stop. 'I love this man.' She thought. 'Not just because of the sex, although that was very nice,' but she knew in her heart of hearts that it was a truth.

"Cooper..." Rebecca suddenly realised that here in the kitchen doorway, she didn't know how to proceed. Her, a world class lawyer capable of stopping judges in their speeches. She tried again. "Cooper my darling." She said in a very low voice, not sure how it felt in her mouth to be saying it. "My darling." She said again softly, looking directly at Cooper, gazing into his deep blue eyes and feeling herself being drawn into the whirlpool all over again. She clutched at his arm.

"Cooper, please. Breakfast. We have things to do. Places to go." She forced her thoughts back on track. There were men in danger out there. They were in danger in fact. Almost by mutual recognition, they both remembered the New World aeroplane out there on the landing strip, even now simmering under the rapidly ascending sun. That meant who ever owned it was coming back here. Rebecca said, "Their aeroplane." Almost at the same instant as Cooper said "The New World plane..." Reality came crashing back. Their personal discoveries would have to wait. They hurried into the kitchen and Cooper soon had some bacon from the freezer, tomatoes from the same source, and bread ... from the same source all sizzling away on the vast top of the stove. Gas meant that it was hot instantly, and the size of the range was something to behold. Rebecca stood back and left Cooper to it. It was obvious that originally it had been a wood or coal perhaps fuelled stove, but converted to gas at some point. It occupied almost an entire wall of the kitchen. Rebecca was totally enjoying watching Cooper. So self assured, so capable. Ok, so they lacked fresh foods. This was a very remote place after all. Obviously he was not here all that often either. So frozen rations it had to be. Oh how he needed a woman in his life - and a house keeper. Rebecca looked about her. This place was vast, and there was no way she would be capable of bringing it back to life on her own. At the very least it would need the help of at least two housekeepers, a couple of gardeners and who knew who else. She smiled at the thought. Perhaps, just perhaps Cooper would be happy in a much kinder climate, in an already established house, with her in it - of course. She smiled. Cooper couldn't take his eyes off her. She seemed to be blocking everything else out of his sight and thoughts. He burnt his fingers on the bacon, he burnt his fingers on the stove top, he almost let the fry pan fall to the floor he was so busy watching Rebecca. He knew he had to concentrate on the problems outside. They were very big problems, and men were in danger. His men, his friends. Finally, he had the light meal served up, and they hurriedly ate, almost reluctant to sit at the table. They drank almost a jug of fruit juice from the refrigerator, and Cooper flung the dishes into the sink.

"Later." He said. "We have to work out what to do. Firstly, a call to the police in Innamincka, to find out what they are doing. I called them last night as soon as I got in. They should have got back to us by now. I need to find out why not. Then I have to get you to the hotel there." He held up his hand as Rebecca started to protest that she wasn't leaving him.

"No Rebecca. It's far too dangerous for you to stay here. We fly out now. Right now, to Innamincka. Then I'll come back and sort this out. Rebecca, I've only just found you…"
Cooper stumbled over the unfamiliar words.

"I don't want to lose you. I. love you."

Rebecca was vaguely frightened. But Cooper was here with her. What harm could she come to, and he might need her. Why would they attack Cooper's property, or his men in fact? Would they attack the homestead if they knew Cooper was here? Almost in answer to her unspoken question a rifle shot rang out, the actual sound of the bullet could be heard travelling past the house then it slammed into the front tyre of their plane with a loud bang and a hiss of escaping air. A second shot smashed the windscreen. Cooper was already running for the rifles Rebecca had left leaning against the large wooden table in the main lounge room. The boxes of cartridges were open on the table, and he could see spare magazines there as well. 'Good girl.' He thought.

"Sorry Rebecca." He said through clenched teeth, "We won't be going to the hotel after all." He picked up the phone. Rebecca wondered how he was going to call anyone. As if reading her thoughts, he said in an aside.

"Wireless telephone. No cables out this way." A big smile lit his face. He pointed to her laptop as he was waiting for the call to establish. "Can you contact your people and let them know what's happening?" Rebecca jumped for her laptop. There had been no other shots, but she was staying low, and out of sight of the windows. Skype was still running, as the computer hadn't been turned off last night. She had momentary thoughts of what could be heard in a far off country with the video link still open to her friend and researcher.

Rebecca started the tone to call her friend to the screen. It took only a moment and Kali was there on the screen.

"What's up Rebecca?" She asked. "Are you still in the Australian outback with that gorgeous hunk?" Kali smiled mischievously. "Yes, I've looked up photographs of him. Very nice." She then saw that Rebecca was looking very worried. "Rebecca…" She started to say.

"Kali, we are under attack! Can you believe it; someone is shooting at us. Well, at our aeroplane anyway. They shot the tyre out on the front, and the windscreen. We can't fly out now." Rebecca suddenly shrieked as a bullet smashed out the far lounge room window across from her. It had gone straight over her head, having come through the wall on her side of the room. Kali was on the other end of the video link jumping up and down in frustration and fear for Rebecca. She was also on the phone to her MI5 contact, yelling about terrorists in the outback, her friend being shot at, and what the hell was his department doing about it.

"Yes now. Right now." She was screaming into the phone. Kali had never felt so useless. Her friend was in grave danger and all she could do was watch. Meantime, Rebecca had dragged her laptop onto the floor under the table and was trying to get herself into focus again so Kali could see her. Meantime, Cooper had dropped the phone on the table and was yelling to whoever was on the other end of the line.

"We could do with a bit of help here James." He turned aside to Rebecca, for a moment he had thought she had been hit, laying there under the table. "It's Sergeant Hurley." Then he went back to the window on the side of the house where the last bullet had entered. He looked carefully out into the cattle yards that took up most of the area about three hundred yards away on that side of the house. There were no cattle out there of course. Wrong time of the year, so what was that buzzard so interested in as it circled lazily in the blue cloudless sky. There was no cover in the cattle yards, but further back, one of the countless sand dunes rose up, its direction almost parallel to the house. It was covered in tufted Spinifex grass, and a gnarled and stunted scrubby bush clung to the very top. Cooper watched that bush carefully for a few minutes and was rewarded when he saw someone's dark blue baseball cap just showing between the lower branches of the bush where it hugged the sand. None of his people had hats like that. Useless out here. Certainly none of the stockmen, and for sure none of the wild men who roamed his place. He moved back into the room and propped a chair in line with the window and rested his .308

Winchester on the chair back. He took careful aim at the bush trunk right beside the very tip of the hat he could just see next to it. They wouldn't be able to see him there in the relative darkness of the house as he took aim and slowly squeezed the trigger. The resulting roar rattled the windows and sent dust flying from every surface. Rebecca reared up under the table and almost knocked her self out as her head hit the underside, letting out a yell as she did so. The bush on the sand dune shook, and chips went flying off it, and Cooper had no doubt that the man who had been laying beside it would not be hearing anything in that ear for days. He was just as likely to have splinters of wood in his face as well. He had been very close to that bush. Cooper waited. There was nothing stirring, but he noticed the buzzard was moving his circling flight slowly further away in the direction that Cooper had run last night. The hidden gunman was probably retreating. Cooper hoped he didn't meet up with Billy or any of his people, or he might not make it back to his camp in any case. Cooper relaxed and went of over to help Rebecca out from under the table.

She stood up and dusted her skirt off.

"Well, that was exciting." She said by way of understatement. She lifted the laptop back to the table and discovered Kali still there waving her arms about and yelling into her phone.

"Kali, Kali." Called Rebecca. "Calm down. We are ok. The danger is over for the moment. The gun man appears to have hightailed it when Cooper shot back at him." She sincerely hoped he had hightailed it, anyway. Cooper was scratching his chin in thought.

"I think the mission was to disable our means of escape. And at that they succeeded. Or him anyway as I think there was only one man. The shot at the house was just a chance to rattle us."

"Well it rattled me and Kali!" Rebecca exclaimed. Cooper

101

leaned into the video shot so Kali could see him clearly.
"Hi Kali," he said with a grin. "Exciting times in the bush, huh." He moved back a little and picked up the telephone he had dropped earlier. He could hear shouting coming from it. Kali was instantly talking to Rebecca. "Ooh, Rebecca. Don't you even dream of coming back here without him? I simply have to get a close up look at that man, and phew, what a man!" Cooper of course was right there, blushing to the roots of his hair. He coughed, Kali and Rebecca laughing lightly at his discomfort.

Cooper was now talking to the Sargent, filling him in on the details. After about five minutes, he got off the phone and turned back to Rebecca.

"Help is on the way. They will be here by dusk." He said. It was still mid-morning. "What's happening with Kali?"

"Kali has her MI5 friends onto it and they will be here shortly as well, apparently. She didn't say how they were going to achieve that but I guess they know where to come to as I've already sent them map coordinates. How they mean to come I don't know." Rebecca was still feeling a little shaken and moved to stand in front of Cooper. He immediately took her in his arms and tilted her face up to him. He kissed her long and hard, not even pulling away when he heard Kali 'whooping' in the background. When they puled apart finally, Rebecca almost panting for lack of breath she turned to the laptop and said with a smile.

"Goodbye for now Kali" and snapped the lid shut. Rebecca slid back into Cooper's arms and gave herself up to the pleasure of his strength and rock solidness. She hadn't felt this way in many years and didn't want the moment to end. It was Cooper who eventually eased her away to arms length and looked at her, his deep blue eyes piercing her soul to the core.

"Rebecca, as much as I am enjoying this.... I feel like I have been on a search all of my life and have now finally found what I was seeking, I'm afraid we have more pressing problems. Right now I would think that those people from New World are going to come back. They have taken everyone else, and you can be sure they won't want to leave us here shuffling our feet." He was looking out of the windows now as he spoke.

"It may well be that help is on the way, but will it get here soon enough? We should get some protection in place. Let's face it, we don't even know if we are being watched right now."

Rebecca was looking at Cooper, her eyes wide in worry. She wasn't exactly afraid, but those rifle shots had been very real, and very powerful. She had no experience of weapons of that caliber, and very little experience with anything smaller. Hand guns were common place in the US, and she had seen and handled a few. Her father had owned a few small rifles that he had kept on their farm in the UK to keep down the foxes and vermin from stealing the chickens and lambs. In fact, her ears were still ringing from the sound of the rifle that Cooper had fired. Just as well she hadn't fired it herself, it would have knocked her flat she was sure.

"What shall we do?" She asked Cooper. "This house is too big to watch all sides. If we can assume that they will come from that direction," here she pointed to the sand dune away out there where the shooter had hidden. "Then perhaps we should watch that side, as it also has the airstrip there, and their plane is still there and in one piece." Rebecca was thinking. "Do you think we could start their plane, maybe? It would be too much to think that the keys were left in it."

Chapter 9

Cooper scratched his chin and thought. Rebecca smiled as she realised that every time Cooper was deep in thought he started to scratch his chin with the tips of the fingers of his left hand. She hadn't noticed when he was kissing her, but he had a short stubble on his chin, and his fingers were setting up a faint sand paper sound that seemed to tickle the sensitive nerves in the side of her neck. She all but gasped out loud and crossed her legs in an involuntary movement that surprised her, and sent a red flush washing across her lower neck. Cooper didn't notice, but went over to the window and looked out. No one about, so he stepped out through the window frame onto the wide veranda outside. Still no movement. He looked back to Rebecca.

"Honey..." He stopped in mid speech for a moment looking at Rebecca. "Sorry." He didn't even know if she liked or wanted pet names. They had exchanged some pretty hot times, but did that qualify him to start going all soft on her? "Rebecca, honey." Dam, he couldn't help it. 'Oh forget it' he thought. "Keep an eye out, and yell if you see anyone. Don't fire the rifle..." He had seen the look of awe on her face as she had looked at the rifle when he brought it back to the table. Someone in awe of a such a weapon would not be able to handle it safely. It was a tool, like a hammer or power saw. Handle with care, and respect, but don't fear it. It was the people holding the weapon that one had to fear. She would be safer - and so would he be, if she left it alone until he could train her properly in its use.

"I'll be back in a moment." With that he sprinted for the New World plane sitting on the runway, shimmering in the liquid heat. Rebecca had never seen anything like this heat. It shimmered over the plains like a vast sheet of water, seeming to float just above the ground. Objects that were embedded in it like windmills and trees, and even the New World place, seemed to be floating just above the ground, in a shimmering moving mirage. She realised that was what she was looking at. This was a true mirage. No wonder the sight of so much water had driven the explorers mad in the old days. It wasn't water, just a reflection caused by the heat. She could see that even men walking through it seemed to have a surreal quality, not really men, but shifting wriggling shapes that sometimes had legs and sometimes didn't and seemed to progress toward her like ghostly apparitions. Suddenly she was bolt upright. Men! She jumped out of the window onto the veranda and started yelling in the direction of the parked plane. She couldn't see Cooper at all. Where was he. Rebecca was normally a very calm person, but she was a long way out of her element in this place, and her comfort zone was non existent.

Suddenly Cooper was right there beside her, his arm around her waist. He was squinting into the distance, looking in the direction that Rebecca was wildly waving her arms in. "Sure enough." He said with a final nod of his head. He helped Rebecca back through the window to the interior, and the semi darkness. All the curtains had been drawn previously, leaving just this one window free. He checked the rifles and took up a position near to, but back from the open window. Who ever that was moving about out on the sandy plains was still a long way off. The heat mirages tended to enlarge and telescope objects toward the viewer, so that a person for example may seem as though they were just over the ridge, but could be in fact miles away. Cooper studied the moving images carefully. It was nearly impossible to tell just how close the people were, or even who they were. They could be Billy's people, or they could be the New World people. He would just have to wait and see who came out of the shimmering haze. He said to Rebecca.

"Their aeroplane is locked, but it won't be any use to them anyway, as all the tyres are flat. I don't know who has done that, but they are. We still have a couple of motorbikes in the far shed, and a camel catching truck. Slow but very strong. However, we are safe enough here in the house until help arrives." Cooper couldn't figure out what the New World people were up to though. The prospecting and digging were one thing, but why take all of his people prisoner and try to keep himself and Rebecca on the station by force. It didn't make sense. They must have known that Cooper would have radio-phones and satellite internet at his disposal so their activities would soon be known. Perhaps they were surprised to find so many people out here on the property, thinking perhaps that Cooper and Rebecca were still in Brisbane. He couldn't understand what they hoped to achieve. Maybe that's how they behaved back in their own Eastern European country. Rebecca had told him that she thought they were Eastern European, perhaps Ukrainian or Uzbeks. It was just as likely that that was how they behaved in those countries. He had watched the TV news and read the papers often enough. Well, it wouldn't work out here, and they couldn't have been thinking of the future consequences at all when they started heavy handing the local people. They couldn't possibly have known about Billy's people either. The day dragged on, and Cooper and Rebecca began to doubt that the strangers would turn up. It was apparent that no one else was turning up either. Not the police from town, and not the people promised by Kali's friend from London. Although that didn't surprise Cooper. He had found that people from places like England, or Europe in general really had no idea of the vast distances and utter emptiness of the Australian outback. Cooper's homestead was probably as remote as it was possible to get in this land of remote places.

Cooper wanted to talk to Rebecca. Any reason would do! He just wanted to talk to her, to hear her voice, to feel the... well, he couldn't describe it. feeling that it gave him. He enjoyed hearing her voice. Like eating a sweet ice cream on a sunny day in the park. She gave him a sense of the joy of life. Was this what love was? Love, the one with the Big L. Maybe it was.

"Rebecca." He said, almost tasting the sound of her name in his mouth. Her lips were so smooth and soft. She didn't try to force her tongue into his mouth - actually, he didn't like that at all. He did like teasing with his tongue and being teased in return, when he was kissing, he loved the feel of Rebecca against him. She had seemed quite tall when he first met her at the airport, but without her shoes on, she was actually quite a bit shorter than he was. Maybe it was just the way he felt about her.

"Yes Cooper?" Said Rebecca. "Cooper? You said my name... What are you doing, away with the pixies or something?" She was looking at Cooper like he was doing something strange. He snapped back to the moment, to the room. He had been daydreaming about Rebecca he realised.

"Ah, sorry. I was... ah, daydreaming?" He said, none too sure of himself. What was going on? Daydreaming like a love struck school boy. The last time he had done that he had been in boarding school, and Miss History - Miss Marmalade actually, had been his first true love. She hadn't known it of course, but at the time he thought he might just stay in sixth form for the rest of his life so he could be with her.

"Rebecca." He said again and coughed. "I think I love you. No." He held up his hand to ward off her refusal, as he was sure she would. "No, don't say anything. Please. I'm not asking you to love me back. I'm just letting you know, that for the first time in my life, I am falling hopelessly in love, and falling in love with you." He paused. "In fact, I'd prefer it if you didn't reply. Not until we get out of this place. I should never have brought you out here. I'm amazed at how stupid a man can be."

He dropped his hands to his side and turned to the window again. This was crazy. They couldn't just sit here. He determined to do something about the situation.

"I'm not going to sit here and do nothing. It's time we took the action to them.

"Rebecca, I love you, and I'm going to fix this. This is not - absolutely not the way I wanted you to experience my home for the first time." He moved about the room, flinging open all the curtains and blinds, letting the light in. He picked up the rifle and headed for the door.

"Wait here for me - one more time honey." He didn't hesitate this time over the word honey. "I'm only going to scout around. You will be able to see me most times. Whoever that was in the heat haze, must have been a long way off. I just want to make sure there is no one closer." He set off toward the nearest ridge. He'd be able to see for miles from up there. Rebecca watched him walking away into the shimmering mirage. Perhaps he was a mirage she thought. Their lovemaking last night had been fantastic, he was so careful and attentive to her needs. She knew her experience was very limited. In fact, she was now forced to admit to herself, she had been hiding in her work. The heartbreak of losing her fiancé had hurt so much. The result was, that in matters of relationships with the opposite sex, she was practically virginal. What must Cooper have thought of her? Her girl friends talked openly of some of the things they did with their boyfriends, often making Rebecca blush. Something she tried to hide from them. She was going all warm and fuzzy just thinking about how Cooper had slowly moved inside her last night. She didn't think it was possible for a person to create so much pleasure in another person. She had thrilled from her toes to the top of her head, even now as she stood on the veranda watching him, she could almost feel him slowly entering her, stroking her breasts, nibbling on her ear lobes with gentle teeth bites. She was becoming very aroused, her wetness thrilling her as much as shocking her. In desperation, to break her mood of delicious introspection

she started to pace up and down the boards of the veranda.
Finally, Cooper stepped back onto the veranda. He took her
in his arms and tilted her chin so she was looking into the
dcpths of his eyes. She couldn't help letting out a small sigh.
Oh how she wanted him. Love, yes, she loved him.

"We are alone for now." Cooper said. His steady look
changed to surprise as Rebecca started hauling at his shirt to
get it out from his waist, fumbling and eventually tearing the
buttons in her haste to get his shirt off. Cooper began
responding, lifting her cotton dress over her head in one swift
motion, her arms coming up and falling around his neck. He
reached down and moved her hips away slightly, she was
pressing into his hardness, whimpering in little gasps. His
hand began to explore her sex, softly stroking back and forth,
her wetness making his tentative entry so much easier. She
started sagging at the knees, and in a single motion undoing
his belt buckle and sliding his trousers and underpants down.
'Oh My God' She thought as she released him from the
confines of his clothes. Cooper's breathing was like a rushing
wind as he fought against the over whelming desire that was
burning through him. He needed the feel of Rebecca around
him, his erection was tingling as he longed for the sensation,
when suddenly Rebecca crouched down and took him fully
into her mouth, drawing him into a dizzying black hole of
rushing sensation. He drew in a mighty rush of breath and
his back arched as Rebecca held him against her, drawing
him ever deeper. He couldn't stand it any longer and tried to
draw Rebecca to her feet so he could make love to her,
entering into her delicious sweetness. She shook her head
violently in protest and he couldn't hold out any longer, his
climax shuddering his body from head to toe as her sudden
movement drove him over the edge. Cooper gave voice to a
primal cry as the orgasm wracked his body, until eventually
he came back to his senses, stroking Rebecca's head as she
rested her cheek against his now spent sex. She slowly stood

up, putting her arms around his waist, she said.

"Now you can call me honey." She smiled. "Now you can sample my... Honey trap." As she took his hand and guided it between her thighs. 'Oh what have I been missing' She thought to herself as Coopers fingers began to bring her alive in ways she didn't think possible.

"Cooper, my sweet love, my gorgeous man. Oh Cooper, yes, oh yes...Do it to me, don't ever stop." Rebecca heard herself, and although she couldn't believe the words were coming from her, she didn't care, Cooper was steadily bringing her to her own climax, right out here in the open air. Not a soul for perhaps a hundred miles. Suddenly Cooper reached down, cupping her bottom in his huge strong hands and lifted her up and carefully guided himself into her. He was hard and huge again, taking her breath away. Rebecca moaned aloud, matching Coopers long sigh as she slid down the length of him, her legs gripping tight around his waist. Slowly their movement built, in perfect synchronicity until Rebecca felt herself climaxing in huge waves of passion, thrashing her head from side to side, biting Coopers lips, his cheeks, his neck as though she wanted to take all of him inside her, while her pulsing contractions were bringing Cooper to a massive veranda shaking climax again. He rested his back against a veranda post and clutched Rebecca to him tightly. He never wanted to let her go. Referral wanted to stay locked to Cooper forever.

"Rebecca, honey honey honey..." Gasped Cooper, "my God. If that's making love, I am never letting you go." He slowly let Rebecca ease down and stand with him, still holding her tightly against him. "This is not just sex talking. I love you more than words can express."

Rebecca clasped him tightly. "I love you too Cooper. But..." The air rushed out of Cooper.

"But?" He croaked. "What? What is it? But what?" He moved Rebecca away slightly. Her naked beauty dazzling him like the midday sun. He was getting hard again. 'No' He shouted to himself, 'I need to find out the but.' Too late, Rebecca had taken his rigid member in her hand and was slowly stroking him back and forth, his knees almost buckling.

"But What!" He almost shouted at the roof.

Rebecca smiled with a mischievous grin, all the while drawing him toward the bedroom, and like a tiny puppy on a leash he followed. They tumbled onto the bed, and Rebecca straddled him, saying,

"But... I want lots and lots of this. It's the way you make love to me. It's in the way you hold me. It's in the way we make love. There is no one in the world but us." She gave up talking, throwing her head back and slowly rocking on him, their dark bushes merged as she rocked on the divine fulcrum, their love melting them into one person.

Rebecca wished, no less than Cooper that their peace together could go on forever. Eventually they were completely spent, and lay together for a long while, just in each other's arms.

Rebecca was first to surface, quietly heading for the bathroom and a quick shower. She finished and quickly dressed, heading for the kitchen to give Cooper some space, and her some thinking time while he showered and changed. She smiled when she heard the washing machine chugging away. That was some man.

"I've put all our stuff in the wash, hope you don't mind." He declared as he came through barefoot into the kitchen. He headed straight for Rebecca and squeezed her in a giant bear hug.

"No more 'buts'?" He teased with a smile.

Coffee was bubbling in the pot, and Cooper poured them a cup each.

"Sugar? Milk?" He asked, realising that he not only had no idea whether she took milk or sugar, but almost everything about her. He would make it his life's mission to find out. Starting with basic fare.

"What would you like to eat? You have everything at your fingertips here." He smiled. "Except fresh eggs. However, I have powdered eggs, that reconstitute very well?" The question in his voice alerted Rebecca that the powdered eggs might not be all that they were supposed to be.

"This is a break in my normal routines like I've never had." She said. "So I guess I can try powdered eggs as well!" She looked at Cooper and smiled. He was still unsure of her it seemed, and with good reason. She was giving no sign that she wanted to stay in this place for one minute longer than was necessary. However, Cooper thought that powdered eggs may be one step too far for her, so he quietly decided to leave the mention of eggs of any sort out of any further conversations. One look at Rebecca told him that she was not a big eater in any case, so he was at a bit of a loss as to what to prepare for a meal. Being a cattle property they had meat of all cuts in plentiful supply. There was tinned and frozen vegetables, and all sorts of spices and condiments. Cooper thought he was a passable cook but didn't know what Rebecca might be used to although what ever it was would almost surely not be on the menu here.

He was about ready to give up the idea and suggest that they just make some soup later on for dinner.

"There is some fresh fruit still in the cool room, if you'd like an apple or pear, maybe? I know it's been a while since either of us managed to grab something to eat." Cooper took Rebecca's hand and led her through the kitchen to the cool room, it's entrance built into the kitchen wall.

The room was well stocked with fresh fruit, and to Rebecca's surprise it was actually very fresh.

"Just an apple for now thanks. Cooper." Rebecca realised that she had been about to use a term of endearment with him. She also realised that the more she watched him, the more she realised just how "at home" he was here. Of course it was his family home, and he would naturally be familiar with the place but there was something else - and it seemed to be flashing at her like a warning signal. A man so comfortable with his surroundings would not easily change them, for any reason. Rebecca had some built in insecurities that she kept hidden well. The strongest one was the feeling of fear that came to the surface at the thought of committing to a man again and having him not come back to her. She knew it was irrational and had even been to a therapist about it. Nothing seemed to cure it. Now it had surfaced again, hammering on her chest as though trying to escape into the open. What if she committed to be with Cooper? She couldn't survive here, in this place. She knew she'd give it a valiant try, but in the end it was too alien to her. It would fail, and once again she'd be left on her own. It would be the same for Cooper, if he threw it all in and came to London with her, for she had to go back. Her career was just starting, and she enjoyed it. What could Cooper do in London? No cattle there. No open spaces. He'd be crazy in a week, once she went back to eighteen hours plus days. "Cooper," she suddenly blurted out "what sort of degree do you have?" She faltered a little. "I know you have done something, I saw it in your profile, but truly, I can't remember the detail."

 Cooper selected a couple of nice apples from the cooler basket, and led the way back to the main room, sitting comfortably in a chair that was obviously his. It just moulded around him as he settled back into it. He was looking at her steadily. He had heard the hesitation in her voice and it shocked him after what they had just been doing. He didn't reply immediately, he was thinking himself that he should take stock of what was happening between Rebecca and himself. She was pouring some juice into a glass and then turned to raise it to her lips when Cooper replied.

Chapter 10

"Agricultural Management." He said calmly. Rebecca was choking on her juice, having had her jaw drop open just as she was swallowing. Juice was running from her nose, and down her chin, she thought it must have been coming out of her ears. Embarrassment didn't even come close to describing how she felt in that moment. She mopped at her face with her shirt tails. What a mess. She looked at Cooper. Surely she hadn't heard him right. There was nothing about any of that in his profile. She had read it in detail, and Kali her researcher hadn't mentioned it. She was going to have to have a long talk with that girl. Rebecca still couldn't believe it.

"You are having me on surely Cooper. Don't even joke about things like that. How can you be qualified in such a thing when you spend your life out here in the wilderness? How do you keep current? I..." Rebecca stuttered to a stop. She had so many questions she didn't know where to start. What did this change? She didn't know. It certainly put a whole new slant on her view of Cooper. She had never for a moment thought of him as a clueless country boy, who knew about cattle and little else. He had been to University, she knew that. But what she didn't know was what he had done there. Cooper handed her a damp face cloth he had retrieved from the bathroom. The look on his face hadn't changed much she noticed. Well, this was going to take some getting used to. Did she have the time and the inclination? This was one heck of a shock. Just when she had decided - well almost decided, to forget the whole thing and let Cooper down gently as she headed for home, and the safety of London and her job, this knowledge turns up. She headed for the spare room to change her shirt. She was shaking her head as she did so. Rough country, rough clothes, nice man, but some rough edges. Or were they? He was more guarded than rough. Yes, she thought. Guarded. Suddenly she looked up and screamed. There was a stark naked black man standing in the back doorway of the house, still clutching his bundle of spears and throwing stick in his hand, he had the other hand up in a sign of peace, palm outward. Rebecca almost collapsed against the wall as she recognised Billy, the man who had taken Cooper on some long journey the day before. She still didn't know the full story on that one. Billy didn't move, just grinned, his white teeth a beautiful flash of white in the darkness of his face. Cooper was suddenly there beside her, rifle in hand and half lifted, when he too recognised Billy.

"Billy, lucky I didn't shoot you!" He said calmly.

"I know you not shoot me boss. You good man. Your woman got very loud voice but." He was grinning from ear to ear again. Rebecca was beginning to wonder if there was some relationship between his unabashed nakedness and his happy disposition. Or was he just crazy? A crazy aboriginal man. Great, that's all she needed.

"Cooper, can you give that man some pants for heavens sake? Doesn't he know what's decent around a woman." Rebecca stalked off to the room to get the clean shirt.

"My women got no pants boss? I had pants, but lost them long time back. No good out here." Billy scratched his head. "Oh yes, those men gone now." He added. He started to turn to go. He didn't like houses at all. They made him jumpy and feel closed in. He didn't understand at all how white men lived in such places.

"Wait, Billy." Billy kept going and finally stopped outside in the yard. "What you mean? Men gone. Which men? Our men? The other men, the strangers." Billy's face was unreadable at the best of times, his dark visage and wild mop of hair, his large and sun wrinkled face making his expression practically unreadable. Like all these men, he rarely looked you in the eye, considering it an insult to the other person to do so. You had to be close family before such

115

liberties could be taken. The sideways glance, the eye-line usually just about at mouth level, this was the closest a man would get with almost anyone to looking them in the eye. They thought the white man was terribly rude going around looking everyone directly in the eye.

Billy thought a bit. "Yes boss, those other fellers. That mob all gone. Pack up truck, let you mob out, and drive away toward. that way." He pointed south. "Your boys be home soon. Dogs here now." With that Cooper heard the dogs coming like a pack of hunting hounds. He had a dozen of more cattle dogs, pure and mongrel, but they were all working dogs, and all related. Like a huge noisy family, they came racing into the house yard barking and growling, tussling each other to jump all over Cooper and Billy, and take turns jumping into the water trough that led out from the windmill. Rebecca stood in the doorway at the back of the house staying out of the way. She watched Coopers easy acceptance of the dogs, the fond cuffing of various ears, and scratching of noses. Billy just stood there and put up with it. He didn't like dogs much, and occasionally had a dingo pup to keep his little group company for a while, but they always ran off to follow their wild ways, just like he and his people, so it never bothered him. Eventually calm descended and the dogs all crawled under the house into the shade, panting with excitement.

"Thanks Billy. You are a good man. You come a long way to tell me this. Anything you need?" Cooper asked Billy.

"Na boss. Got all I need." Billy waved his arm in a wide circle out toward the desert. "Men here soon. Well before dark." He simply turned and trotted off toward the south. Back to his people.

Cooper came back into the house. He eased past Rebecca who didn't move from the back door. She followed him with her eyes though. 'What was going on in that head?' She asked herself. Her heart began to ache. He was so... so at

116

home here. So comfortable. Did she have the right to ask him to follow her into the unknown? Into places where he, like Billy in the house, would be uncomfortable, and probably end up hating her for it. Almost certainly would. She decided she would have to put a stop to it right there and then. They must not get close again. She must not get close again. The pain was too much. Their little fling had been nice. More than nice, and she did love him, but it couldn't possibly work. It would only bring misery to both of them in the end. She came back into the main sitting room, and Cooper was standing at the table jingling the gun safe keys. He had locked up the rifles again. The danger was gone it seemed for the moment at least. The men were coming back and there were things to sort out. He was just about to say something to Rebecca when suddenly he heard the unmistakable sounds of a large helicopter approaching at speed.

"Well, better late than never." He commented to Rebecca. Together they went outside into the afternoon sun to observe a large military helicopter slowly settling onto the runway in a huge cloud of dust. A group of heavily armed soldiers piled out first, followed by someone of rank judging by the gold braid on his shoulders, and finally a civilian in a dark suit, reflective sun glasses wrapped around his eyes. As he fastened his jacket Cooper had noticed the gun in the holster under his arm. So he was no office worker. The armed soldiers fanned out along the runway, and two of them were closely inspecting the New World plane. The others slowly approached Cooper and Rebecca. The armed guards first. They all stopped about twenty feet from Cooper and Rebecca and remained motionless. It was impossible to read their expressions, their faces were masked behind protective helmets and visors, and the all black garb presented a slightly confusing shape even in the bright sun. The officer and the civilian approached Cooper and Rebecca. To both their surprise, the civilian addressed Rebecca.

"Ma'am, do I have the pleasure of speaking to Rebecca Boucher?" His voice was pleasant enough, but had an edge of steel that spoke of absolute authority. He took off his glasses and squinted in the bright light. His eyes flicked to Cooper and back to Rebecca. She was thinking that he had nice brown eyes, with early signs of crow's feet lines at the corners as though despite his glasses, he had spent a lot of time in wide open places in far away countries. Rebecca nodded and answered.

"Yes, I am Rebecca and this is..." She began. The man addressing her interrupted her.

"We know who he is." He closed his mouth, snapping his words off like a man biting the end off a Havana cigar. "We are interested in talking to him." With that he gave a small signal and the surrounding guards moved in and before he knew it, Cooper was being hustled off toward the helicopter. He had been just about to protest about being spoken of in the third person while he was only a few feet away, right next to Rebecca in fact. Now he was considerably more worried than a mere insult had made him. Cooper was a big man by any standards, but he found himself being propelled along by men who were like mobile tanks on legs they were so big. His protests fell on deaf ears, the soldiers ignoring any attempt at conversation. They politely but firmly bundled him into the seating area of the helicopter and strapped him in. He looked down and found himself actually locked in. There was a stainless steel locking system on the belt harness. His mouth was hanging open in surprise that was quickly turning to rage.

"What the hell do you think you are doing? I own this place. This is my property, and you have no rights here. You have no right to do this to me. It's not me you need to detain, it's those scum who have been trespassing on my place for months now." His voice trailed off as he realised that the soldiers were not paying the slightest attention to him. He yelled out so the others with Rebecca could hear him. "You over there. You, Sunglasses man. What the hell do you think you are doing? I'm addressing you, and your gold plated mate. This is my place. I demand you release me immediately." His voice trailed off as he realised that they were ignoring him. He began to worry a little. He had been expecting a friendly greeting and a discussion about the intruders. He had not been expecting this, and that was a fact. Only one guard was near the helicopter now, the others having gone back at a brisk walk to stand in a line stretching way at an angle from the two men talking to Rebecca. Rebecca was looking toward Cooper and waving her arms about. Cooper couldn't hear her, but had no doubt that she was reading them the riot act. Or he hoped she was, she was a lawyer after all. Cooper remembered that fact and smiled. He would be ok. There was obviously some misunderstanding. They had only just arrived and couldn't possibly be aware of the situation as it really was. They certainly didn't know what Billy had told him only a short while before. Cooper sat back in the seat and tried to get comfortable. The seat belts had been pulled pretty tight, and it wasn't all that easy. The men who he had shouted at completely ignored him. 'What was new?' He thought to himself. Everyone was ignoring him. Vague thoughts of being spirited off to Guantanamo Bay flicked through his mind. He shook his head, think himself stupid for thinking such thoughts. He had done nothing wrong. Well, not really. Rebecca had been more than willing as he recalled. 'What are you thinking?' He almost said aloud. They weren't worried about any relationship he may or may not have with Rebecca. Any woman for that matter. These men were here on serious business, and somehow he was right smack in the middle of it - and on the wrong side of it it seemed. He would just have to wait and see what happened.

Rebecca meantime was stamping her foot in frustration. "I'm telling you, he and I arrived here together. We came from Brisbane on his plane, over there." She pointed to the damaged Cessna. "Someone shot out the tyres and the windscreen so we couldn't fly it out." She drew herself up straight and tried to look as cool as she would in a court. "I am a lawyer. An attorney at law if you want the American equivalent. I belong to a London firm of great prestige, and good connections. Our New York office is equally well established, and with equally good connections. Unless you want a whole ship load of trouble descending on your head, I demand that you release my ... um. Cooper. You must release him. This is not a battle field; this is his home." Rebecca realised that neither of these gentlemen had given their names. She launched into them again.

"The very least you could do is introduce yourselves. You obviously know who I am, and who Cooper is. May I ask who you are?"

"Sorry Ma'am," replied the suited one. "My name is Special Agent Mitterrand. I'm with the US Embassy here in Australia. This is Captain Fielding. Australian Intelligence. ASIO to be exact." He paused. We have been watching the activities of the... intruders, for some time. When we were alerted by MI5, our friends in the UK, we thought it best if we got here ASAP." He pronounced it a-sap, which made Rebecca smile. Just like in the movies. Really, who were these people? The British would never behave in such a rough and cavalier manner. She didn't know about the Australians. A rough lot from what she had seen so far. Rebecca was not impressed, and it showed on her face. She may have been out of her comfort zone dealing with Cooper's domestic arrangements, but this she knew about. This was her territory. Rebecca went on the attack herself. Come in here and throw their weight around would they.

"Was your mother one of those hippie people?" She asked

the Agent specifically.

"Beg pardon Ma'am?" He blinked.

"That's a hell of a first name. 'Special Agent'..." Rebecca wasn't smiling. She wanted Cooper out of that helicopter. "Would you mind telling me just why you have hustled him off and restrained him in the helicopter? You do know there are laws against illegal detention." Her face was set, her lips in a thin line. She had been prepared to welcome these people as rescuers until they had shown their otherwise aggressive intentions. If not aggressive, certainly unpleasant, and not the least bit friendly.

"Miss Boucher, we know exactly who you are, and we know who your friends are, including those in MI5. The fact is that we have been watching the activities of the New World people for some time. They seemed to think that they had escaped our notice, and could hide out here in the middle of nowhere, using this place as an illegal dump for their nuclear waste. The small radiation proof transport pods someone in their organisation has invented is of great interest to a lot of the world's nuclear energy companies. Fortunately, they chose to try to secret the material here, rather than go through legal channels. We are none to sure what Mr Anders' involvement is in the operation. It is his property after all." Agent Mitterrand looked back at the hapless Cooper. He turned back to Rebecca and said.

"Ok, we'll take your word for it Miss Boucher. I do know your credentials and respect them. If you say he had no part in this operation, then I'll accept that, on the proviso that should that prove to be wrong - you will be personally responsible. I'm sure you know what that means." The Agent signalled to the men near the chopper to let Cooper free. Cooper wasted no time in getting out once freed and marched across to where the agent and the Captain stood. He was about to give them a piece of his mind when he caught Rebecca's eye. The slightest shake of her head alerted him, and she breathed a sigh of relief when instead of launching into a full scale outraged volley, he drew a deep breath instead and simply said.

"Thank you for having the good sense to realise that I am not one of the bad guys." Cooper turned away and went to stand next to Rebecca.

She took his hand and squeezed it. She may still have reservations about this man, but she had no intention of letting these people take him off to who knew where, perhaps never to be seen again. It was bad enough the 'bad guys' where on his property and shooting at him, he didn't need the friendlies doing the same thing.

Apparently Agent Mitterrand had decided that he may have been a bit hasty in grabbing Cooper, because he now smiled depreciatingly and said,

"Well, lets put that behind us shall we? From where we were, some considerable distance away, it didn't look good. We didn't want to take chances. So Cooper," he continued. "What can you tell us about these people?"

Cooper scratched his chin with a fingernail. Rebecca smiled, she was getting to know Cooper well she thought. That was definitely a mannerism of his. Cooper looked at her in slight puzzlement. He was momentarily distracted by her sheer beauty. Even out here in the harshness of the outback, and she definitely not dressed in her best clothes, she was still like someone out of a top fashion magazine. It must have been quite disarming to be against her in a court of law. Cooper looked at the two facing him, Captain Fielding and Agent Mitterrand. Special Agent he corrected himself.

"I think we can do this inside, rather than out here in the blazing sun." He could feel the heat, so he guessed that Rebecca would certainly be feeling it. "And for what it's worth," he continued, "I'm told that the intruders have gone from their camp away there to the south. Apparently they upped stakes and left in the night. They set my workers - my

friends, free before leaving. They should be here soon."
Agent Mitterrand was looking slightly confused.

"How do you know this?" He asked with a sceptical note in his voice. Cooper pointed away to the nearby ridge. Billy, the nomad aboriginal, stood outlined on the ridge, one foot resting on his other knee, standing one legged, his spears in his right hand grounded in the sand for balance. He was like a dark statue, his lean body unmoving. Just watching. He had appeared just after they had let Cooper back out of the chopper.

"He told me." The agent looked from Cooper to Billy and back again. There was disbelief in his face.

"There are still nomads in this region? Aboriginal people living traditionally in the desert?" The question in his voice sounded disbelieving. "We have no knowledge of these people. How many are there? Where do they live? How long have they been out there?" He snapped his mouth shut. This was bad, he thought. A whole group of people he now had to report on, that previous to this encounter he had no knowledge of. He turned to the captain.

"Captain Fielding, do you have any knowledge of these people? Did you know they are out here?" He shook his head in disbelief.

"Well, yes actually." Drawled the very Australian Captain Fielding. "We have known about them for years. It's their country after all, so it's only... um, polite? To know about them. No one thought they had any interest in the doings of foreigners. We may have been wrong on that score." The look in his eye told Rebecca that he actually had no real sympathy, if that was the expression needed, for the Special Agent in his company. It was a working relationship then, not a friendship. Rebecca noted this with interest. Meantime, they had all moved to the shade of the big house. The armed escort included. Cooper looked at them. They must have been sweltering inside all that black heavy clothing and

123

protective jackets, close fitting helmets and webbing and packs that seemed to hang from every part of them. How on earth they kept it under control if having to move fast he couldn't even guess?

Cooper had a cool room full of drinks of all sorts, including large milk churns full of water kept for drinking. He said to the captain.

"Do you think your men could relax a little? There are no armed rebels out here after all. There is no one to be protected against now. Even previously there was only one armed person shooting at our aircraft. Please, sit yourselves down. Take it easy. I can get you cool water, soft drink, beer? What will it be gentlemen?"

The captain told his men to stand down. Meaning Rebecca supposed that they could relax. It didn't take long, and the men had removed their heavy battle ground equipment, and sat easily on the many chairs and benches scattered along the veranda. They didn't say much Rebecca thought. Probably something to do with training. They all opted for water, Cooper returned first with a basket of tin cups, then went and fetched the large milk churn full of cool water. He wheeled it out on a small trolley, and invited the men to help themselves. Cooper then got a large coffee jug going, and it didn't take long and there was coffee for any who wanted it. Soon everyone was relaxed in the shade on the veranda.

Agent Mitterrand asked Rebecca to explain her presence on the property. He asked politely, and Rebecca thought it wouldn't hurt to bring him up to speed as it were. He and the others had come to their rescue after all. She told him the full story, of the approach by the potential buyer of Cooper's property, leading to her flight out to Australia and her eventual arrival on the cattle property as Cooper's guest. Their finding of the place deserted, and Billy's trek with Cooper to show him what was going on. Neither of the men interrupted, and eventually Rebecca came to the present moment. The agent had been making notes, and Captain Fielding had been listening keenly. They both looked out toward the sand ridges, but Billy was no where to be seen. Agent Mitterrand asked Cooper,

"Do you think the aboriginal people will talk to us? To Fielding and myself that is?" Cooper shook his head slightly. "I very much doubt it. They don't like us much. They tolerate me and my men, because we've grown up here, and know to leave them alone. Billy; not his real name by the way, that's the one you saw on the ridge over there only came to me because he didn't like what the New world people were doing to their country. He needed to check that I wasn't involved. A bit like you I guess. When he discovered I wasn't involved, he took me to where they were holding my workers. One of their team was speared in the leg for his troubles, and one had a warning spear thrown to within inches of him when it looked like he might be coming our way. Billy and I were hidden just in the lee of a sand ridge above them. I didn't know myself that they are a full social group out there until today. Or at least yesterday when a couple of Billy's women came in and stayed with Rebecca while I was away with Billy. But talk to you? I'd be surprised. I've been here all my life, and in that time, I've only every come across the station hands talking about them. Until yesterday, I'd never met Billy, or to my knowledge, any of them."

Agent Mitterrand made some notes then said. "Well, we will have to try at some point. These people could be very important for the security of the country. Such first hand intimate knowledge of the country would be invaluable. Perhaps it depends on how much they want paying."

Cooper's jaw dropped open, then he started laughing. "Pay them?" He gasped through his laughter, now so hard that tears were streaming down his face. "Pay them. Agent Mitterrand, what are they going to spend it on out there?

What could they possibly want that money could buy?" He continued to chuckle and wipe his cheeks. It showed him just how little outsiders understood the lives of these ancient people. "I'm sorry Agent Mitterrand, but it's just not on. If they want to talk to you, and I understand the importance, and help you - then they will do it in their own time, and on their own terms. Terms you may not actually like."

Agent Mitterrand and Captain Fielding conferred quietly together for a few minutes slightly away from everyone and then came back along the veranda.

"Ok Cooper - may I call you Cooper? and Rebecca?" He looked at them both seeking approval for first name use. He continued. "We'll leave that for the time being, anyway. We need to find out where the New World lot have gone. But where do we start?"

"That's easy." Said Rebecca. "They went south, according to Billy. There is only one road in that direction according to Cooper, so they must be on it. Their plane is here, and useless. Unless they had air transport somewhere along that track further south, they are all in that huge truck that Cooper told me about. Should be easy to find, and you may call me Rebecca, if I have your first names?" She raised a quizzical eyebrow.

Agent Mitterrand nodded. He didn't smile much Rebecca thought. He also didn't answer her, but changed his address to her.

"Miss Boucher, then I gather yourself and Mr Anders will be happy enough to stay here, while we go and try and locate them. I'm most curious to pinpoint exactly where they are. I doubt they have actually escaped, so I'm sure they will be found." It sounded as though it was more of a command than a query, but Rebecca wasn't arguing, and nor was Cooper. Now that they appeared to be safe from direct attack he had some things he wanted to talk over with Rebecca, and it needed privacy.

"More than happy Agent Mitterrand." Rebecca replied.
Cooper just looked at him and nodded. He was capable of
showing courtesy to guests, providing food and drink as
necessary, but he was still smarting from being bundled into
the helicopter and was not at all ready to forgive and forget
so easily. At a signal from the captain, the men were on their
feet and kitted up again in moments, and headed out to the
helicopter. The captain followed them, and finally, with little
more than a nod of his head, Special Agent Mitterrand
followed them. Rebecca was not sorry to see him go. They
had arrived too late to do anything by way of help and
caused more trouble than they had averted, actually. Cooper
watched them go, the chopper lifting off in a cloud of dust
and heading away to the south, low against the horizon. He
had given them some features to pinpoint their search for the
camp site, and from there they should be able to track the
vehicle south if they wanted to. He didn't want to see them
back particularly. Cooper looked at Rebecca.
"I'm pretty sure that no one meant any actually harm. No
one in New World that is. If they had wanted to, they could
have done a lot of damage the moment we arrived. There
was something else going on." Cooper moved over to be
close to Rebecca. She was wearing a light cotton blouse with
buttons up the front, looking almost like a very chic cow-girl
shirt. Her jeans were painted on, and he noticed her feet
were encased in strapped sandals of the kind that were
jokingly referred to as Jesus sandals. He smiled. She looked
such a picture of little girl glamour, and country girl chic that
his heart began to thud against his chest wall. She was
beautiful and everything he wanted in a woman. Intelligent,
fit and healthy, a wicked sense of humour and stunningly
beautiful either in or out of her clothes. He had trouble
keeping his hands off her. He was beginning to think that
they had maybe gone too far already, but he had to put a
stop to their getting together. It was a path filled with danger

and misery. She would never fit into his world, and he knew she thought he would never fit into hers. Essentially he was a cowboy. Albeit a very rich one, and she was a big city lawyer. The biggest city actually. The two biggest cities in the world. New York, and London. Oh she knew he had that university degree, gained after long years of hard struggle studying at university. Degrees were not easy to do, but although a lot of work, it had come reasonably easy to him. He had wanted to get his study out of the way, get his degree and get back to the property to help his father. He had managed it too, but his father hadn't lasted much longer and Cooper found himself rattling around the vast homestead with no one to share the joy of the place with. The result was obvious, and now that he looked around him, the house looked drab and weary with the sunshine of Rebecca standing in the middle of the room. He had never noticed it much before, the long familiarity had allowed the deterioration to sneak up on him. Well, it could be fixed and fixed quickly if he had a reason. He knew he didn't have a reason, because he knew equally well that Rebecca was out of there the moment she could manage it. Just like the others. Had they seen this too, and like Rebecca just not said anything. Suddenly it came to him. That was what her comment about the chickens was about. Nothing to do with actual chickens, but a comment more gently put about the lack of any home comforts about the place. Not even fresh eggs. No children. No flowers. No greenery of any kind. Well now that he could see what was revealed to him, he could fix it.

"Rebecca." He stopped and looked down into her eyes. He felt he was drowning in vast pools of deep green ocean. Her eyes seemed to change between brown and a deep green depending on her mood. "Rebecca. I know you have to go back to London. I know I am not..." He had to swallow to clear the knot in his chest. "I know I'm not what you want in your life. You think I wouldn't fit with your lifestyle. The city confines. Your friends and family. What would I do for a living? I won't like it but I have to let you go back to your own part of the world, the things you are familiar with. Your career for one thing is very important." His face was so sad, Rebecca had to stop herself from bursting into tears. She clutched at his arm, shaking with emotion. Not bothering to answer, she reached up, stretching on her tip toes and kissed him. She held on, and as her kiss began to melt him she could feel his lips responding. He circled her with his strong brown arms and held her close. His passion was rousing, he couldn't help it and Rebecca could feel the surge of him against her. She clung on as though drowning in a turbulent sea. She felt the storm inside her. She knew if she said anything she would immediately weaken and give up any hope of going back to England just to stay here with Cooper. She un-linked herself and bit down on her lip to stop it trembling. Cooper slowly dropped his arms to his side and Rebecca fled into her room, the door swinging shut behind her. She buried her face in her pillow to drown out the sounds of her sobbing.

Cooper was bitterly disappointed. There was nothing he wanted more than to be with Rebecca, but if she didn't want him, there was nothing he could do. He just didn't see how a relationship could work. A long distance relationship was totally out of the question; the distances were too great. He had to stay and continue with the cattle property. He owed it to his father to keep the dream alive. It had meant that his hard won degree languished in it's frame on his study wall, unapplied and almost forgotten on a day-to-day basis. He had managed to keep abreast of modern developments in his particular field, as the nights were long and solitary out here, but what could he do with it out here. Cooper began to pace about the house, in and out of rooms, along the wide verandas, out into the yards and sheds. He was taking stock of what he saw. not just counting sheds, but looking at them. Looking at the house, really looking. Looking at the house yard, now almost indistinguishable from the surrounding countryside that stretched away into the shimmering distance. Sand ridges that had always seems mysterious and beautiful to him now looked to be exactly what they were. Dangerous and slow moving destroyers of landscape. Were they coming closer to the house with each passing year? He could do measurements on that, and research through old family records and photographs to find out.

What he saw now as he found his way back to the house did not please him. He decided he really needed to take absolute stock of his situation and act on it. If he was to stay here - let alone invite anyone else to stay here, the place had to be brought back to it's former grandeur and soon. Inside and out, the whole house and its surroundings needed a complete make over. That would require a woman's touch, and he had only one woman in mind but that woman was clearly not interested in staying here. What a quandary. Cooper was intelligent enough to see that his life was at a crossroads. Cooper mounted the steps onto the veranda and turned to face the yards again. He lent against the supporting post and stared into the distance. He supposed Rebecca was still in her room. He had heard her sobbing through the thin panel walls. The house was very old, and had been built in the old tongue-and-groove timber wall style, and never modernised in over a hundred years. Thin walls let the sound travel. He felt wretched - it was the only way of putting it. He had once again caused Rebecca unnecessary hurt, but he couldn't let her go on thinking that he could just go back to London with her. He could not equally expect her to give up all she knew to come and live out here in this wilderness. Certainly not if the place looked like this. He realised that he was in something of a state of shock over his new insight into where he lived and had been raised up all these years. This place was still his fathers house. Practically nothing had changed and yet his father had been dead for years now. Cooper smacked the veranda post in frustration. Suddenly his mind was made up. He knew exactly what he had to do. Rounding on his heel he marched back into the house and into his study. He picked up the phone called and straight through to Toowoomba airport and ordered a service plane to come out and fix his now crippled aircraft, and they should bring tools to repair the New World plane and take it back to Toowoomba. There were other places he could have organised this with, but he had accounts at Toowoomba, and it was just easier. They would come straight out in a small jet, his runway was suitable, and he bank account was never questioned. Next he called British airways and booked a flight one way, one person to London for two days' time. Name: Rebecca Boucher. Departing Brisbane, direct flight. His next call was to a building firm in Toowoomba that he had used before, and that he knew were familiar with working on projects on remote properties. They were to arrive by the end of the week, using a charted plane and carrying all they could fit on board to start refurbishing this place immediately. The plane was at their disposal for as long as it took. They had an open account to get what they needed. Their only rider was that the house was to retain its heritage character and basic layout, and where possible original materials. In other words, he wanted it to be a restoration as well as a modernisation. electricity was to be provided by the latest state-of-the-art technology, and they were to hire a team on sub-contract to start with the outbuildings, and work their way into the house. Repairing, pulling down and rebuilding where needed. Gardeners were to be hired and put on the job. There was plenty of accommodation between the house and the stockmen's quarters, and if any was lacking - truck it in. He had been an hour on the phone by the time he smacked his palms together and declared himself ready. The first team would be here in the morning. They were left in no doubt that if they couldn't do it, he would immediately find someone who could.

For the first time in a long time, Cooper felt good. He checked his watch. He still had time. He called his old professor at the university and arranged to see him in three days. The day after Rebecca left. He realised he hadn't told her yet that she was going home. The chartered plane would be here in a few hours to take her back to Brisbane. He called the hotel and booked a room for her, and one for him. Now all he had to do was tell Rebecca. He paled at the thought. He knew he loved her as he had never loved anyone before in his life, but he also knew that some things had to be done in this life. Sending Rebecca home was one of them. She was undoubtedly a fine lawyer, and would only go to waster out here. Wither away like a wilting rose in the heat. A sweet English rose. He almost jumped to his feet and went out into the lounge room to find Rebecca. He had left her alone for some time and hoped she was ok. He needn't have worried. The stockmen and others were back and gathered around Rebecca on the veranda. She was positively glowing with the attention these rough gentlemen were showing her. She looked up when Cooper stepped onto the veranda. The men all stood up, dusting off their jeans and slapping their hats on their legs. Rebeca was smiling and happy. Cooper welcomed the men with handshakes and heartfelt sentiments about their safe return. The foreman took Cooper aside a little, away from Rebecca and said to him.

"I'll have to talk to you a bit later Cooper." He looked aside at Rebecca. "It's not pleasant." Cooper understood. The man was a bushman, one of the old school, and there were certain things you didn't say in front of women as far as he was concerned. The others were looking at them standing slightly aside, and their laughing banter quieted down. To cover up the moment, Cooper stepped back to join them and looked at Rebecca.

"I have some good news for Rebecca." He said. "You're returning to Brisbane tomorrow, and London the day after. You will be home in a few days, this horrible adventure behind you." He could see she was stunned. "I'll have a new aircraft here later today, and if mine isn't fixed, then we return to Toowoomba with the repair team and fly on to Brisbane. It might be a good idea to pack - if that's necessary." He forced himself to ignore Rebecca's look of shock and hurt surprise and turned to his men. "There will be building teams here by tomorrow, for as long as it takes they will be working here. All other work, apart from absolute necessity will stop. That has priority. You are all to work with them. If anyone is due, or wants a holiday, that's ok too. You young ringers can go home and see your folks..." He paused. "Oh yes. Full pay. your wages continue in any case. Charlie here will be in charge in my absence as usual."

Even in her state of mild shock, Rebecca recognised the actions of a born leader in the way Cooper had organised everything. She could sure use some of that in her office. She lowered her head and hurried into the house. She was determined not to let Cooper know how hurt she was. He was treating her like a cast away rag doll. Oh how it hurt. Yes, he was escorting her to Brisbane, but she expected nothing less than that in any case. But the speed and finality of it all. Home before the end of the week. It was hard to believe.

Some time later Rebecca had her small bag packed and had showered and changed into her travelling clothes. She looked stunning. Cooper stopped in his tracks, crossing through the lounge room. He was riveted by her beauty. He couldn't believe he was sending her away. After everything they had said to each other. All that had happened together. He had to. He knew it.

Chapter 11

Rebecca was holding herself on a tight rein, fearing that if
she looked directly at Cooper, she would start crying again,
and surely she had done enough of that on this recent
emotional roller coaster. The steady whistling sound of a jet
aircraft approaching broke the silence. They both looked
toward the door, neither really wanting to move. The plane
circled once and touched down, taxying almost up to the
house. It was quite a large plane, obviously designed as a
work horse. Large cargo doors were built into the sides and
within minutes these had been opened, and a team of men
began to pile out and started unloading right there on the
edge of the runway. Cooper looked at it with satisfaction
and turned to Rebecca.
"We are flying back in with this plane on it's return to
Toowoomba. It will take too long to repair my plane if
indeed it can be done here, and I want you safe and on your
way today. I'm sorry for the short notice Rebecca but it has
to be this way. This is just no place for you, and I am so sorry
that I brought you out here into this..." Here he swept his
arms in a wide arc, "This run down eye-sore. I don't know
what possessed me. I made an error, and hope you will
forgive me." There was little else he could say. Rebecca was
distraught, but she wouldn't say anything. She couldn't. She
struggled not to show any expression on her face. She had
fallen heavily for this man, for the first time since her earlier
loss, she had let her guard down. She thought he had felt the
same about her, he had certainly given all the signs. Now
here he was sending her out of his life. He was being a
gentleman and escorting her back to Brisbane, and for that
she was thankful. She was quite capable of managing the
trip herself, but it meant she could spend some more time
with him. As hurt as she was, she was not willing to let go
completely. She didn't understand his sudden change of
heart, it had been nothing she had done herself, so she could

at least spend the next few days until her departure from Brisbane International trying to discover what it was that had suddenly made him draw away back into himself. Rebecca had a vague idea floating around in her mind, but she didn't want to think that something as material as 'how things looked' could affect him so badly. It could be the reason for the sudden and unexpected flurry of building and repair work that was about to happen. Even now he was head to head with the leader of the repair team, and the aircraft people who had arrived on the plane. She could only admire his force of personality. Soon he was finished with them, and the plane was unloaded.

Rebecca was not unhappy to be leaving, her experiences here had not been exactly pleasant apart from the interludes with Cooper of course, but the rest of it... The rest of it she could have done without. She had already decided that this property was not a place where she wanted to spend much time. A holiday would be fine, if the house were liveable, for a few weeks. It was not an option on a permanent basis however, and she thought that Cooper had suddenly realised it as well.

It was time to get back to her real world and leave these dreams behind. Rebecca picked up her bags and moved to the edge of the veranda. She stood looking about at the dry dustiness of the barren landscape. Apart from the few men working on shifting supplies nothing moved in the heat. It was actually quite depressing.

The team of men had arrived in good time, and it seemed that Cooper would be able to take Rebecca back to Toowoomba in the aircraft that had arrived today, and from there to Brisbane tomorrow. The jet was soon unloaded, and the head of the repair team informed Cooper that the repair team would take at least two days to make his plane safe enough to fly back into Toowoomba. The jet was returning almost immediately, and if Cooper and Rebecca wanted a lift into Toowoomba, they should board now.

Cooper came over to Rebecca and spoke quietly.

"Rebecca, it's time to leave. I'm sorry your stay here has been so unpleasant. I'm really sorry. I have..." He paused and swallowed. "Come to think very highly of you. I had hoped that we may have had a happy time here, even though it was essentially a business trip. The surprise that lay in wait for us, then the sheer danger of being shot at, and lastly my own realisation that in it's present condition this property is barely fit for human habitation."

"Cooper, you can't be held responsible for the actions of those criminals. That could not possibly be your fault. As for this house and property, well, you have now seen it as I first saw it. But Cooper, you know I love you." She paused. "Yes, I do. For that reason, I would be happy anywhere where you are. Repairing and refurbishing a house is a simple task. You just never had any incentive I guess?" Rebecca wiped the back of her hand across her eyes.

"Cooper, what would I do here? I'm not a housewife. I'm a lawyer, just beginning a well planned career. Even if the house was a palatial mansion, I could not live here."

Cooper nodded, looking at his feet.

"I know this Rebecca. Truly, nobody realises it more than I."

He picked up Rebecca's case and held her hand as she stepped down the front steps and joined him walking out to the jet. He didn't let go of her hand.

He felt that there was nothing more to say. He knew he should be saying something though, he could feel it in his bones, but what? His steps slowed as he thought abut the dilemma. He wanted Rebecca to stay, but he wanted her to go for her own sake. He knew she wanted him, but he knew also that staying here was not an option for her. It was unresolvable, something that a chat over a cup of tea would never resolve. He shook his head in resignation as the options played over and over in his head for the hundredth time. Rebecca too seemed lost in her thoughts, her steps slowing to match Coopers. The whine of the jet engines starting did nothing to hurry them along. The pilot was watching them, and knew something was happening, so he took a great deal of care to ensure that the engines were just idling over, warming up in preparation for departure. Rebecca's heart ached at the prospect of losing Cooper but she could do nothing about it. She had a career to return to. People were relying on her, and if this was what love still held for her - more heartache, then she thought herself better off out of it. She was determined not to be hurt again and the sooner they got underway the better. She straightened her back and lifted her chin. She stepped out ahead of Cooper and almost marched to the steps leading up to the aircraft door. Cooper could only follow, now with surprise etched on his face at the sudden shift in Rebecca's demeanour. By the time he entered the cabin area, Rebecca was seated and belted in. She was in a single seat, so all he could do was take a seat across the wide aisle from her. The plane was essentially a workhorse, and not particularly designed for passenger comfort. They would be barely able to converse on the return journey, but Coopers glance at Rebecca's face told him that casual chat was probably out of the question, anyway.

Cooper signalled the pilot who then began the full take-off procedures and soon had them lifting into the cloudless sky and turning to make a direct line for far away Toowoomba. In this plane it would only be a short journey of around an hour, perhaps a little less with favourable winds. There was nothing to do but settle back and try to work out what had happened. The short and passionate interlude had seemed so full of promise, yet like a fire of hardwood coals with water poured over it, had hissed and sputtered into coolness in a very short space of time. As he mulled over the events of the last few days, he kept coming back to the involvement of the people from New World, and the involvement of the special services departments of both Australia and the UK, and the US it seemed. So item one. Cooper checked on his fingers. Rebecca was certainly a lot safer if she was no where near his property. These people were a clear and present danger to anyone on the place. Even though they had apparently fled south, and that had yet to be checked, it meant nothing in this day and age of instant communications. The Federal Police and military types who had turned up and tried to take him had also gone south in some haste, and not bothered to let him know where they had gone, or what they were doing. To be expected he supposed.

Cooper drew a small note book from his shirt pocket and listed item one.

One. Rebecca's safety. Paramount. Remove her from the property and his life.

With this one line written, he lapsed into a state of introspection. How could he remove her from his life? Dam it, he loved her. He was no school boy and thought he recognised the signs of loving someone when he felt them. He turned to look at Rebecca, sitting some few feet away across the aisle - she may as well have been on the other side of the world so great did the distance of those few feet feel. The noise inside the body of the plane did not encourage conversation. There was very little in the way of lining or soundproofing. Only the pilot's cabin and instrument area had been kept intact and soundproof in the interests of safety during flights. The two pilot's seats, and a small space behind them for an engineer or navigator with his own desk and instrument panels. Cooper flung off his seat belt and stood up as best he could in the low ceilinged cabin. He beckoned to Rebecca to join him and indicated the cabin where the pilot was. There was only the one on this short trip. No one else was in the flight deck cabin and the door was propped open.

Rebecca sat for a long moment just looking at Cooper. Her eyes were brimming with tears, but he chose not to say anything or indicate that he noticed. He looked forward again and noticed out of the corner of his eye that Rebecca was dabbing at her eyes with a small white handkerchief. He kept his gaze resolutely forward for a few more moments, then again held his hand out to Rebecca and said "Please Rebecca. I must talk to you." His words were only half heard in the noise, but she could read his lips well enough and see the pleading in his eyes. She fumbled with her seat belt and struggled to her feet when it sprang free. Cooper moved forward, holding onto the seat backs and reaching out for Rebecca's hand. She kept her hands to herself. She was not going to let him touch her again. She knew the damage that would do to her resolve. She was aching all over as though she had been in some sort of accident, but knew it was a form of mourning for what might have been. She knew the feeling well and was determined that she would surmount it this time and move on. She just had to get her feet back on the ground and put some distance between herself and Cooper. This time it would be her choice. The plane cruised through the thin air as though on ice. Not a bump or dip marred it's course. The air outside was thin and cold, but cloudless as far as the eye could see. The browns and reds of the landscape below unchanged even as the sight disappeared over the far horizon. Rebecca turned her gaze back to Cooper, and her heart lurched. He looked to be so much a part of this land. She could see the blue of the vast sky in the blue of his eyes, the brown of the landscape in the changing browns of his hair and the sun shine in his tanned brown arms. He could as easily talk to the dark skinned people who inhabited the silent regions of his vast property as he could to her, a pale city dweller from one of the biggest cities in the world. She almost sobbed aloud as the injustice of life struck her almost like a blow to her body. She struggled to collect herself. She did not want him, Cooper, to see her insecurities in her eyes. She had to do this. They were not good for each other that was plainly obvious. They would end up destroying each other if one was forced to concede to the other simply so they could be together. Life had set them on different paths, and they were neither of them capable of changing that course. Or so it seemed. Rebecca preceded Cooper into the tiny cabin space, the pilot watching them as they tried to fit in. The biggest problem was Cooper. He just wasn't built to fit in that cabin. Rebecca sat on the edge of the control console in the centre between the two pilot seats, in a spot that the pilot indicated to her. It was apparently a small surface used as a step - or in this case, a small uncomfortable seat. Cooper squeezed himself into the navigator seat, his knees almost touching Rebecca's. The pilot adjusted his headphones making sure they were clamped on his head and looked forward, busying himself with a full aircraft instrument check. He knew when discretion was called for. Cooper closed the connecting door and immediately most of the sound stopped, leaving just a slight whooshing sound of the air rushing past the aircraft as it sped eastward. The engines were a long way back now, slung on either side almost under the tail. Both Rebecca and Cooper were looking at their knees, just millimetres apart. Cooper swallowed. He had never felt so helpless in his life as he struggled to find the right words to say to Rebecca, who sat there looking at him with her steady brown eyed gaze, clear now of tears and almost clear of any expression at all. She was not about to make it any easier for Cooper. If there was blame to apportion, she was going to blame Cooper for bringing her to this place. Leading her to trust him, to hold her, to protect her yes, but if she had never set foot on that dusty forsaken place she would never have needed protecting, anyway. What hurt her the most though was that she had trusted him with her deepest feelings, with her very body, with her heart and her body. A heart that she had never opened to anyone, ever, for a very long time. She couldn't raise her eyes to meet Cooper's just yet.

She remained silent, the silence dragging out into minutes. The pilot kept himself busy scribbling notes in his log, and catching up on details he had forgotten he had to record. Finally, Cooper drew a breath and said to Rebecca.

"I had to get you out of that place. I'm sorry, but your safety is very important to me. You were in danger there." He paused, and into the pause Rebecca fired back.

"In danger from you Cooper. From you. No one else." Her eyes flashed and her chin came up. Her lips were pressed into a thin line. Her heart was thumping in her chest and she was beginning to feel foolish perched on the tiny step of the console. If Cooper wanted to make excuses for his sudden wish to be rid of her now that he had had his way, then at least he could be honest with her. He wanted her off the place and out of his house so he could get on with the renovations and rebuilding, no doubt for the benefit of some local girl he had in mind. Someone who wouldn't mind living out there on a place that appeared to be less fertile than the surface of the moon.

"At least be honest with me Cooper." Rebecca was short of breath she was that tense, and her words sounded less than pleasant, but she was beyond caring.

"You want me off the place and out of your house. Indeed, you want me on the other side of the world as far away as you can place me in as short a time as possible, and it's nothing to do with New World, but everything to do with you and what you want." Rebecca caught her breath in a sobbing hiccup as she tried to steady herself. She was on the verge of shouting. She felt like screaming at him in frustration and hurt.

"I... I..." Words failed her, and she suddenly stood up and

fought past him and out of the cabin, back to her seat where she strapped herself in and looked out of the window, not seeing a thing. Her chest was heaving as she tried to breath deeply to calm herself. She was as much shocked at her own feelings as anything else. She had not been so close to losing her self control ever. Not even when Jake - there. She had used his name. Not even when she had been told he had been killed in action. Then, that time, she had simply stood there looking at her father as though he had suddenly started speaking Chinese. His words after that first statement had simply flowed through her. Her mother's tears had looked like stars glistening on her cheeks, but Rebecca had simply withdrawn. She had surfaced some weeks later and got on with her life as though nothing had happened. People stepped around her, and no one mentioned her state of being ever.

In courtrooms her cool was legendary. Many of the grey haired older lawyers and the hot-shots up and coming had tried to break her cool and failed in their attempts. Now here she was trying to control herself because of this man. She looked at her hands, and her fingers were shaking. She clutched her hands in her lap.

Cooper sat immobilised in the small cabin. He wanted to tell her he loved her and that she could ask him to do anything at all in the world and he would make it his life's mission to try to do it. He wanted to tell her he loved her beyond reason. He wanted to tell her he didn't fully understand himself why he had made the sudden decision to get her off the property and essentially out of his life. He knew the house was a broken down relic of the grand home he had been born into thirty odd years before. The whole property in truth should have been abandoned years ago. He knew that now, but didn't know how to explain to Rebecca that he now saw his own home as others must see it. He would spend what it took to fix it, and make it all new and grand again, but when he looked out to the far horizon, he realised with some shock that it would make no difference. None at all. Rebecca would not be there and he would be. Same empty shell of a man in the same empty shell of a house. Flies and thirsty cattle for company. He knew then what he had to do.

He looked back into the cabin to see Rebeca with her head resting on the headrest, her eyes shut and her head slightly turned to one side. She appeared to be sleeping.

Cooper reached over and tapped the pilots shoulder and indicated he would be climbing into the co-pilot seat. The pilot, Stephen, removed his headphones and lifted some charts off the seat so that Cooper could get into the seat.

"Stephen, can we get clearance to go direct to Brisbane Domestic Airport?" Cooper asked.

The pilot raised his eyebrows.

"Hmm. Maybe. I'm not sure Cooper. Our flight clearances are in and out of Toowoomba only."

"Call them up, ask for the supervisor, and the Australian federal police supervisor to be ready when you call back." Cooper set his jaw and determined to make sure he got to Brisbane without delay.

"Tell them I have word on Agent Mitterrand and Captain Fielding." He watched as the pilot Stephen called up Brisbane control and relayed the message. Cooper couldn't believe it when Brisbane called back within minutes. The pilot put the speaker on, bypassing the headphones.

"Brisbane control to aircraft QA142 from…" The voice hesitated. "Central western Queensland. Please state your business."

"Brisbane," Cooper replied. "Do you have the AFP there, the Australian Federal Police? Or military?"

"Yes. Both." Came the terse reply.

"Good. Brisbane, I'm requesting permission to come directly into Brisbane Domestic, bypassing Toowoomba. I have a passenger on board who has to be returned to the UK on the first available flight. We should be in Brisbane in about sixty minutes if permission is granted. If you have contact with either of the men previously mentioned, tell them that the delicate cargo that they encountered recently with the man Cooper is the … cargo… in question." Cooper released the button and waited. The aeroplane whispered on into the gathering gloom below them. The day was drawing in down there. The early lights of Toowoomba could be seen in the haze away out on the horizon now.

Cooper picked up the mic again.

"Brisbane. We are approaching decision time." Cooper didn't want to give anything away on an open air channel. He was learning fast that the people of New World had resources beyond his comprehension, and as well the local Royal Australian Air Force base would be on their flight path if they proceeded to Brisbane. He didn't want to overfly that place uninvited. Indeed, he was probably on their radar even now.

Brisbane would know what he meant. The minutes ticked away. Stephen looked across at him and pointed to the airspeed indicator and the fuel gauge.

"Brisbane is do-able Cooper. But there will be nothing spare for waiting up here. We go on or land in five minutes."

Cooper nodded and watched the clock on the console. With one minute left and the red second hand looking like a dagger in the lights of the console, the radio crackled into life.

"QA142, cleared to land. Runway 4. Do not taxi. Land and hold. Acknowledge." The speaker gave a squawk of static as though clearing its throat.

Cooper grabbed the mic. "Acknowledge Brisbane. Runway 4. Land and hold." He let out a breath.

The speaker squawked into life again.

"QA142. Cargo is cleared for departure eleven fifty nine pm.

Formalities handled this end."

Cooper breathed a sigh of relief. Just in time. He nodded to Stephen and gave a grim smile.

"You ok to handle this Stephen?" He asked.

"No worries boss." Said Stephen with a grin. "Do it every day." Cooper very much doubted it. Within a few minutes the pilot was engrossed in checking his on board radar, answering the radio calls coming in, and the headphones now firmly back in place. He was entering the very busy airspace of a domestic airport, as well as it's accompanying international air port, and the air force airbase now just to their right. His attention would be wholly on the job at hand.

Chapter 12

Cooper carefully eased himself back out of the cabin and took his place in his seat in the body of the plane, across the aisle from Rebecca. He looked at her and saw that she was still asleep. Good. No more shocks for her until they landed. With only a few hours to wait after that, she would be on her way. Cleared on tonight's flight direct to London's Heathrow. He was determined to stay with her whether she liked it or not until she stepped onto the actual aircraft taking her home.

"Home." He said aloud. Rebecca stirred. She couldn't have heard him though he had spoken aloud. Perhaps he had spoken a little louder than he intended, the noise in this part of the aircraft played tricks on the ears. Rebecca's eyes were open, and she was looking at Cooper. Just looking. He felt slightly uneasy. He decided to brave it.

"Rebecca, we are flying directly into Brisbane. We land in a few minutes. From there you will be taken directly to the International terminal, to catch tonight's flight to Heathrow. You will be home tomorrow." Cooper smiled with what he hoped was a friendly confident smile, but felt to him like a sickly grimace. He didn't feel confident at all. In fact, he was feeling decidedly uneasy at the suddenly impending departure of Rebecca.

"What did you say?" Asked Rebecca. "Did I hear you correctly? Brisbane. In a few minutes?" Her voice rose an octave. "On my way tonight?" She drew a breath. Then added. "I can't wait." Her tone not indicating any such thing at all.

The small jet began its descent into Brisbane, the lights of the city sweeping beneath it then disappearing into blackness as the plane swept out over the bay next to the airport itself, and they began the sweep around to come in from the north, and land on the runway assigned to them, one used mostly for cargo planes and maintenance purposes. Well to one side

146

of the huge international runways. As Rebecca looked out of the window, she could see a massive Air India jumbo coming down almost beside them, it's landing gear hanging down like the claws of some gigantic bird of prey. They dropped onto the tarmac and rolled to a stop. The plane rocked slightly and stayed where it was. Rebecca looked at Cooper, her eyebrows raised.

"We were told to roll to a stop and hold." He said by way of explanation. He got to his feet and went to the cabin again and looked out of the windscreen. He patted the pilot on the shoulder in thanks. Speeding toward them on a service road was a collection of cars with lights flashing on them in multiple colours. The aircraft was surrounded in seconds, and the pilot having already dropped the entrance steps, the first person through the door into the cabin was Agent Mitterrand. He bounced to a stop just inside the door like a long lost friend, a smile of welcome on his face and with a boisterous shout welcomed them to Brisbane.

"My friends! Welcome. So glad to see you again. You won't believe my news. Rebecca, Cooper. What an amazing 24 hours. I am a little surprised to see you both here so soon. I had thought that maybe..." Here he stopped and looked from one to the other. "Hmmm, apparently not. I'm not often wrong you know." He looked rather sternly at them, his mouth set in a thin line. "We'll see." Neither Rebecca nor Cooper had any idea what he was getting at.

"Come, come, we can't sit here all night. The airport people are having fits as it is. Travelling light, I see. Good. Let's go." He turned back to the door, then said over his shoulder. "Your pilot, Stephen? He can park the plane for the night, these people will help him out and so on. You won't be going back with him. Either of you." With that he rattled back down the steps and walked briskly to the ubiquitous HUMV, black of course. Rebecca looked at Cooper. She couldn't help smiling.

"Is that the same person we met out at the station?" She said. "I find it difficult to believe."

Cooper scratched his chin with a finger, in what was now a familiar gesture to Rebecca.

"I guess so. Although I have a feeling all this bonhomie may be a show for someone. Can't imagine who though." They made their way down the steps, a little nervous when they saw the heavily armed team waiting by the vehicles. Rebecca couldn't help taking hold of Coopers arm with a nervous grip and walking as close as she could to him. His very bulk was reassuring, the darkness and glittering lights all about with a cool wind keening across the open spaces was a scene that generated its own tension. She literally clung to him with both arms as the gigantic shape of a jumbo jet roared past them only seemingly yards away, it's engines howling like banshees from hell, with a bone shaking rattling roar of machinery at maximum strain shaking the ground beneath their feet. Cooper looked at the dark shape hurtling past them and gripped Rebecca with his arm around her waist. She was so tiny! He still wondered at her frailty. He held on to her in case she was blown away by stray jet wash. How on earth could he let her go? The jumbo lifted away further along the runway and the engines changed pitch as it picked up speed now that it was loosed from the ground. The undercarriage was coming up when they lost sight of it in the darkness. They hadn't taken a dozen steps when another huge aircraft was screaming toward them on its take off run. It was time to get out of here. What ever was in store for them had to be better than this? This was cold, noisy, and definitely terrifying.

Cooper ushered Rebecca into the open door of the squat vehicle and climbed in beside her. He was not going to let them separate him from Rebecca. Something was happening, and he was going to protect her whether she wanted his protection or not. Once settled, the Hummer

rolled off onto a side road and the whole convoy made directly for a huge gate in the perimeter fence. The gate rolled open enough for the vehicles to barrel through and closed behind them immediately. The Hummer that they were in was midway in the convoy of about a dozen, and they peeled out across the road with lights flashing and sirens screaming into the night forcing all other cars onto the grassy verge that filled the wide spaces along the airport approach roads. They were circling back around to get to the front entrance of the International Terminal, it being impossible even for them to cross the busy runways. They came to a stop in a flurry of vehicles, with cab drivers and bus drivers waving their arms and shouting. It all went quiet though when the armoured Special Services men piled out of the Hummers and stood facing the crowd of irate civilians in a semi-circle out from the vehicle that Rebecca and Cooper occupied. Special Agent Mitterrand opened the door for Cooper, a faint smile playing about his mouth.
"No good having the power if you can't abuse it now and then?" He said in a half question. "You shouldn't have too much trouble at check-in." All eyes were on Rebecca and Cooper as they walked rather timidly into the departure concourse. Agent Mitterrand showed them to the VIP departure area, and into the quietness of this supposedly exclusive lounge. He wasted no time, because the flight to London was imminent, and he knew he had a mission to complete.
"Cooper," he said. "I want you in London with Rebecca. On tonight's flight. Can do?" He didn't sound like he would take no for an answer.
Cooper was startled, it was the last thing he had expected to hear. It made no sense, and in any case he had business to attend to here.
"Nope, sorry. No can do." Cooper replied immediately. "In fact I want the work aircraft turned around immediately, so

149

we can fly back to Innamincka. So I can fly back to Innamincka. Rebecca of course is going home." He held up a hand. "No good arguing about it. That's the way it is." The agent looked at Cooper long and silently. His face was not a happy face thought Cooper. Too bad. He had things to do and he could see no point in his going to London with Rebecca. She probably wouldn't want him to, anyway. He looked at her and could not read her face at all. She was just standing there watching the exchange between him and Mitterrand, her face giving nothing away.

"Listen to me Cooper. This is not a request. I..."Agent Mitterrand started to say, but Cooper again interrupted.

"Last time I looked, this was a free country. That means that I can - and will, return to my own home, on the plane that I chartered myself. What ever your problem is, it's none of my business and so you can work it out yourself. If Rebecca needs help back in London, her friends in MI5 will I have no doubt, provide such help." Cooper reached out a hand to Rebecca to shake her hand.

"A hand shake Cooper?" She asked in surprise. "We are going to part on a handshake?" Her expression was almost still a mask, but Cooper could see the beginning of tears in the corner of her eyes. Cooper turned his back on the agent, and stepped up close to Rebecca, taking her in his arms. He was instantly transported into a world of light as he felt the heat radiating from Rebecca like a tidal wave. He hadn't been prepared for such a reaction and it stunned him. His arms tightened around her as he looked down into her eyes. Oh this had been such a mistake. He should never have touched her. The feel of her in his arms jolted him to the core. Her eyes were like drowning pools, and he felt as though he was being drawn down into their depths. Her lips seemed an impossible distance away from his, and without thinking he lowered his head and touched her lips with his. He knew in that instance that Rebecca felt as he did. Was as surprised as he was. Her breath was hot on his face as he drew his face back slightly and she sighed softly

"Oh Cooper." He clenched her small body to his and whispered in her ear,

"I will see you in London... my dearest. I will. But I have to finish things here. I can't just walk away, I... I love you Rebecca Boucher." With that he gently released her and stepped back. His head was swimming. He had not meant to say anything like that. He was going to be firm but polite and bid her farewell as a good friend. They had only known each other a short time after all. Now? Now he had fired up his emotions again, and from the look on Rebecca's face, hers as well. Rebecca left her hands trailing down his arms until finally she held his hands in hers. She looked steadily at him, oblivious to everyone else.

"I love you too." She said simply, a faint smile on her lips. She dropped his hands and turned to go through the lounge to the departure area. She didn't need the others to escort her from here. She knew the way, and had her passport in her hand, and her carry on bag on her shoulder. Her suitcase had already been taken through directly from the VIP lounge boarding controls. She didn't look back as Cooper stood there watching her walk out of his life. Her back was straight, her shoulders back and head held high. The picture of cool self assurance, in her dark skirt and pale blouse, her shoulder length hair shining from the lights of the lounge. Agent Mitterrand and his assistants seemed a little confused as to what to do. This was not going the way he had planned. Not at all.

"Cooper," he said. "Rebecca could be in trouble back there. She has upset those people by not completing her brief. They may try to harm her." He spread his hands.

"Agent Mitterrand, I am sure Rebecca's friends in London can look after her. Now they know the type of people she has come across, they will be at pains to watch out for them. Me being there will only cause unnecessary confusion. In any case as I told you. I have things that need attending to here. I am about to wind up my interests in Innamincka. It may even be handed back to the traditional owners, and from that point on it's up to them. I would not like to be in the shoes of anyone from New World trying to intrude on their land." Cooper folded his arms across his chest. A pretty bold body language statement if he'd ever seen one he thought. "Make of that what you will Agent Mitterrand. Now if you would be so kind, please escort me back to the jet, and locate my pilot. I wish to get back to Innamincka. I know that he has night flying clearance and is being paid by me. We can call ahead and have the landing lights on for our return. Thank you for your help in expediting Rebecca's return flight. I do appreciate that." Cooper waited now for the agent to respond. He could see that he was in deep thought. Cooper had no idea what had been happening regarding the intruders on Innamincka, but if they were still there after all, then his men would sort them out this time. No one out there would be caught napping again. Mitterrand looked at Cooper. "Fine, I concede that you should want to go back to your own place. It's commendable that you may be handing it back to the traditional owners, but it's not my business. My business is stopping foreign nationals using Australia for their own purposes, uninvited. We can deal with them when we find them on this occasion. Meantime, with you and your men out there, it adds a level of difficulty to the operation." He walked up and down, every bit of his impatience showing in his steps.

"Cooper, in that case, can you talk to the native people there? I don't mean you station hands; I mean the ones who have gone back to the bush. Or probably never left it from what I can see. If we have their help, we can be off your place in no time at all. We wanted to talk to them, but can't even find them. There appears to be no trace of them."

Cooper smiled. "If they don't want to be seen, they won't be." He said. "Fine. Ok, I can do that. I don't want to unhelpful. I just have my own business to attend to. Will you return with me on my plane, or do you have some other transport?" Cooper was remembering the helicopter, and his momentary detention in it. Agent Mitterrand was recalling the same thing it seemed.

"Er, we have our own transport thanks. My aid here will escort you back to your jet and locate your pilot. You should be fuelled and on your way before Rebecca has even lifted off. I'll maybe see you out at Innamincka by dawn, if we need to return there." With that he turned and strode off into the restricted area. The guards never batting an eyelid as he passed through.

Cooper and the assistant made their way back out of the terminal, and to Coopers surprise the Hummer that they had arrived in was still occupying centre position in the arrivals parking bay. Much to the consternation of other motorists and coach drivers. No one however was arguing with the heavily armed team standing rock solid, their black kit making them look like something out of a science fiction film. Everyone climbed back into the vehicles and they roared out of the terminal area, the tourists no doubt having a real tale to tell of their journey through the Brisbane international terminal.

Rebecca meantime was by now in the actual departure lounge, waiting to board. The time seemed to have just slipped by. She felt as though she was in some kind of strange trance where things went on around her without actually involving her. This was not good she thought. "Snap out of it." she said aloud. A couple of people looked at her, but no one really took much notice. Just another passenger venting their frustrations over some travel problem. Rebecca was not sure of herself, and this was a new thing for her. Cooper had turned her otherwise stable world upside down.

His parting kiss just now had really rocked her. She was aware that it had also affected him, but still he had parted from her and was determined to go back to his place in the outback. She could see no other reason for him to be doing up the old house, then that he intended to re-establish it as his home, rather than just the house where he lived. Ok, so that's the way it was she mused, and gathered her few belongings and headed for the gate. She didn't look back.
.....

London was wet. Wet and cold. There was snow in the air. Rebecca could feel it as she got out of the taxi and crossed the pavement to the front entrance of her offices. It felt a little strange as though something had been moved. She stopped and looked up at the building, at the doors, at the man standing by the doors assisting people in and out of taxis. His role was probably redundant these days, but the building owners kept him on and Rebecca liked the style it seemed to give the place. It set it apart from the rows of blank offices along the street. She was about to continue inside through the vast revolving glass doors when a reflection in the glass as it came past her caused her to stop in her tracks. The door was in danger of knocking her off her feet as it continued its revolution, and she had to step back quickly to avoid it.

"Are you all right Miss Boucher?" Asked the doorman solicitously. Rebecca just nodded to the man. She could have sworn she had seen Cooper walking past behind her as she had approached the doors. She looked around, but there was no one in the street even remotely like him. It was still early, and the few people on the street in the central business district of London were hunched down against the wind and the rain, some struggling to hold onto umbrellas that threatened to whirl away in the next gust. She took a last look and shook her head. This would have to stop. She had been home for some time now, home from Australia and the searing heat of the Outback. There had been no word from Cooper and she had seen no need to contact him. He had made his position perfectly clear, and she was determined to remain above the school girl business of chasing him. But it was strange, she thought as she made her way into the building and to the bank of lifts in the foyer. This was not the first time she thought she had seen him. It was very disconcerting, and just when she hadn't thought about him at all for days on end, suddenly there he was. Or seemed to be.

Of her client there had been no communication at all. His account had been settled in full through their company offices, and no communication had been made other than that. That in itself was very strange, and it had been mentioned in a couple of meetings. Rebecca had given a full account, both written and verbal in her first meeting after her return. She had reported everything to her partners. "Well," she thought with a smile. "Not quite everything." She could feel her skin prickling as she sat down at her desk, the memories of her love making with Cooper flashing through her mind. She flushed slightly, the coloured tinge climbing up her neck to her hair line as her nipples hardened. Rebecca jumped up again and started opening filing cabinet draws, rearranging the things on her desk, and finally making coffee.

Chapter 13

One of the partners put his head around the office door and looked at her.

"Coffee time? Mind if I join you?" He swung into the office and plunked down in a spare chair.

He blew gently on the coffee that Rebecca handed him.

"Your Australian?" He said with a questioning inflection. "Tell me about him." James Links had been a partner for a few years now and had been the youngest partner until Rebecca had come along. Rebecca was a little surprised at the rather direct approach to this subject.

"He's not 'My Australian' James." She retorted. Perhaps a little too sharply. He looked up at her.

"Sorry Rebecca. I didn't mean..." He said softly.

"No of course not. I didn't mean to sound so sharp, sorry. Just a bit preoccupied. Well, yes, the Australian. I haven't heard from him of course. The last I heard was when I left Australia in the middle of the night. He was at the airport with the intelligence agent. Last I heard he was going back out to his property. It wasn't being sold. Apparently it was never being sold, he just wanted to see up close who was showing interest in it. He had had intruders on the place, and there was some sort of nuclear material involved as I understand it. I haven't heard from the client either actually. Their account was paid, and that's the last I've heard."

Rebecca was sitting in her chair now, rocking slightly, her foot pressing on the floor.

"Hmmm, yes." Said James. "Actually I was asking about the man himself. What did you think of him? What was he like as a person?" James blew gently on his coffee.

Rebecca was looking at James, trying to figure out where this was going. She didn't want to ask outright just yet. It might have been just idle office chatter. James having a lull in his busy schedule, perhaps. He didn't sound like he was prying, or worse, fishing. He just sounded interested in Rebecca's view. In any case, if he needed to, he would tell her what his interest was about.

"Well, let me see. What can I tell you? I was only there for a few days overall, so I hardly had time to get to know him, really." Her cheeks coloured. She hoped James hadn't noticed. "He was nice enough I suppose. Tall, good looking. Very well off financially. A bit lonely I think. He lives out in the Australian outback, a long way out. In fact, I think it was almost in the centre of the country. I've never seen a place so lonely and desolate." She was easily able to describe Cooper's good looks, his lovely face and his so soft lips. His brown hair that seemed to change colour as it reflected the bright Australian light. His fingers that left little trails of sparks across her skin as he trailed them across her stomach. His muscular physique that seemed to ripple under his sun browned skin as he moved. Rebecca thought she had put Cooper into the back of her mind, but this question had opened up a door that she would have preferred to keep shut.

She smiled at James. "In short - he's very nice." That was as far as she was prepared to go. James would not be interested in the details that she had just been recalling. As it was, she was sitting here in her London office with her lower stomach fluttering and very small electric currents flickering through her secret places. It was all she could do not to squirm in her seat. The attention light on her phone started flickering, and she snatched it up.

"Yes." She almost yelled. Relief at the distraction flooding through her. James smiled and rose from his chair. He didn't mention to Rebecca that he had been advised of the presence of the old client being back in town, as well as the presence of Cooper, by friends in Whitehall whose business it was to know these things. He placed the coffee cup back on the tray on the side cabinet and with a finger wave to Rebecca left her office. He looked to be deep in thought, and

Rebecca wondered again at the reasons behind his seemingly innocuous questions. There were clients waiting for her in the reception area, and she had to attend to them. Cooper was shelved again. She had to go and earn her living. The day moved along and Rebecca kept busy with the various things that made up her day. There had been no more probing questions from James or anyone else for that matter. Her office had a steady stream of visitors, and suddenly the day was finished, it was time to leave. She sat back and twiddled with a pencil that lay on her desk. It was only early in the evening yet, and Rebecca didn't feel like going home. Hitting the speed dial button on her desk phone she called Kali. It took a few moments and her research assistant and friend came on the line.

"Kali, are you finished for the day? I'm heading down to Vertigo 42 for a drink, if you care to join me?"

"Vertigo? Sure. I love the view, and the food is not bad either. I could use a snack. and a glass of red. I'll meet you at the lifts. Leaving now?"

"Right now." Replied Rebecca, rising from her desk. She picked up her grip, and headed for the lifts. This was just what she wanted. A relaxing drink, something light to eat. Maybe. It was a bit early for dinner at about seven. She needed to talk girl-talk with Kali. They didn't have far to go, both buildings being right in the London square mile so it was an easy walk along the busy streets, and there was the destination. Whisked up to the forty second floor, the bar and restaurant was busy, but not packed yet. Mostly after work types like themselves. Rebecca decided to perch on a seat near the windows, Kali beside her, and sip their house red. She had already made a reservation for two earlier in the afternoon, hoping that Kali would be free. It was that kind of place. Maximum security in the foyer and reservation only entry. The lights of London glittered below them and around them in the many buildings of the City.

She loved this place. Kali eased back and admired some of the men in the place. There was no fear here of being hit on by anyone looking for a pick-up, male or female, but there was no harm in looking. She smiled and raised her glass of red to Rebecca.

"Here's to Cooper." She said. Rebecca nearly spilt her drink. "Where? Not here surely." She looked around in alarm. Kali was laughing helplessly.

"Oh Rebecca, of course he isn't here. I was only toasting his memory because I have noticed these last few weeks that you have a certain far away look in your eyes a lot of the time." She put down her glass.

"Want to talk about it?"

"No, I do not want to talk about 'it'." She replied, emphasising the it. "There's nothing to talk about. honestly." The truth of the matter was that she had been spending far too much time thinking about Cooper and it had even been affecting her ability to work.

"Hmmmm." Was all Kali said. She swirled her drink.

"Then you won't mind if I talk about him." She added.

"Fine, go ahead Kali. Means nothing to me." Rebecca could feel the salt of the lie on her tongue. She placed her glass of Shiraz on the table. Heywood Estate, Australian Shiraz. Kali looked from Rebecca to the glass and back again, a faint smile on her lips.

"So the Australian Shiraz is just accidental is it?" A throaty chuckle escaped her as Rebecca looked at the glass then back at Kali.

"Oh, ok then. I do think of him a lot. In fact, I actually miss him a lot. He's the first man who's come into my life in a very long time. It feels like months since I've been back, but in fact it's only been six weeks." Rebecca was looking at Kali, but her focus was suddenly inward, although her gaze was still on Kali. She coloured slightly, the heat rising up her neck to the roots of her hair.

Kali chuckled again.

"From what I saw on Skype, you have good reason to remember him" She said. "He is one hunk of a man. I am assuming from what I saw and heard, that you weren't sitting around discussing the weather." Kali was ordering some more drinks, and snack foods while talking. It could be a long session if she could get Rebecca started talking. That girl needed to talk too. It was obviously troubling her friend, and Kali was determined to draw her out. She leant across and tapped Rebecca's fingers. She had gone really quiet. Kali frowned slightly.

"What's up Rebecca. Gee, I'm sorry if I have upset you. Really, I am only trying to get you to talk to me, get these things out in the open where you can deal with them. Good heavens, you look like you've seen a ghost!"

Rebecca turned the biggest eyes Kali had ever seen on her. Kali raised her glass and took a large sip of wine to give Rebecca time to think about it. Rebecca looked like she might need a moment, but then she said.

"Kali... " Then in an almost whisper, "I'm late!"

Kali choked on her wine, hastily grabbing at her napkin to catch the spraying red droplets, the rest running down her chin. She had heard the expression about someone sitting there with their mouth open in surprise and realised she was now doing exactly that.

"Rebecca! you don't mean..." She looked around to make sure they weren't being overheard. "Late, as in ... late?" She whispered in shock. "Are you sure? Of course you're sure. Stupid question. When did you realise?"

"Just now. I just did the sums when I realised how long I've been back. Oh My God!" Rebecca slumped back in her chair and took a long sip of wine. She looked at the glass. She looked at Kali. She reached out her hand to Kali.

"Kali, I can't." She wailed. People turned to look enquiringly in her direction. Kali was gripping her outstretched hand in support. Kali was shaking her head slowly.

"Rebecca, get a grip girl. So you are a little out of sync. Sometimes travel does that. Other things too. Have you been feeling well? No..." She whispered again. "Morning sickness? And in any case, I assume that you of all people would have used protection." Kali was sure her friend was at least that sensible in this day and age.

Rebecca went as white as a sheet. Kali was getting worried, and a couple of the chic young things nearby were looking at Rebecca with traces of concern starting to show on their faces.

"No." A very long pause. "None at all, ever." Her voice was very husky as though she was struggling to keep in the raging emotions that were flooding through her. Most of her adult life, she had repressed any overt emotional response, and now it felt like they were about to burst forth in an overwhelming flood. She sat back in her chair and fanned her face with her table napkin. A waitress appeared at her side.

"Are you feeling ok miss? Can I get you something?"

Rebecca looked at her and smiled faintly.

"No, I'll be ok in a moment. Just some bad news. Or maybe good news. I don't know." She said.

The waitress looked at her in puzzlement for a moment and moved away.

Kali sat forward again and said.

"No need to get all upset. You can't know right now. You just need to do a test or something. You will probably be ok in a day or two. This sort of thing happens a lot to people. Timing gets thrown out." Kali shook her head. "No protection!" She exclaimed, in disbelief.

Rebecca's colour was coming back, and she nibbled at the little canapé she had taken from the plate in front of her.

"Champagne I think Kali. I think I'm in shock. You are right of course, it's not likely, and anyway I can check easily enough. It was rather stupid of me I know, to leave myself unprotected. I don't know what I was thinking."

Moments later the Champagne arrived, and the flutes were filled. Rebecca tipped hers back like she had not had a drink in years. Her glass of red abandoned on the table. The waitress took both the red glasses away. Kali kept looking at her friend. She seems to be coming around to her old self again. Back in command of her emotions.

Rebecca was thinking again about the rather strange questions put by James earlier on that day.

"What would James be asking about Cooper for do you think?" She asked Kali. "Earlier on today he came into my office and asked outright, what I could tell him about Cooper."

Kali shook her head.

"It does seem rather odd for James to be asking questions about Cooper. It wasn't even his brief, so he had no involvement at all. I'll see if I can find out tomorrow." Kali smiled. She was very good at ferreting out such information. They ordered a light meal from the menu and finished the champagne about the same time as the meal. The place was getting a little overcrowded now, so they decided to leave. It was another work day tomorrow in any case. Rebecca wanted to stop by a chemist and had to swear to Kali that she would phone and tell her the results as soon as she found out the result of the pregnancy test. Rebecca was sure that it would be negative but she couldn't help feeling apprehensive, remembering that she had been so foolish as to have sex with Cooper without protection. She hurried home, having the taxi wait outside the chemist and then taking her on to her door step. She lived close to the city and usually caught the tube train. Tonight though, she wanted to be home and indoors with her thoughts. Cooper figured large in those thoughts. Was she prepared to share any news with him? She didn't know. She did know that she just wasn't prepared herself.

She sat for a long time on the edge of the little foot stool she kept in the bathroom, staring at the tell tale read out on the plastic holder. She wasn't particularly focused on it, just staring in the general direction. Her thoughts were on the other side of the world. What was Cooper doing now, it must be day time there now? Was he out working on his property? In town on business? Should she phone and let him know? Or was it really nothing at all to do with him now? He seemed to have made his position perfectly clear by not contacting her at all. He had practically carried her onto her departure flight from Australia, and she didn't think his reasons for having her leave really held water. He must have realised that she would never leave her position in the firm to move out and live in that remote wilderness. He must have known equally well, that he would not consider moving to London - or even England, because of his deep attachment to his home. So why did he seem so intent on distancing himself from her so absolutely, when even knowing all that, didn't really stop them from forming some sort of close relationship? So the positive result on the little card strip held its own set of concerns. Some hugely emotional issues, some purely practical. She pushed herself to her feet and walked back out into the unit. She felt a little aimless, and couldn't seem to think of what to do next. This was most unlike her, and she was very aware of it, but couldn't help herself. Kali would be of some comfort she knew and picked up the phone and dialled her number.

"Kali?" The phone trembled slightly in her hand. "Can you come over for a bit please?" She stood looking at her feet. She looked at her flat stomach. She was proud of her looks, her shape, her fitness. Was it all going to change? Kali was silent for a bit then said.

"I'll be there in ten minutes." She hung up.

In no time she was ringing to be let in to the unit lobby, and on her way up. They stood in the door hugging for a long time, then with a sniff and a wipe of her eyes, she stepped back into the unit and Kali followed.

She looked at Kali and smiled weakly.

"Well, it looks like my life is about to change rather radically." She showed Kali the test kit result strip. "I'll get a doctor's opinion of course but it looks pretty positive to me."

"What will you do?" Kali asked. "I mean, I know you only just found out and haven't had a moment to think about it at all. I just wondered really what you might have thought about Cooper and his position in this situation."

"I haven't had a moment to think, really. I seem to be unable to focus at the moment. I'm not going to be able to come into work in the morning., that much I know. As for Cooper... do I tell him? Can I tell him? I just don't know. Perhaps he does have certain rights in this. Well I know that he has - did have - some involvement in this." She smiled. "Some very nice involvement, actually."

Kali smiled.

"That's better. It's nice to see you smiling again." Kali was very pleased. If Rebecca was able to smile about even some part of this, then she would be alright. Kali was not about to offer any solution one way or the other. She would however support her friend in what ever decision she made for herself. What Rebecca couldn't possibly know was that Cooper had not forgotten her at all. He had been very busy with the repairs and updates to his house and yards, and not a day had passed when he hadn't been thinking about her. The work had progressed well, and he had thrown money at the problems like he had never done before in his life. He wanted his place sparkling again. The number of aircraft coming and going with supplies and building materials, furniture, white goods, machinery and so on had made headlines in the Toowoomba daily paper, and was the talk of the social group behind the cattle industry of the entire region. It hadn't taken all of his time though. He was going to change his entire outlook and primary career. He had been sent to boarding school and then to university by his parents, and his father had been happy to leave him there until he finished. Cooper had not given it a second thought. All of the children of the station owners of the outback went to university. Most never went back to the land, and inevitably the properties went in to decline and were taken over by multinationals and put under managers. His place was one of the few left in private hands. Which made it extremely valuable. But his time at university had not been wasted. It was that degree that was now going to be his life. He felt he had discharged any filial duty to his father now, and it was time to map out his own life before it was too late.

Chapter 14

How often had he passed the telephone in the hall? How often had he reached for the phone on his office desk? He couldn't count, but each time he had stopped himself. Rebecca was there just a phone call away, but he still hesitated. What was it. Distrust of her? or himself? He was not really sure about her, even though he was about as sure of himself as it was possible to be. Determined, resolute, and perhaps even stubborn to a degree, when it came to women he had actually had very little experience of them. His mother had died when he was very young, and although he had enjoyed his time at university, the study had generally kept everyone busy, and the social activities had seen little chance to form deep relationships, anyway. In the remote parts of the country where he lived, the nearest neighbour was an hour away by plane, and there were no daughters in any case. The country dances of his father's day were a thing of the past now, and so he had been feeling increasingly isolated on the place for some time.

Cooper reached over and picked up the phone. It was time to get back in control of his emotions. He was behaving worse than a teenage boy worried about making a mistake. He had to go to London, anyway. If he was to finish this mission, then he had no choice. He had decided to find out what Agent Mitterrand had wanted him in London for, and it was an idea that caught his interest. More importantly, he could see Rebecca again. Cooper put the phone to his ear and dialled Rebecca's office number. He realised he didn't have her private number, nor even her mobile number. So London was ten hours behind. He checked his watch. The call tone sounded for what seemed an interminable time. It should be about eight in the morning there. Maybe too early, but then an office like that would surely have early starters. Suddenly there was a voice on the line.

"Rebecca here."

Cooper nearly fell off his chair. He was momentarily lost for words and blurted out.

"Rebecca, it's Cooper. Can you talk, do you have a minute?" He smacked his forehead. What a goose. Calling out of the blue and then saying something as banal as that.

"I mean; do you have time to talk given that it's your work day there?" Cooper realised that he still wasn't making a lot of sense. He started again. Rebecca still hadn't said a word, but he knew she was there, he could hear her breathing.

"Rebecca, have you heard anything from New World? Have you heard anything from MI5 or whoever your contacts were? I've heard nothing, seen no one. In fact, I haven't heard or seen anything from Billy or his people here either. They seem to have disappeared." Cooper waited for Rebecca to respond. One way or another.

Finally, she replied.

"No Cooper, not really. I've not actually heard from anyone at all. New World paid their account some weeks back, and that's that." She paused and Cooper could hear her draw a breath.

"This is the first time I've heard from you too. I thought..." She stopped mid-sentence. "Never mind, it's not important now."

Cooper had the definite feeling that something was wrong. Her voice had a resigned note in it, as though she was tired from thinking about things. It was not like her at all. She had a naturally upbeat look on life. A glass half full kind of girl. Her feisty nature usually kept her in charge. This rather quiet, almost submissive sound was something new.

Something was wrong. Cooper realised he had no way of finding out.

"Rebecca." Cooper began again. "Is something wrong? Are you unwell?" He asked.

"No, not unwell." She replied. "Cooper, I have to go. Please don't call again." The phone line clicked in his ear and she was gone. Just the hiss of static on the line.

He held the phone in his hand as though it was a snake about to bite him. What the hell was going on. He had behaved rather badly when she was here, he knew that. Packing her off on the plane like some discarded girlfriend. Making matters worse by not calling her at all in the ensuing weeks. He shook his head. He was not a man about to take being hung up on.

He hit the redial button. He would apologise to her whether she wanted to hear from him or not.

The phone rang for some minutes then with a click there she was again.

"Yes?" Was all she said. Very unusual. Cooper frowned.

"Rebecca, please let me apologise to you."

Rebecca interrupted with, "Cooper, you are about to be a father." Then the phone went dead. She had hung up again. Cooper had dropped the handset as though it truly had bitten him. He stepped back from the desk, staring at the handset laying on the floor of his office. He couldn't think straight. He had a reputation for being Mr Unflappable, but this had hit him right between the eyes. It was impossible. Well no, he realised it was eminently possible, he had not taken any precautions, and it seemed that neither had Rebecca. Indeed, it had not even crossed his mind. He bent and picked up the handset and hung it on the cradle. This was something he had not counted on and the news had momentarily caused him to be unable to think. He flopped down into his office chair and stared out of the window. He had not planned on children entering his life at any point. Of course he had thought that being married to Rebecca would be wonderful, but at this early stage his thoughts had not extended past that possibility to the natural outcome of such a union. Now it seemed that having a child was coming first. Did he even want a child? Well, this couldn't be attended to long distance so the only thing to do was fly to

London and talk to Rebecca face to face. Anything happening here on the property would just have to wait for his return, or carry on with out him. What ever was going on here he didn't seem to have any control over anymore anyway, and the rebuilding work was almost complete on all the outbuildings, and the builders were now starting on the main house. Maybe it would be a good thing to get out of the place for a few months. The decision made, Cooper started packing a few things right there and then. He was a man of action, needing no long decision period. He had to go to London, and the subject was very important, so with nothing really holding him, the best time was right now. While packing, he carried the phone with him, and within minutes had his flight booked, and accommodation arranged through a travel agency. He could be in Brisbane, and off to London on the evening flight day after tomorrow. He didn't need to rush, there was an aircraft on the runway near the house. He carried his suitcase through to the lounge room. He had decided on only one case. It was easier. A carry on holdall for his immediate needs, and a suitcase. Travel light and fast. He was a frequent flyer with Singapore Airlines and travelling first class ensured him walk on check-in with a very minimum of fuss. Being Australian, he needed no visa for England, just the current passport. Ready to go.

Cooper looked at the cityscape far below. He'd only been to London once before, and that had been many years ago, in his gap year he supposed. there was nothing familiar, and although he recognised some of the landmarks, that was only from seeing them in movies, the local TV news, and documentaries and the like. How would Rebecca react to him just turning up on the door step?
He found his way to his hotel by cab. He didn't see the sense

in trying to rent a car and find his way around because of the traffic if nothing else. It was just after midday, and he needed to relax and let the tension of the trip ebb away. As tough as he was, that journey took it out of anyone so he did little else but put his suitcase in the room, thank the porter and head down stairs to the nearest bar. Cooper needed a drink, and he needed to collect his thoughts. Now that he was here, what was the plan? He couldn't just bowl up to Rebecca's office could he? Could he? No, if she was in any sort of state, and he could imagine she was, that was the last thing he wanted to do. He was still not sure of his own feelings on the subject, other than he had to know what Rebecca's plans were. He realised that he was faced with the prospect of having an heir to his father's property. It was something else that had never crossed his mind. That he would marry, have children, and they would become the heirs to the Anders cattle empire. Now here was exactly that situation right in front of him. Well, tomorrow he would try to see her. He still only had her place of work to go to. He had no other address, so bright and early he would go to her office and find out once and for all what her plans were. He raised a hand to the barman to order a whisky, and just leant against the bar waiting for it to be mixed. Whisky and dry, and he didn't care if it was the house special. Cooper raised his eyes to catch his reflection in the mirrors behind the bar and slicked his long hair back over his head. He looked a bit of a sight he realised and determined to go back to his room and have a shower and change as soon as he had finished his drink. It was getting on to late afternoon now, and he wanted to make contact with Rebecca today if he could.

Suddenly, in the corner of his eye he caught sight of two men who had just come into the bar. He nearly dropped his drink as the barman handed it to him. It was the same two men he had seen in the hotel in Brisbane, he was sure of it. He almost turned around, but instead steeled himself to follow their progress in the mirror. They must have known he would see them, but seemed oblivious of his presence. He didn't look his usual cool well dressed self he admitted, and he had let his hair grow longer over the past weeks, and sported what was probably a fashionable two or three-day growth of stubble on his normally smoothly shaven face. In fact, he thought, he looked positively disreputable. Which may explain the rather tart response of the barman to him. He looked somewhat out of place in this very swish hotel drinks bar.

'Good, perhaps they haven't actually recognised me.' Cooper thought. 'So what are they doing here? It's too much of a coincidence.' He sipped at his drink and kept his eyes down as one of them came to the bar to order.

The barman was there instantly. 'So...' Thought Cooper. Sure enough, when the man ordered two mineral waters, he put them on his room. "4162 room please." He said, and there it was, that sibilant East European accent. There was no mistaking him now. Cooper was a hard man to hide, but his presence there was unexpected it seemed, so no one was looking out for him. His current slightly dishevelled state must have been just enough for the pair to place him beneath their notice. All thought of cleaning up in his room disappeared as he sipped his whiskey and carefully watched the pair. They in turn weren't trying to be inconspicuous, but occupied a large table near one of the window walls in the bar. The busy cityscape seen through the glass was a fantastic sight to Cooper, used as he was to horizons so far away that you could see the curve of the world. 'Perhaps I could get used to this view.' He mused. The barman was looking sideways at him from along the bar. Cooper didn't want to raise any undue attention, so he kept his head and shoulders slightly slumped forward, resting his arms on his elbows and signalled to the barman. The man carefully finished polishing the glass he had in his hand, placed it in the rack and rather casually came along the bar to stand in front of Cooper.

In a manner that shouted slight disapproval, without being overtly rude - a skill any good experienced barman mastered early in his career, he said to Cooper.

"Would sir like another whisky?"

Cooper looked at him from under his lowered eyebrows and placed his room key-card on the bar. The barman didn't flicker an eyelid, but the next whisky appeared in front of Cooper as though by magic it came so quickly. The key-card was gold, and only four of them existed. This one was number one. There was one for each of the apartments that took up each of the four quarters of the buildings uppermost guest floor. Cooper meantime kept a careful eye on the two thugs who sat over by the wall talking quietly between themselves. Cooper wanted to make a call, but didn't want to use his mobile. He had an idea that Agent Mitterrand had it tracked, and probably bugged, so although he actually didn't mind him knowing where he was, he didn't want him listening to his calls. The barman was still close by, and Cooper only had to look his way and he was there.

"How can I be of service sir?"

'That's better.' Thought Cooper and said.

"Can I use your house phone to make an outside call please?"

"Of course, sir. Just press 0 first for an outside line." The man placed the phone on the bar next to Coopers right arm.

'Good, perfect.' He thought as he turned slightly away from the men. He desperately tried to recall Rebecca's office number. He looked at the barman.

"Do you happen to have a phone book? I need the office number of the firm of lawyers Willet, Barber, Links and Boucher."

"I can do better than that sir," he reached behind him and plucked a card from a little card holder. "Which partner sir."

The man smiled. Cooper was surprised, and his face showed it.

"Regulars, sir. Their offices are just around the corner."

"Thank you, really." Cooper said.

"Glad to help sir, in fact if you are in here about six, one or the other of them, sometimes all, will probably be here after work." This was even more startling.

Cooper picked up the phone and dialled Rebecca's number direct, right there on her card.

The ring tone was slightly different but ringing none the less.

"Rebecca Boucher, how can I help?" She said.

Cooper was nearly speechless, but quickly gathered himself. "Rebecca, it's Cooper. Please listen. Don't hang up." He could hear her breathing quicken.

"Yes Cooper. These long distance calls will be costing you a fortune. Really."

"Not long distance, I'm in the hotel just around the corner. Apparently it's the regular haunt of your team. Can you meet me here...? Please." He knew that the two men were just sitting over there, and he knew Rebecca would not want to see them but a plan had formed in his mind. It meant Rebecca had to walk in here unsuspecting.

Rebecca was still hesitating. He could hear it in her silence. Finally, she replied.

"I can meet you there in ten minutes if you like." Rebecca was not hesitating because of any wish to not meet Cooper, but rather stunned surprise that he was here in London, and just around the corner at the Metropole. Nothing for months, now he was here in person. Did he think he was going to step back into her life just because of some misguided feeling of having to do the right thing. 'How quaint.' She thought. She would manage quite well enough alone thank you very much. She was quite wealthy, with a fantastic career ahead of her. There was no reason why with the help of good nannies she couldn't continue just as she was.

"Good, and Rebecca...." Cooper hesitated. "Can you ask your friend from the... Firm... to meet you here. Urgently. Like now if he can." Cooper hung up.

Rebecca stood looking at the handset. That was different. He had obviously meant her friend in MI5, the organisation often referred to as The Firm by those connected with it. He had had a warning tone in his voice as well. Rebecca was very very good at reading people. It was one of the reasons she was at the top so young. Something was up. She didn't think Cooper was the sort to cry wolf, so perhaps he wasn't here for the reasons she thought. She speed dialled her friend Kali. Kali answered immediately, she must have had the phone in her hand.

"Kali, who is your friend in MI5?"

"Benjamin." Kali replied.

"Can you ask him to meet me in the Metropole immediately? Something is up. Can you join me? We can go together, Cooper is there and has asked me to meet him there - with Benjamin. He thinks Benjamin is my friend."

"Give me a few minutes." Kali hung up. She was in the building and was in Rebecca's office in less than five minutes. They gave each other a quick hug as Kali looked at her friend. Rebecca was quite pale. Kali didn't ask, but just looked at Rebecca.

"It's ok Kali. I'm just a bit surprised to find Cooper here. I thought I saw him this morning as I was coming in, and suddenly here he is. He is also asking that Benjamin meet us there. There was something in his voice..."

"I called Benjamin on my way to your office. Luckily he was in, and can be at the Metropole in thirty minutes. He is very curious about Cooper I must say." Kali walked in a circle, thinking.

"Can we... Stall? Just to give Benjamin time to get there. No wait. Cooper doesn't know me. I'll go now, you come over in

fifteen minutes. Benjamin should be close by then. Ok?"
"Kali, are you sure?" Rebecca was worried for her friend.
She needn't have been.

Kali grinned from ear to ear.

"Sure I'm sure." She bounced on her toes. Kali was very fit,
and the tight jeans and faux leather jacket she always wore
over a tight fitting pull on vest showed clearly just how string
taught fit she really was. Dark short hair and dark and
intense eyes gave her a real look of ... danger, if seen in
passing. Kali didn't talk about her personal life, not even to
Rebecca much, but Rebecca knew she worked out a lot, and
was often in the company of a very big man, with the spring
in his step of a martial arts specialist. Rebecca smiled.

"Sorry Kali. I just don't seem to be able to register things
properly at the moment." Rebecca shook her head.

"Ok, then, give me ten minutes and then start over. How will
I know Cooper? I never did get a clear look at him past you
on Skype." Kali gave a throaty chuckle. Rebecca coloured a
little and replied.

"Just look out for the Australian."

Kali left with a flicking wave of her fingers. "Ten minutes."
And was gone. Rebecca collected her grip and her coat, ran
a brush through her hair and did a double take at her
reflection in the mirror. She rarely wore much in the way of
makeup, not really needing it, but now! OMG she thought.
She found her lipstick and smoothed just a little colour on
her lips, and just a touch of colour base on her cheeks. She
stood back and looked. 'Hmmm, not quite like a corpse now,
but close.' She resolved to start modifying her diet. She
would never make the distance, she thought, if she was being
drained by something as trivial as someone turning up
unexpectedly. A quick shuffle of some paperwork and an
unnecessary desk tidy, and the ten minutes was up. She set
off for the Metropole. The lift swished to a stop, and the
doors opened, and there beside was one of the partners.

Willet - James Willet. Senior partner. He looked at Rebecca as though seeing her for the first time that day.

"Something upsetting you Rebecca? You look terrible. I do hope you aren't getting something." He said.

Rebecca laughed, a slightly brittle laugh, and swallowed. "Sorry James. No, I haven't caught anything. Not as such, just been a bit busy with a case that is particularly troublesome. I'll be fine, thank you for asking." They travelled down in silence. Rebecca was struggling to hide the giggles. Did being pregnant count as 'catching something'? She hoped no one else was going to comment on her looking terrible. She felt bad enough as it was. The lift opened into the foyer, and James Willet strode away to the reception desk with a "Take care." In Rebecca's general direction. He had his own problems.

Rebecca headed for the street, wrapping her coat tightly around her and pulling her fur cap down over her hair so her ears were covered. It looked cold outside. She lowered her head and stepped out. The cold bit into her like a knife, finding any chink in her covering to sting bare skin. It was never like this in Australia she thought and headed down the street. What was she going to say to Cooper? Other than he was not under any obligation to her.

She was convinced that she didn't need him in her life. He was nice. Very nice in fact, but she was in no way willing to give up what she had worked so hard to achieve over the last few years. Cooper wanting to walk back into her life would undo everything. Child or no child. He would have visiting rights, the whole deal in fact, just she didn't come as part of the package. She would have to make sure he clearly understood this, right from the get go. She put her head down against the biting wind and struggled forward. The hotel was not far, but in these conditions it may as well have been at the North Pole. Finally, the building shone out across the wide street, the lights all on to display a warm welcome to travellers out in the gathering gloom. It was not particularly late, just dark. 'This is crazy!' Rebecca muttered. She pushed through the massive revolving door, into the warmth of the vast foyer, the plush understated grandness of the place always pleasing to her senses. She realised Cooper hadn't said which bar he was in, and she hesitated a moment. So it had to be their usual, because he had rung from there, and she only ever went to the same bar which was the one here on the ground floor, around past reception. A nice comfortable day bar, evening drinks, casual, oriented toward the after work office crowd. There was a small restaurant in the other direction from the bar. Nice. She thought she might eat there tonight.

Cooper was unmistakable, sitting slightly hunched over at the small bar. Unusual, she thought. He also looked as though he hadn't yet changed from the trip over, nor even shaved. Rebecca hesitated, her eyes fixed on Cooper. Something was wrong, she could feel it. Then she saw that Cooper was watching her in the mirror behind the bar. His right hand was on the top in front of him, his index finger pointing to his left, so that only she could see it. She involuntarily looked left and immediately spotted the two heavies from New World. She missed a step, and her heart missed a beat. What was Cooper doing, getting her to the bar? He must have known they were there; they had obviously been there some time. She didn't know what to do suddenly. She was rooted to the spot, one foot slightly forward as she had been about to cross toward Cooper. Suddenly she nearly jumped out of her skin as an arm went about her shoulder and a strong voice said softly.

"Hello Rebecca, Kali tells me you may be needing some ... assistance? I'm her friend from the Firm. You can call me Charles." He looked down at her, a faint smile on his lips. "Shall we go and talk to Cooper? Kali will be with us momentarily." He had not so much as glanced at the two men, both of whom were slowly sitting back down, having half risen at Rebecca's entrance.

Rebecca was feeling distinctly out of control, and she didn't like it one little bit. She approached Cooper, Charles still with his arm draped casually across Rebecca's shoulders. Charles spoke quietly in Rebecca's ear, leaning down slightly. "Forgive my familiarity Rebecca. Give me a little laugh please as though I've made a small pleasantry." Rebecca did so, almost without being able to stop. The two men at the table were focused intently on her and Charles. Cooper still just sat there, still looking vaguely like he didn't belong in this place. The two men ignored him. Rebecca and Charles reached the bar beside Cooper, but Charles totally ignored him, as did Cooper to Charles and Rebecca.

The two men sitting over to the side had their heads together in whispered conversation and didn't notice the arrival of three others all wearing neat grey suits, dark ties and highly polished shoes. They weren't particularly big men but the air of menace about them was unmistakable. They sat down at the same table as the two Eastern Europeans, much to the surprise of those two men. Their focus on Rebecca and Charles had allowed the newcomers to insinuate themselves into the scene almost unnoticed. The two henchmen went to rise, but a quietly spoken "Sit," from one of the men in the grey suits had them both back in their seats. They were boxed in really. They had been sitting with their backs almost to the wall so they could see the bar area clearly, and the arrival of the three now had them fairly effectively trapped there. Cooper was watching this and now stood up, stepping around Charles to Rebecca's side he brushed his hair back and said.

"Thanks for coming to see me Rebecca. I wasn't sure you would. I... We need to talk. This situation is under control finally. Cooper glanced at Charles. "I don't think I've had the pleasure." His outstretched hand was taken in a brief shake

by Charles and introductions made. Charles said.
"We've been looking for this pair for a while now, and your arrival seems to have brought them to the surface. We'd love to find their boss as well."

"Upstairs," Cooper smiled. "The bar tender here knows the room number. Just ask him." Cooper took Rebecca's elbow and invited her to step away a little with him.

"Rebecca, what can I say? I had no idea of your... Situation. Under the circumstances I will of course support you financially as well as, as well as... Our child." The normally self assured Cooper stumbled on the last few words.

Rebecca wasn't impressed. The look on her face said it all. Even in his current state, he was very much a man, and Rebecca had to struggle to keep the look of him out of her thoughts. She had already determined her course and it didn't involve Cooper in any way, not financially, not physically.

"What do you mean? Under the circumstances. There are no circumstances. None that involve you directly any more at least." Rebecca lost her sharp tone half way through the sentence. It was after all not Cooper's fault that he had only just found out. She hadn't known herself all that long.

"Cooper, can we save this for later please?" Rebecca glanced across the room at the men sitting in a circle almost, around the two heavies from New World. Charles had let Rebecca and Cooper move aside slightly, but now encouraged them to move back alongside him.

"Cooper, Rebecca, I have to thank you for drawing these people out. We had actually lost track of them in Australia. I know, I know, but we are stretched very thin at the moment. Budgets and all that. It seemed that the native people who live on your property Cooper, harassed them all the way nearly to the border of their country. The intruders ended up getting out on foot to a support vehicle that came to collect them. The local people had disabled their truck."

Charles chuckled at the memory. "Do you know, they speared the tyres of the truck. Such ancient weapons, and they still disabled a modern vehicle. There's lessons to be learnt there." All the time, Charles had his attention on the others across the room. Soon the team who had come in with Charles stood up, indicating to the two that they had literally cornered, that they needed to accompany them. Charles nodded to the one in the lead and turned back to Cooper and Rebecca.

"Would you mind waiting here please for a while? I hope to be able to have Usman Abbas accompanying me when I return. I would rather that you were somewhere open and in public - as we are here."

Rebecca looked around for Kali. She had left the office ahead of Rebecca and was supposed to be here.

"Have you seen Kali?" She asked Charles.

"No." He replied as he left. Cooper was looking about the room. He hadn't seen anyone else enter the room in the time he had been there, but he wasn't surprised. After noticing the two thugs, he hadn't been looking for anyone else. Rebecca couldn't help smiling. She was thinking back to the circumstances where Kali had certainly got to know Cooper, if not actually face to face.

"Yes Cooper, Kali knows you, but I don't think you really know Kali. Do you remember the laptop was open with Skype running one day back at your home…? Kali was on the other end of the link."

Chapter 15

Cooper had the good grace to blush slightly and twirl his drink. He remembered only too well. Suddenly he felt like he had been travelling for days, and he was very aware of his current state of dress and appearance. He looked across the room. The others were in heated discussion. It was then he noticed a dark haired young woman sitting in the shadows created by a tub of palms in a little used corner of the room. He touched Rebecca on the shoulder. The touch sending waves of emotion through him.

"Is that Kali?" He asked quietly. Rebecca looked across to where he was indicating. Surprise lit up her face.

"Of course it is. Kali!" She called out. "What are you doing over there? Come join us." Rebecca stepped forward to welcome her friend over, and to introduce Cooper. It was just like Kali to wait in the background until she was invited in, or was actually needed. Her purpose after all had been to make sure the way was clear for Rebecca. Finding the people from New World on the scene had given her the idea that it may be better to wait and watch and not let on that she knew any of the players in the room.

Introduction were made as Kali looked Cooper up and down. 'Well,' she thought. 'He looks a bit rough.' Rebecca saw the slightly raised eyebrows.

"Kali, Cooper has not long landed, he's just arrived from Australia. We got caught up in this business, and he hasn't had time to unpack even." Rebecca checked herself. What was she doing making excuses for Cooper? Was it her fault? No. Nobody but his. She turned back to Cooper and asked. "Have you unpacked yet?" He was a bit flustered, but answered politely enough.

"Not yet Rebecca. Obviously." His speech was a little clipped. It was just too much.

"I'm going up to my room now. I don't care what Charles wants us to do. You two can join me if you like, or wait here for reasons that Charles couldn't be bothered to explain to us." Cooper turned and started to leave. Rebecca took hold of his arm.

"Wait Cooper. Do you think we should wait here, really?" Suddenly she shook herself slightly. "No, we are coming with you. Kali?" She looked at her friend.

"I'm with you Rebecca." Kali replied. They both turned and followed Cooper who was by now half way across the room. Nobody looked across at Charles and his team. Cooper was in no mood now to be bothered with something what was no longer his problem. He was also feeling very guilty because he had asked Rebecca to come to the bar, knowing full well the men who had rough handled her in Australia were right there in the same bar. Well, it had to be brought to a head, and this had been as good a time as any. Now finally it looked like the powers who looked after that sort of thing were back in control. She had been perfectly safe in any case. He would have seen to that. Now finally he could relax a little, although it looked like Kali was going to stick to Rebecca like glue from here on. Well, so be it. They were obviously good friends, and Cooper had things to talk about, that he was sure a good friend would need to know about, anyway. It was apparent that Kali had come ahead of Rebecca now that he though about it. That meant she was watching out for Rebecca, and it also meant that Kali's first loyalty was to Rebecca. They seemed to be very close, and it would do him well to remember that Kali apparently knew all about some of their most intimate moments. He noticed Charles hurrying after them, his hand raised as though asking a question. Charles caught up with Cooper who had now stopped in the entrance.

"Charles?" Cooper said in question. Charles stopped a few feet from Cooper so that he could keep the others still in the room in full view.

"Cooper - thank you for your help." He said rather stiffly.

"Without your warning, delivered as it was, we may never have caught up with this team. Not just these men, but their boss. He's also in our care now, up in his room. We had... other team members go up there directly we arrived." He looked at Cooper, perhaps expecting congratulations. Cooper was not about to congratulate anyone.

"You mean," he said. "That even when you entered the bar you knew where they all were? Then what was the meaning of that little charade about the bar tender knowing the room numbers?"

"We had to know. I had to know. Just exactly where in the mix you fitted. You see, Mr Anders; we haven't been at all sure about you. About your exact position in this whole thing. Then we find you here, in London, in the same hotel as the people who have been trespassing—supposedly—on your property in Australia. People we have been trying to keep track of for some time and who have proved to be very elusive. For good reason. Considering the activities they have been involved in."

Cooper was dumbfounded. Finally, it came home to him. They had suspected him all along, and probably still did. Both the Australian agencies and the London agencies had thought he was directly involved. It had only come into the open when Rebecca had stepped unwittingly into the mix. The New World corporation had made a mistake when they had sent her out to talk him into selling his property, so that they would then have full access to it. Full access that meant in that remote place, not a soul would have had any idea what they were up to. No one that is apart from the local tribal people, and Cooper doubted that they would have been taken into consideration in any plans that New World were making. The whole sorry thing began to make sense to him, and it reaffirmed some of the resolves he had already begun to formulate, even before he had left Australia to come and talk face to face with Rebecca.

"Well." Stated Cooper. "I don't think you need worry yourself on that score Charles." Cooper had noticed the use of his surname by Charles, an obvious ploy to formalise the situation, and Cooper was having none of it. "Rebecca, Kali. Are you coming?" Cooper turned away from Charles and continued on. He took a few steps then turned and looked over his shoulder at Charles.

"Thank you for intervening in any case, but I assure you - for what my assurances are worth, that I knew nothing of these people. At least, I knew nothing of their intentions." Cooper continued on through the lobby toward the lifts. Rebecca and Kali trailing along behind. Kali stopped half way across the lobby and put her hand on Rebecca's arm.

"I'll stay here in the lobby, or the bar. I'll wait for you down here Rebecca. You don't need me to accompany you with Cooper. Honestly." Kali turned back with a last look at Cooper, standing at the lift doors, waiting for the lift to take him to his room. Rebecca simply nodded and went to join Cooper. The lift arrived and together they stepped inside. Within seconds they were exiting the lift on the twenty fifth floor and heading for Coopers room along the quiet hallway. Neither had said a word since they had left the bar area, and Kali had taken her leave. Cooper was trying to sort out his emotions, and Rebecca seemed to be in a daze. It was enough to keep them both quiet.

Cooper swiped his key card and they entered his room. His suitcase lay unopened on the bed where he had flung it earlier in the day, and he opened it and started putting his things into the cupboard's hanging space, and onto the night stand beside the bed. He didn't have much, he had left the house in Australia in a hurry, figuring he could buy what he wanted in London, past his basic needs for the first day or so. Rebecca stood with her hands folded in front of her,

184

watching. Cooper seemed to have forgotten her presence and in the end she had to beak the silence.

"Cooper..." she paused for a long moment. "Cooper, what are you thinking. Why invite me up here to your room, then just busy yourself in silence. Am I so hard to talk to?" The last was said in just above a whisper. "We need to talk, but first, you need to clean yourself up. I'm sorry - but you look little better than a tramp." Cooper swung to face her, his face unreadable.

"So you care what I look like do you?" He said. "I thought you only cared about yourself in the end." He knew he was being harsh, and he knew he had just insulted Rebecca, but he was tired and beyond caring. He strode into the bathroom and closed the door behind him. He needed a shower, that much he knew, and a shave. And a haircut. He looked at himself in the mirror. He looked closely for the first time in days. 'My God!" He thought. 'No wonder people were staring at me and not wanting to sit near me.' He shook his head and stepped into the shower, the hot water steaming up in a cloud that quickly filled the bathroom, the glass partition steaming over and little rivulets of water trickling down the glass, forming a myriad tiny tracks on the glass. Much like the tracks of lizards in the sand dunes back home he thought. He had taken his razor into the shower with him. This was going to need some heavy duty scraping he thought, so he lathered up his hair with the hotel shampoo, letting it run down over his bristly chin. Finally, with the stubble on his chin softened enough with the heat of the water and the shampoo he set to work. He soon had his face cleaned up, all trace of stubble gone. The haircut would have to wait, but at least he would look half way presentable again. It felt good to be 'Spring Clean' again he thought. He let the water cascade from his shoulders and stream away down his body, his head tilted back so that the shower ran directly into his hair, then out and away. He felt a change in the air temperature and opened his eyes. The shower door was open and Rebecca was standing there watching him. Just silently watching him, her eyes looking steadily at his as he opened them. He wasn't embarrassed, they had been far too intimate for that now, but he was surprised.

"What is it Rebecca?" He asked. He could not read the expression on her face, and so far she had not said a word. She turned away from him finally and went and leant against the sink.

"Cooper, you have to understand that I never did have marriage or children in my life plans. We enjoyed each others company and both of us are responsible for this baby. But I never expected you to have to marry me because of it. I don't expect it now. Regardless of what you or others may think. You have your life mapped out in the Australian bush, and I have mine mapped out here in London. I'm not changing, and I doubt you would want to, so there's an end to it." Rebecca folded her arms across her chest and looked at Cooper, now out of the shower and towelling himself dry. Her heart was racing and her stomach was tingling at the sight of his lean hard body., but she steeled herself as she had done many times in court, and would not be distracted. Cooper combed his long hair back and stepped into his underpants. He still hadn't said a word, just letting Rebecca say what she had to say. He could see that the sight of him had affected her, but he could also see her determination to deny her feelings. He was secretly pleased that she could still find him attractive, because if his plans went right, then she would be his for the long term. He still hadn't told her of the plans he was formulating. Indeed, he didn't have a full idea himself yet, but it meant major changes in his lifestyle if he could pull it off, and it did all hinge on Rebecca. So Cooper waited. Suddenly, Rebecca turned and left the bathroom, and without stopping left the hotel apartment. She had said nothing. The door swung shut with a soft click behind her. Cooper stood looking after her, poised in the act of pulling on his trousers. He tried to collect his thoughts. Caught completely by surprise, for a moment he couldn't take it in. What was she doing? She couldn't leave now, just... walking out like this, nothing resolved. He stumbled and almost fell as distractedly he tried to get his other foot into his trouser leg. Finally managing to get his trousers on and zipped up he reached the door of the apartment and flung the door open just in time to hear the hiss of the lift doors closing and the lift itself descending. He turned back into his rooms searching for his phone and keyed it into life. Suddenly he stopped. Dam it, he realised he still didn't have her personal number, so he couldn't call her.

Cooper reached for the room extension phone and pressed Reception.
"Come on, come on!" He shouted, just as a voice came on the line.
"Reception, how can I help?"
"Quickly, the lift coming down has a young woman in it. Please ask her to stop. To wait in the foyer for me. Hurry man" Cooper had heard the soft chime of the arriving lift in the background. He slammed the phone down, and dragged on his shirt, socks and shoes, still hopping in the struggle as he headed to the lift to try to catch up. Half dressed, he almost fell into the lift as it's doors opened in front of him. The doors closed, and the lift continued to ascend. He almost shouted in frustration, as he realised he had mistakenly jumped into the rising lift car, instead of waiting for the descending one. The couple already in the car looked at him worriedly as he struggled to tidy his clothes and run his fingers through his hair.
"I'm so sorry." He offered. "I'm late for a meeting..." It was

187

the best he could offer as he realised the lift was going all the way to the fifty-fourth floor. He leaned back against the wall and closed his eyes in frustration. This whole day was not going well. Finally, the lift arrived back on the ground floor and Cooper emerged into the foyer. He had given up the chase, fully expecting that Rebecca was by now far away. He looked around in the faint hope that she might still be there, then turned and took the lift back up to his floor, and went back to his room. He reached into his pocket for his room key card and realised with a groan that it was on the little table right by the door - on the inside. He was locked out. Could this day get any more frustrating he wondered? There was nothing for it but to return to reception and request another key card.

Cooper was crossing the foyer when he almost ran into Kali, hurrying from the small bar where they had met earlier.

"Cooper, have you seen Rebecca?" She asked, grabbing his right elbow in her hand. She sounded agitated, her voice rising slightly. "Isn't she with you?" Cooper shook his head and said.

"Kali, what do you mean? She left me about ten minutes ago now, either to return to you down here or to return to the office, or even home. I have no idea, really. One minute we were in the shower talking, and the next minute she just up and left the suite."

Kali raised an eyebrow at the mention of the shower, but was too concerned to pause on it.

"No, she was supposed to come back to me here, not go off on her own just now. Charles and his team have some sort of problem, and I need to locate Rebecca... And she isn't answering her mobile either. Cooper, I don't think she made it down here to the foyer, or I would have seen her."

By now Cooper had stopped in his tracks. He looked carefully around him. He was very tall, and could see over the heads of anyone in the area, giving him unrestricted sight of everyone moving in the foyer. There was no one he knew, and certainly no sign of Rebecca. What was going on he wondered? She couldn't have just disappeared. Although Charles and his crew seemed to have done. Cooper headed to reception and picked up another key card from the girl there.

He was about to turn away when she held up an envelope with his name on it.

"Mr Anders, this message was left for you just a few minutes ago by a European gentleman." She passed it to Cooper.

He opened it and scanned it quickly, and passed it to Kali, his mouth set in a grim line.

"So that's their game is it?" He smacked one fist into the palm of his other hand. "We'll see about that when I get my hands on them. They will regret the day they crawled out from under the rocks." He went to the lounge to see if Charles might be in the bar area. There was no sign of him, and indeed the whole room was empty.

"Kali, enough pussy footing around with Charles and these criminals. They must be close, probably have someone watching us to see what I do. Can you raise Charles do you think?" He asked. "I want his help, but obviously don't want him to be seen with me." He stood in the middle of the room, trying to think what to do. He only had minutes. The note had been very brief. "Be in the third level car park in five minutes, alone, if you want to see Ms Boucher again." What did this mean? See her alive again? It certainly had that ring to it. Kali was on her mobile and obviously had Charles on the other end. She was flapping her hand and pointing to the phone and mouthing 'Charles', while nodding her head in response to whatever was being said. Finally, she ended the call and said to Cooper.

"Charles said to go down to the car park and meet with who ever wrote the note. He will be close by, but out of sight. I have to go with you. The note did say they wanted you alone, but even so, you can insist."

Cooper just stood there for a moment. What was happening? Everything was going wrong. He felt like he was being led around by the nose. It was time to take charge. He was not a man to be pushed around easily, and although he felt somewhat out of his depth in this environment, he was strong enough to forge ahead, anyway. With a smack of his hand on his thigh, he strode across to the lift to go down to the car park. Kali could come along if that's what she wanted, but he now didn't care either way. He stepped into the lift and Kali hurried after him. He pressed the button for the basement garage and they headed down. Assuming someone from the gang who had taken Rebecca wanted him for some reason, he had little choice. He was acutely aware that he was unarmed. He could only hope that Charles was on the ball.

He stepped from the lift with Kali a step behind. The third level was almost empty of cars. Cooper couldn't imagine where Charles and his team would be, there was no cover, and the lift was not really suitable. He slowly scanned the few vehicles he could see. If these people were there they had to be in the black Audi S8 with darkened windows that was parked some three bays directly opposite the lift. The half dozen other cars were all clear glassed window types and didn't appear to contain anyone. Cooper hooked his thumbs into his belt with his legs slightly apart and waited. It was their move. Kali stood beside him, almost vibrating with anger and tension as she raised herself onto the balls of her feet repeatedly, as though getting ready to take off at any moment.

Cooper was growing impatient with this game and began to stride toward the dark car. As he did so the rear window slid down and a voice commanded,

"Stop there. Do not come closer. Just listen. You have caused me a great deal of trouble over that worthless piece of desert in Australia. All you had to do was sell it to me. Ms Boucher simply had to facilitate the sale. But no, you both had to jump into bed with each other at the first opportunity and complicate things beyond all reason. Now I can never set foot there again in that country. I have lost millions of dollars already, and now the authorities in this country are forcing me out as well." The voice stopped. Cooper still hadn't seen the man responsible for it, and he still hadn't seen Rebecca. They were both too far back in the darkness of the interior of the car.

"Where is Rebecca? What have you done with her?" He shouted at the person in the car. "What have you done with the woman I love? If you harm her I will hunt you down like a rabid dog. Let her go now or by God I will start on you here and now." As he finished, two men got out of the front of the car, deadly black pistols in their hands. The driver and a passenger. They were gigantic! Cooper had rarely seen such big men, but it was the guns that stopped him in his tracks. It crossed his mind that they weren't going to be able to make any quick get away now that the driver was out of the car. So if he could disarm these two, he still had a chance.

"Well scum?" He shouted. "What is it you want? I couldn't care less for your petty problems. Just let Rebecca go, I know you have her there. Let her go now and I won't harm you." Cooper kept his eyes on the two bodyguards. The pair looked at each other. Surprise evident on their faces. What was he talking about? 'Harm them.' They were armed, he was not. They didn't move, however; they hadn't been told to. Cooper started forward when he heard Rebecca suddenly scream out.

"Cooper no, he has a gun." He stopped in his tracks. Rebecca was ok. She had risked everything to warn him. He had no idea where Charles and his team were, but their presence would be welcome any time soon. The man in the car spoke again.

"You are a foolish man Mr Anders; do you know that?" He paused. "You could have been very rich, but now you will have nothing. Your home will be worthless, and your girlfriend here will be gone."

The window of the car started to slide up, and was just about fully shut when there was a deafening roar of a large caliber gun shot and the glass of the window shattered into a million diamond fragments, spraying out in a great arc of razor edges that caught one of the guards across the side of his face. He cried out in pain, the blood already streaming down his neck. His companion was looking at the car in surprise and didn't see Cooper coming. He went to the ground with a thud and lay still, his gun skittering under the car. Cooper kicked the other guards gun away and hauled open the car door. Nearest to him was a large man in a pin striped business suit holding a blood soaked trouser leg and staring at his shattered knee in silent surprise. His mouth formed in a silent O, the pain not yet overcoming the shock. Rebecca was pressed back into the farthest corner of the seat, holding a huge silver Colt 45 in both hands, pointing its wavering barrel in the general direction of the wounded man. Her eyes were as big as saucers in her face and Cooper could see in that instant that she was only just holding it together. Her face was as white as a sheet, and she was holding her bottom lip in her teeth, staring at Cooper. The man in the car with her, Cooper didn't recognise him, was trying to deal with the blood and the pain of a shattered knee joint so he was no trouble.

Cooper quickly moved around to the off side door and reached in to help Rebecca out of the car. He carefully took the Colt from her shaking hands and lowered the hammer slowly, passing it to Kali who was by now at his side. Rebecca stepped out, holding on to Cooper to steady herself. She no sooner stood up straight than Cooper had to grab her to himself as she started to faint into unconsciousness. He wrapped his strong arms around her, supporting her easily in his embrace. He could smell the scent of apples in her hair. At that moment two black Humvees roared down the ramp and screeched to a stop at the front of the car, men in full armour spilling out and surrounding them all. Charles slowly got out of the lead vehicle and came over to Cooper, still supporting the unconscious Rebecca and shielding Kali. The bodyguard who had received the shattering glass shards to the face was leaning against the door trying to stem the blood flow, his companion was still out for the count, and the business type in the back of the car was now alternately moaning and calling for an ambulance.

"Well, it looks like you may have things under control Cooper. Messy, but under control. I have to hand it to you." He turned aside and spoke to the team commander.

"Can you get a couple of ambulances here ASAP?" He looked at the man in the car. "Get your medic to attend to that one in the car now please. We don't want to lose him. There will be enough paperwork as it is." He looked without compassion at the person in the back of the car. The man's face was as white as a sheet, and he wasn't looking good at all.

Charles looked at Cooper and Rebecca, Kali peeping out from behind them both. He was scratching his chin, obviously trying to piece the situation together.

"I'm not too sure I should start asking questions at this stage." He said aloud. "However… firstly. Whose gun is that?" He pointed at the silver Colt in Coopers left hand. Cooper lifted his chin toward the man in the back seat of the car, now being attended to by the medics. They had cut off his trouser leg, exposing the mess that had been his knee. He wouldn't walk properly on that leg again if indeed he didn't lose it below the knee. Cooper looked at him without a flicker of sympathy while the mans eyes burned into Cooper like a demon. 'Tough.' Thought Cooper, 'but he had it coming.'

Rebecca had surfaced again and was struggling to regain her composure. She had been very badly frightened by the experience and had been sure that her life had been hanging in the balance until the opportunity had presented itself to grab the gun.

"Charles," she said. "I'm sorry, but when I grabbed the gun in his hand, it was momentarily pointing away from me, and it… just went off. The bullet smashed into his leg and must have bounced off something and flew upwards smashing the door glass. He dropped the gun then, and I grabbed it up and pulled the hammer back just like they do in the movies." She looked at her hands, one hand looking very red and with scorch marks near the thumb joint. "My hand is burnt!" She said in surprise. "And… my ears hurt. I am having trouble hearing anything." Cooper smiled and held her close again. She might be tough in the courtroom, but was obviously not used to dealing at the sharp end of rough crimes. A medic came over and took a look at her hands. He put some antiseptic on the scorch marks but otherwise she seemed ok. "You will be ok in a while Miss. It's just scorch marks from the gun going off while you had your hand wrapped around it. Your hearing will return fine in an hour or so." The medic looked at Charles.

"Boss, do I write this up?" He said, with a non-committal expression on his face.

"Don't worry about the paperwork until we debrief back at the office." Was Charles' reply. He looked again at Cooper and the two women.

"Cooper and Kali, I'd really appreciate it if you both escorted Rebecca home. To her home - not the office. I will meet you there later." He signalled his driver, who had arrived in the office limo along with the ambulance. "William, take these people to Rebecca's address please, then return to the office. We should be finished here by the time you get there."

Rebecca, Cooper and Kali climbed into the limo, and the driver whisked them up the ramp and out into the traffic. Rebecca was laying back in the seat, her head against the soft leather headrest. Kali sat in the little single seat just in front of her, with Cooper next to Rebecca, holding her hand. The car wound its way through the traffic, William the driver was very experienced with city traffic. He knew where Rebecca lived, her apartment was not far from Hyde Park and he knew the area well. Kali turned around in her little seat, it was one of those little fold down things that were attached to the side panels especially for secretaries and others who needed to be in the vehicle with who ever was in the rear seat. She tapped on the dividing glass, and William slid the panel back.

"Yes Miss Kali?" He asked.

"Please pull over and drop me off here William. I would prefer to find my own way from here." Kali was feeling like an intruder, and although she was worried about her friend she also knew Rebecca well, and knew she was strong enough to get over any shock from the recent events. Rebecca needed to be left alone with Cooper. The car cruised to a halt outside of a well known coffee house. "How is this Kali?" Asked William.

"Fine thanks William. If Charles wants me, he knows how to contact me." She replied. With little more than a flicker of her fingers she left the car and went directly into the coffee lounge. She realised she badly needed a coffee, and something to eat. She had not had anything to eat all day and was starving. The limo eased back out into the traffic, which easily gave way to it. The flag staff on the front, with a small pennant fluttering from it told everyone else on the road that this was an official vehicle, and people knew to give way to it. Cooper noticed and thought aloud to himself. "Courteous lot these British." Rebecca just smiled. She was rallying quickly, but was enjoying the attentions of Cooper here by her side, and thought that there was no reason why she shouldn't continue to do so for as long as possible. She gave a small sigh. 'If only things could be this way forever.' She thought.

Chapter 16

Here she was back home in London, and with her big strong Australian by her side, and she was the one discharging huge pistols at strangers. She giggled at the incongruity of it all. She put her hand to her mouth, surprised at the giggle, and she could see the look on Coopers face. He too was surprised. Concern and surprise chasing each other across his open, handsome face. She reached up and stroked his jaw. His stubbly whiskers felt like sandpaper, but nicer. Shaving in the shower was tricky. Cooper cupped her hand in his, holding it to his cheek.

"Are you all right Rebecca?" He asked with worry in his voice. "I hope that the shock won't affect you badly in any way." He looked down at her abdomen then back into her eyes. She saw the look and blushed slightly. 'So he is worried' she thought.

"I'll be fine Cooper. I recognise the shock for what it is, but other than that I'm unharmed. Thanks." She kept her hand in his though and closed her eyes. The peace of the quiet air conditioning sounds almost lulled her to sleep. All too soon the car arrived at the kerb side of her apartment tower. William looked around at the passing pedestrians, just as a precaution. He didn't really expect anyone would be on watch. The person who had snatched Rebecca in the hotel had seemed to be acting on his own although undoubtedly had something to do with New World. He stepped from the car and held the door open for Rebecca and Cooper to alight. Cooper helped Rebecca out, keeping his hand on her upper arm to support her. She was still as pale as a ghost, and his concern was obvious. William waited until they were inside the building, and the huge glass doors had closed behind them before departing.

Rebecca was in a quandary. On the one hand she thought that she really didn't want Cooper in her life. She was sure he had turned up out of some idea of duty to her and the unborn child. Yet here he was, still helping her and showing all the signs of a real father to be, concerned for his woman and child. By the same token, she didn't want to feel obliged to marry Cooper just because they had conceived a child together. Her thoughts whirled around in her mind. That she loved him was in no doubt, but could she take the time out to have a child and marry, with a husband and family that would surely intrude dramatically on her current life style? What would he do in this huge bustling city? He would be like a fish out of water here in London. There was no doubt that he could find suitable work, but would that keep a man happy who was used to being in the wide open spaces doing just as he pleased. No nine-to-five man this one. Rebecca looked up at Cooper as the lift doors opened and smiled. He was very special, and she knew it. She would be crazy to let him go. Even crazier if she actually forced him away. She made up her mind on the spot. Time was of the essence, and as she didn't think Cooper was going anywhere anyway, regardless of what she wanted, she was happy that the decision was made. She really started to relax. The lift doors opened, and she fumbled in her grip for her keys. Cooper hung back a little, uncertain as to whether he should come in with her. Her apartment door was right in front of them. "Umm, Rebecca, do you want me to come in with you? Perhaps you need to get some rest rather than talk. I've no doubt Charles will be in touch soon enough to sort it all out." He leaned in and opened the door for her and stepped back to allow her access. The colour was back in her face he noticed, but she still had a far away look in her eyes, and seemed to be only half hearing what he was saying.

"Rebecca, I think I will sit with you a while. You don't look at all ready to be on your own. Come." He entered the apartment, holding her gently by the hand to lead her in.

She was looking at him intently, and it was he thought, a little unsettling. She hadn't said a word so far. Cooper looked about him, the apartment was beautiful. Spacious, and bright, the weak afternoon sun streaming in through the wide windows. It would be dark soon he thought. There was a long settee in a well type area by the windows, and he guided Rebecca to it and sat her down. He piled cushions up near her so she could relax back on them if she wished and lifted a coffee table into place by the settee within easy reach of her. She was following his actions with her eyes, but still seemed content to remain silent. 'Well that's ok.' He thought. 'Hell of a thing having a Colt 45 go off in your hand.' He smiled at Rebecca and went to find the kitchen and the coffee. It didn't take long, and soon he had a couple of steaming cups on the low table, with some sugar cubes and milk in a small jug that he had found in the 'fridge.

"Rebecca, you don't have to talk at the moment, I understand you probably won't be feeling like it after recent events. However, before I leave - before you tell me to leave - I must tell you that I will leave very reluctantly. I will not go easily, nor quietly. This child is our child. Not just yours. I don't just have a duty to help raise it, I have a right. I have a right to love it's mother... I want to give the child everything, but the best thing I can give it is to love its mother. You Rebecca. I love you with all my heart." Cooper was kneeling on the floor by Rebecca's side, her hands in his by now as he looked intently at her. Suddenly he drew a breath. She was crying. Tears streaming down her face.

"Oh my God!" He exclaimed. "What have I done? Rebecca, I'm so sorry. I'm so sorry. I should have waited; you are in no state to be listening to me running on."

Rebecca put her arms around Coopers neck and drew him to her.

"No Cooper my dearest. I could listen to you all day. I'm crying for happiness. I've just realised as we came home here how much I really do love you. I'm happy for you to have any part you like in the raising of our child."

Cooper rested on his knees. He was a little stunned. He hadn't expected Rebecca to come right out with such a statement. Perhaps she was affected by events more than either of them thought. "Rebecca, hush my dear. I'll call a doctor for you. I think you may still be suffering from shock." He got to his feet and picked up the phone, suddenly realising that he had no idea how to get hold of a doctor. This was a disaster. How did he expect to help raise a child when he couldn't even call a doctor?

"Rebecca, I'm sorry again... do you have a number for a doctor.?" Before he could answer, the phone in his hand rang, and he automatically answered it.

"Charles here. Is that Cooper. Good? I'm on my way over. Be there in five minutes. Don't leave the apartment."

"Charles," Cooper interrupted. "Send or bring a doctor with you please. I'd like Rebecca checked over properly." Charles rang off and Cooper went back to kneel again by Rebecca. He searched her face for signs of trouble, but she seemed fine now. The tears had stopped, which was a good sign he thought.

"Charles will be here shortly and bringing a doctor to give you the once over." Cooper didn't know whether to smile or frown. Rebecca said,

"It's ok. I'm ok. Really, I'm ok now. I don't need the doctor. Really."

Cooper shook his head.

"It's too late anyway now. Charles will have one on the way. I wonder what Charles wants, anyway?"

Rebecca struggled to sit up straight again.

"Well. I did shoot a man in the leg. I don't know how I'm going to talk my way out of that one. Self defence I suppose." She shook her head and frowned in thought. Things just kept happening. Getting in the way between her and Cooper. She really needed to sit quietly with him and talk about what they were going to do. He obviously loved her, but how did he see his future role with her? Rebecca couldn't even guess. Was he seeing himself as the visiting father? The live in father? Well, that would mean marriage, and he hadn't even mentioned that option out loud. Did he want to get married? Did she want to get married? Truly. She loved him - she knew that, but did it necessarily mean marriage? That was a lifetime commitment. What of her career, and his for that matter?

Cooper stood up and went to the wide windows overlooking the London skyline, thinking to himself as he watched the slowly changing light as the day moved on. He trusted his love for her, and her desire to know all of him. He knew that if he did nothing he was risking what they had each day, he kept the secrets of his life inside. He knew that facing her he was facing himself, so he had to accept what he was and where he had come from, and what he was to become if he was to be fully accepted by her. It was a pity that Charles was going to be here so soon. That was to be expected though he thought, given the circumstances. There were questions to be answered and as Rebecca was a lawyer, no one would know it better than her. So much turned on his decision he almost couldn't face it, but he knew he had to. He had to be strong, and firm. Rebecca and the child needed him. Would need him. He didn't believe for one second in the seemingly new ideas that a woman could maintain a vibrant career and bring up a child on her own at the same time. She would need help, and a shoulder to lean on. The door chimes sounded just as Cooper was turning back to Rebecca, his mouth opening to say something. Rebecca was watching him in expectation, he could see it plainly in her face. With a hiss of frustration, he redirected himself to the door, spreading his hands in a 'what can we do' gesture that brought a fleeting smile to her face. Cooper swung the door open to see

Charles standing there waiting to be welcomed in. A person Cooper took to be the doctor beside him.

"Come in Charles, come in. What's the bad news then?" He shook hand quickly as the doctor was introduced.

Charles came over to the lounge where Rebecca was sitting. He was smiling broadly.

"Rebecca my friend, how are you feeling? I do hope you are well." He looked at Cooper.

"Rebecca, I could use a Scotch; what about you Cooper?" He looked back at a surprised Rebecca.

"Yes, I know it's a tad early, but you do keep the finest blends I know, especially the one produced by our Canadian friends. Single malts get far too much press, and I can tell you your Canadian Club is perfect for a congratulatory toast in the late afternoon." Much against Coopers ideas of what was needed, Rebecca got up and soon had some glasses, ice and a decanter of Canadian Club whisky on the coffee table in front of them.

Charles held up his glass, the ice cubes tinkling together.

"Did I say toast? I did, didn't I? I believe there will be a wedding soon?" His eyebrows raised to emphasise the question in his voice. He held his glass toward Rebecca who responded with hers, the soft clink soon joined by Coopers. While Charles and Cooper took appreciative sips of theirs, Rebecca sniffed appreciatively at hers and then just held the glass in her lap. Charles looked at her silently, then at Cooper.

"Ahhh, I am right after all." He looked at Rebecca. "Truly. Congratulations." He smiled at Rebecca. "So I guess you will be taking some time off soon?" He added.

Rebecca placed her untouched drink on the table in front of her.

"Soon enough for that." She said with a smile, and a glance at Cooper.

Charles jumped to his feet and gulped his drink down. "Nice whiskey that!" He said, turning for the door.

"Oh, by the way, the reason I came by." He said. Rebecca went white and caught up Coopers strong hand in hers.

"There will be no... repercussions - from the little fracas recently. You weren't even there. Of course Cooper is living there at the hotel, but he neither heard nor saw a thing. Isn't that right Cooper?" Charles turned at the door, his eyebrow raised as he looked pointedly at Cooper.

"Well, must go, we have some people to escort to the Russian embassy so their medical staff can take care of their own nationals. It seems one of them injured himself messing around with a gun. Nasty things. Guns that is." He sailed through the door smiling. A 'Ciao' floating back to them as the door closed.

Rebecca looked at Cooper, now sitting beside her on the lounge. He was shaking his head and smiling. He looked again at Rebecca and rose to his feet.

"I'll just wait here until the doctor has checked you over." Within minutes the doctor was on his way down to re-join Charles.

"Rebecca," he said. "I should go back to my hotel and clean up a little. You will be ok here now; it seems that Charles has taken care of everything - although you did a pretty good job yourself. If it's ok I'd like to come back later this evening, we could maybe have a meal somewhere nice, and talk a little. What do you think?" Cooper was looking hopefully at Rebecca, his face open and happy. He had come to a decision and it was shining in his eyes.

Rebecca handed him her set of door keys. She had been clutching them in her hand all this time.

"Of course Cooper, I would like that. When ever you are ready, just come back and let yourself in. I need to freshen up, and rest a little as well." She lay her head back and closed her eyes for a moment. Moments later - it seemed like only moments, she slowly opened her eyes to a darkened room, only the faint light of the city glow penetrating the gloom. It took a moment before she realised she was in her own bed, the covers pulled up to her chin. The night stand clock glowed eight pm. She sat up, trying to clear the fog from her brain. She had no memory of coming to bed, no memory of undressing. The last thing she had done was ask Cooper to come back for dinner. Which must mean soon! She needed a shower. That would clear her mind and bring her tired body back to life. She swung her legs off the bed and stood up, heading for the shower, only then realising that apart from her knickers she was naked. She blushed faintly at the thought of Cooper carefully undressing her and tucking her into her bed.

The needles of the shower spray stung her back into life, and the water cascading through her hair made her feel halfway human again. She finished and towelled herself down briskly and went back into her bedroom to find something to wear to dinner.

Niggling at the back of her mind was the question of Cooper. Could she share her life with him? Could she share her child; their child actually she conceded? She realised with a start that the answer was surely yes. Was that what Cooper wanted? She thought it was. She didn't think for a moment that he would have it any other way. Could she, could he, surmount the logistical problems that would come with such a union? She knew for a fact that she could never ever live in the remote outback on his Australian cattle property. She couldn't even think how she would raise children in such a forbidding place.

Cooper caught a taxi directly back to his hotel and went straight to his room. It was time to make decisions and stop waffling about. He got onto Skype on his laptop and called his house back in Australia. He knew the manager would be there although probably asleep at this time. It must have been the very early hours back there. Cooper was paying the man to do a job, and that was a 24/7 job. The call was answered by the manager after what seemed an interminable time to Copper. Stanley was the mans name, and he sleepily said.

"Yes, Stanley here. Cooper, what's up?"

"Stan," Cooper replied. "Is the work nearly finished? All of it."

"Just about." Replied Stan. "I can send you photos if you like. Do you want them now?"

"Yes, send the lot please. Is the outside finished? The yards, the gardens, the power turbines and solar farm?"

"Yes, the wind farm is up and operational, and it's not visible from the house. Neither is the solar farm. You have enough power being generated here now to power a small town. With the new types of batteries available now from that US company, Tesla, your supply is guaranteed for years to come. Not that we get many cloudy days here, but the winter nights can be a bit long, but as I say - power to spare and then some."

Stan got busy sending batches of photos via the Skype file upload. Cooper made some notes on a pad he kept by the laptop, and took a mouthful of San Miguel, a beer he was beginning to like.

"Stan, the gardens and lawns? Is the walled garden finished and ready for planting?"

"Yes Cooper, all done. I can't imagine what you want a walled garden for out here though. You certainly don't need to keep the warmth in, which is the usual reason for a walled garden."

"No, that's true," replied Cooper, "but what I do want is a garden that is secure from kangaroos, dingoes, and people. The boundaries should be as I wanted - at least twenty yards away from the actual garden edges. Have you started the soil treatment? It's mostly sandy loam, and needs a lot of nutrients to get it started, not to mention the water softening from the artesian well. That stuff is nearly brine, and no good for the garden." Cooper scratched his chin in his now familiar manner.

"I can tell you Cooper, the teams you have had here have been working like Trojans. Seriously, I've never seen the like of it. I do hope you are keeping track of costs? I've seen the accounts I've been sending to your city office. I doubt Toowoomba has seen the like of it in a long time. Some of the suppliers are struggling to keep up to the demands." Stan had another batch of photos ready, but the transmission was interfering with the quality of the video link, so he held off.

"Well, if they can't supply our needs, go further afield and find others who can. Europe can supply what we need easily. Italy, Spain, Greece will jump at the chance to supply building materials. Germany for house materials." Cooper brushed his hand across his forehead. "Stan, what ever it takes, I want that place finished and ready within the next two months max." Cooper was not smiling, and Stan just nodded.

"It'll be done Cooper. It may take another team of men or two?" Stan didn't sound too sure.

"So put them on. Just get it done." Cooper said firmly. He scribbled more notes.

"So the outside is almost done. The yards and lawns, trees and shrubs, flower gardens. Shade trees. Secure fencing of at least two acres around the house and grassed and watered and planted with trees and flowering plants as far as can be seen from the house. I want that whole area watered on an automatic sprinkler system. It has to stay green all year round. Which reminds me, how is the work going on the underground water cisterns? We don't get much rain, but when it does it buckets down, and I want to catch that and keep it. We can't keep using the artesian bores, their levels are dropping and the government is going to shut them off all together one day. Apart I hope from house bore holes. So we have to be ready. Those underground cisterns have to hold at least a year's supply of water. More if we can do it." Cooper could see Stan fidgeting on the other end of the line. "What's up Stan? Something not right there?"

"Well, the work on the cisterns is slow going. The local heavy equipment operators are struggling with the concept. Not sure how to proceed." Stan looked at Cooper, obviously looking for guidance.

"Stan, I just finished saying. What ever you need, get it. You have everything at your disposal, and a whole world of resources to draw on. If the locals can't handle it, put them on the road building, and get a team in from Brisbane or Sydney to handle it. They have built road tunnels down there, so a couple of big water cisterns shouldn't be a problem, regardless of where it is. I want that done first thing in the morning. Your morning. ok?"

The cross checking went on for another hour. The house and all of it's surrounds were covered. The house would be unrecognisable now. Every mod con was in place, and some that seemed to have no useful purpose. Lined and sealed, with evaporative cooling, and air conditioning both installed. The place was rapidly looking like a sprawling palace, and that's just what Cooper wanted. A palace for his love, Rebecca. He knew she was adamant she did not want to live and work there, but Cooper had other ideas anyway, that would not go against her wishes.

The last thing to arrange was staff. They had to be in place by the end of the next month. Thirty days plus what remained off this one.

"Ok, thanks Stan. That's excellent. Great work. It couldn't have been done without you. One last thing. Can you get your wife, and one other of the ladies out there, to see to the hiring of staff? Two head gardeners, and four garden labourers. The head gardeners of equal rank. They look after the grounds and the walled garden where the household veg and fruit will grow. What ever they need will be supplied. The same ladies will also hire house staff. Cooks, and house keepers. One cook, two house keepers. They are to be here every day, but of course with weekends off. Friday nights to Sunday nights. If there is no one in residence, that is, myself or Rebecca, then they stay on, and just keep the house tidy and maintained. They must be able to look after guests as well. This is permanent work. If you can't find them local - go international. If your ladies who do the interviews aren't comfortable with them, regardless of qualifications, then they don't get hired. And no mad cooks. You know what camp cooks can be like, and chefs have a reputation for being somewhat crazy. However, the cook or chef must be male, and married with a stable marriage. His wife will work either as an assistant to you, the manager, or to your permanent staff. She must not work in the house or with the cook. They will gang up and end up trying to run the house. It always happens. It may be difficult, but no single cooks or chefs. The other house staff can be, and indeed can be local girls if you find any suitable. It's up to you and your wives."

Cooper sat back, satisfied for the moment that he had covered all the ground. One last thing came to mind.

"Before you go Stan. The sheds and workshops, and station hand accommodation..."

"All done Cooper. Half a mile away from the house and fenced and landscaped. there's never been a station hand's set up like it. Nor a workshop for that matter. We're living in luxury. My house is just a little toward the house from the sheds and quarters. The wife is very happy, and so is the wife of the under manager, their place is right by the station hand's quarters. Oh yes, the aircraft landing strip has been moved now too. It's much further away from the main homestead, and newly surfaced, and big enough to land a 747 if you wanted to." He smiled in satisfaction. Everything was looking good.

"Excellent Stan. Good work. Ok, get an early start, I'll contact you again in a day or so. Anything comes up, email me, or phone me direct if it's urgent." Cooper wasn't finished yet, but his next call would have to wait until business hours in Toowoomba, many thousands of miles away. There was nothing further he could do for the moment. It was now also too late where he was to make any business enquiries locally. It didn't matter, the important bit was done. It was now getting on in time, so Cooper had a shower and changed his clothes. He also shaved. He hated having stubble on his chins, it looked scruffy, and felt terrible. He couldn't understand the latest trend that had young men looking like Euro Trash, with a few days' stubble on their chins. It was particularly scruffy when you had fat balding old businessmen adopting the same look. Ready at last, he headed for the foyer and reception.

"Excuse me miss." He asked the receptionist. "Can you recommend a nice restaurant in the area, quiet preferably, no resident rock bands please." He smiled. The receptionist picked up a couple of brochures and handed them to Cooper. He sorted through them quickly. At last he had one he thought suitable. The Hawksmoor Guildhall looked just what he wanted. Easy going charm with a relaxed atmosphere.

"Looks nice." He said to the girl behind the desk.

"That's perfect. I've been there after work myself. Nice place, I'm sure you will like it sir." She smiled.

"Thanks." replied Cooper and left the front door of the hotel, the concierge calling him a taxi as he came out. He would be back with Rebecca shortly, and he hoped she had had time to get some rest. He was a bit worried about her. He knew she was a strong young woman, but she had been through a lot in the last few hours, and it may have finally caught up with her. He hoped not. He called the restaurant and booked a table for two. Somewhere to the side slightly of the main dining area. He needed some quiet so they could talk. The taxi glided to a stop outside of Rebecca's apartment building.

Chapter 17

Rebecca wondered what Cooper had in mind. She had a few things to say herself, but was not going to be rude or pig headed about what she wanted. She was in fact none too sure about the big picture, but she did know she wanted to raise her child herself. If Cooper was to be a part of that that was good. Excellent in fact, but if he wanted some other arrangement, then he would find out just how determined she could be. She sat on the edge of the chair in the dining room, at her table. She was ready for dinner, and now just awaited Cooper's arrival. Her hands were steady, and she felt good. The shock of the day's events was already behind her. She had dealt with violent crime in her work as a lawyer, but never of course first hand. Some of the people though were very rough to say the least. She was no stranger to violent people. She tapped the table in front of her. If, just if, Cooper moved to the UK, what would he do for a living. How would he spend his time? She had no real idea of his wealth, other than he didn't seem to have to work at anything on a nine-to-five basis. His cattle property was almost self managing, with the team of workers he had there already. So she supposed that he must be reasonably well off. Which was a good thing of course? She had guessed this anyway when she discovered early on that he had turned down the offer to buy his property for what seemed to her to be vast sums of money. Only someone with no financial worries in the world turned down offers like that. So he was secure anyway. Always a good thing in a father and potential husband. She shook her head. There it was again, the word husband slipping into her thoughts. Never mind. Cooper hadn't said a thing about that and probably never would. Oh well. She smiled. It was not an unpleasant thought, but there was a lot against it ever happening, on both their parts. She was not about to give up her career to go and live in the bush. She would live in the English country side, in a suitably appointed home, on some acreage, but that was the limit. She started to day dream about stately homes. Now that would be nice. There were more than a few available on the market of course, but way beyond her means. Maybe in a few years' time, if her career went the way she wanted it to. She was not exactly on the bread line as it was, her parents having left her rather well off, and her London apartment was worth what she considered being a small king's ransom. But no where near enough to buy one of those old country estates with what was often referred to a the 'family pile' sitting on it, built in Edwardian or Georgian times. Times when there seemed to be a lot more money about than there were these days. She shook her head to clear the dreams and got to her feet. The thought of living in a stately home with a husband and children was very attractive and lingered in her minds eye. Her smile gave away the futility of such thoughts. The door chimes sounded, a soft tinkling that penetrated the apartment without a raucous clanging or ringing frightening the wits out of everybody. She pressed the speaker button, knowing that it had to be Cooper. He had the keys, so why didn't he just come on up and into her apartment?

"Yes?" She said into the speaker, giving nothing away in case it wasn't Cooper. She needn't have worried.

"It's Cooper here." He said. "May I come up?"

"Of course Cooper, unless you want me to come down. I am ready, and we could go directly to dinner." She replied.

"Of course. Excellent idea. I'll see you in a moment of two. I'll wait here in the foyer."

Cooper released the button and moved over to lean on the watchman's desk.

"Nice evening for stepping out, sir." The man said. "Rebecca is a lovely girl, is she not.?" The look on his face told Cooper that this was more than a casual comment. The man was doing his job, and Cooper was after all a stranger.

"She is a lovely girl, and I hope to make her my wife. Although I'd appreciate it if you kept that little fact under your hat for the moment." Just at that moment the lift doors opened and Rebecca stepped out, looking ravishing in a long pale dress that seemed to make her shimmer with vitality. Cooper's mouth went dry. 'My God' he thought, 'she is beautiful.' The building watchman winked at him.

"No worries, sir. Discretion is my middle name." He went back to his paper. Rebecca came up to the desk and nodded to the man. She knew him well of course and didn't need to talk to him every time they passed in the building.

"Shall I call a cab?" She asked Cooper.

"No need, I did that as soon as you said you would meet me down here. It should be waiting outside now." He took Rebecca's elbow in a gentle hold, not at all possessive, but steering her directly away from the desk bound watchman. He didn't want the man giving anything away, even accidentally.

Within a very few minutes they were installed at their table is the spacious restaurant. The soft chatter of people enjoying themselves in nice surroundings was quite muted in the open space of the room. They had a perfect table just to one side of the room, so they would not have people pushing past them and waiters clattering around them all evening. Cooper didn't mind the lively buzz of a busy venue, but tonight he wanted Rebecca to hear him clearly. A bottle of Prosecco appeared on the table in front of them, two glasses half filled with the sparkling dry white wine. Perfect as an apéritif. The table was small, and intimate. Their knees touched under the table as they both sat forward in their seats like eager school children. Neither withdrew, enjoying the discrete touch. Cooper sipped his wine after touching his glass to Rebecca's. He smiled almost shyly and put his glass down. Not a man for retiring from a decision, he reached into his pocket and drew out a small ring case in his huge hand. Rebecca watched him quietly, her eyes growing bigger with each moment of realisation.

"Cooper!" She said, with a small note of alarm in her voice. He was already committed, and hopelessly in love. It was do or die he thought.

He took her left hand in his huge hand and opened the ring case with his other hand's fingers. He slipped out the ring, glittering in the quartz down lights above their table. The large emerald centre piece shone with a green lustre only matched by her emerald eyes, the setting of diamonds surrounding the emerald sparkling in a million points of light, reflecting in her wide eyes like fairy dust.

"Rebecca, will you marry me? I love you so much I can't live without you now." As he was saying this, he was slipping the ring on her finger. She was too surprised to pull back. Too surprised to say no. Too surprised to protest. Too surprised to realise that this was what she truly wanted. She looked at the ring, truly beautiful. No ostentatious rock, no minuscule glittering semiprecious stone, this was such a beautiful ring, she would have chosen it herself. Tears prickled her eyes.

"Yes." She whispered. Then again slightly louder. "Oh yes. Cooper..." She couldn't go on. There was a scattering of quiet applause from women at the surrounding tables. Cooper blushed. He actually blushed, Rebecca smiled at the mans' humanity. This was one of the reasons she loved him. Truly loved him. He was not afraid to show his emotions. He held both of her hands in his and looked into her eyes. His eyes smiling at her. She loved that. She could see his smile in his eyes. He gave her all of him, every time.

"Plenty of time for talk." He said softly, as they sat back in their chairs, and sipped their wine together. Rebecca couldn't help admiring the ring on her finger. It was so perfect. She didn't know why, but it just seemed to say to her, how perfectly Cooper knew her likes and dislikes as though they had been together for years.

"But Cooper. My dearest. What about... what about?" She couldn't continue. Cooper held a finger to his lips and smiled.

"It's all sorted my love. It's all sorted. Let's order, and over the meal, when you feel a little better, I can tell you the rest. You mustn't worry about a thing. Your work future is safe and secured. So is mine." He smiled enigmatically and bent his head to the menu.

Suddenly waiters swooped on their table, the Prosecco was whisked away along with the glasses.

"Scusi scusi." Murmured the head waiter. "For your enjoyment, compliments of the house."

A glittering silver ice bucket, beads of cold condensation on the outside containing a dark green bottle of Dom Pérignon appeared on the table along with two lovely Champagne flutes. They were quickly and expertly filled.

With a murmured "Enjoy." He backed away and was gone. Rebecca and Cooper looked at each other and they both smiled, Rebecca giggling a little. She toasted her glass toward Cooper.

"Cheers." She said. Thinking how Australian that sounded. The waiter appeared with note pad ready to take their order. Suddenly Rebecca was starving. She realised it had been hours, days even since she had eaten. They both ordered and the waiter left. Cooper leaned forward.

"Now, where shall we set up home? Of course you keep your apartment. You will need that when working in London, but I've a mind that something in the country would be nice. What do you think?" He sat back for a moment. Waiting for Rebecca to take it all in. He was worried that he may have said too much in one sentence.

"In the country? Where in the country?" She had visions of some ancient farm house in the wilds of rural England.

Cooper pulled a magazine page from his hip pocket.
"Well, I thought something like this. Big enough to keep me busy, and although seemingly in the country side here, far enough out to give us the space when we need it. It's pretty small in terms of acreage I'm sorry, but it should be comfortable enough."

He handed the torn out page to her. She nearly choked on her greens. The place was... it was. a country estate. In Suffolk it seemed. It was a country mansion. Someone's 'family pile' that was up for sale. Rebecca couldn't believe her eyes. Then she saw the price listed on the bottom of the page. She squealed and dropped the paper into her dinner, quickly retrieving it complete with food stains starting to seep through. It was listed in the high millions and listed at some four hundred acres. 'Not big' he'd said. That was massive in English terms, and in the ancient county of Suffolk a rare thing. Cooper was laughing quietly.

"You like it?" He asked. "I hope so, because we already own it. We can move in any time we like." He hesitated a moment. "When we are married of course." He smiled and added "There will be chickens too."

Rebecca was speechless. She was more than delighted, but speechless. Finally, it dawned on her. He hadn't mentioned his place in Australia.

"But what of your place - your home. Your Home. In Australia?" Rebecca had a sinking feeling in her heart. What would he say?

"All fixed up my love. You won't recognise the place now. But you needn't worry. We can go back on school term holidays. Christmas times. Whenever you like. The place will continue to be managed by, well, my manager and his team. I don't need to be there." He smiled rather shyly. "I'm very rich by the way. You should know that. I hope it doesn't change things."

Rebecca shook her head. This was a fairy tale. She felt like she was in a fairy tale. It couldn't be happening. She jumped to her feet.

"Excuse me a moment Cooper." She grabbed her purse and headed for the lady's room. Neither of them noticed half the women around them head for the same destination. Cooper wasn't worried. Rebecca hadn't frowned, and he knew already that when she didn't like something he said, she frowned, just a little line appearing between her eyebrows. She was back soon enough from the rest room and took her place.

"Cooper, what can I say. You have taken care of everything. Everything I've ever dreamed of. Our child will have - no. Our children will have the perfect father. They will never want for a thing." She sat back in her chair, the worries of the past few months falling away from her.

Cooper had one more surprise for her. Like a magician he pulled an envelope from his pocket and handed it to Rebecca. She looked inside. Two tickets to the Amalfi Coast, and a reservation for a wedding chapel on a startlingly blue lake shore.

"Oh, we can invite who ever you like. I've booked out the hotel nearby for our visit and for the duration of the wedding and reception. That is, if you want to. You may have other plans. We can - I don't mean to take over everything - make other plans. We can just go out there for our... wedding honeymoon." He stopped. Rebecca was looking at him steadily. 'Ok, he was used to being in control of his life. But the wedding?' She thought that might be something she wanted to be involved in the planning of. Cooper sat back. 'uh oh' he thought as the little frown line appeared between her eyebrows.

Rebecca smiled again and sat back. Now she knew what worried Cooper. She decided she was going to have fun getting to know him if it took the rest of her life. She picked up her fork and popped the baby mushroom into her mouth. Cooper sat there nonplussed. One minute frowning, the next minute eating as though nothing had happened. It seemed the wedding he had arranged was ok. Of course Cooper still had a lot to learn about Rebecca...

ABOUT THE AUTHOR

Robert and his muse Liz, live in Suffolk, in the United Kingdom with two crazy dogs. He has dual citizenship with Australia and the UK and has travelled and worked in China. He was born and raised in Australia of an English (Lancashire) mother, and Scots father.

The Author's Website
http://www.robert-chalmers.com/